NYT & USA Bestselling Author
TIJAN

Cover image designed by Lisa Jordan
www.lisajordanphotography.com.au

Edited by Jessica Royer Ocken

Proofread by Chris O'Neil Parece, Paige Smith, and Elaine York

Interior Design by Elaine York/Allusion Graphics, LLC
www.allusiongraphics.com

DEDICATION

To my readers!
To the Aaron in my life.

CHAPTER 1

Emma

"There's a man watching you." Theresa nudged me with her elbow behind the table. As soon as the words left her, a hush fell over the group. We were at Joe's for drinks after work with our coworkers, and all eyes turned my way.

I didn't want to look, so I didn't. Picking up my beer instead, I shrugged. "It's probably paparazzi—"

"It's not."

My words died in my throat. Theresa had become a good friend. She knew what I went through—the real story, not the story every media outlet was reporting—and in the beginning, she enjoyed the attention. Everywhere we went, the reporters were there. Carter Reed was their obsession. He was gorgeous with wolf-like blue eyes, chiseled cheekbones, and broad shoulders that tapered to a thin waist. Even though he was usually photographed in a business suit or a tuxedo on the way to formal events, I knew thousands of women's mouths watered at the thought of what he looked like underneath those clothes. Carter was gorgeous, which made the reporters and their audience love him. But what really made them salivate for any shred of information about him was his association with the Mauricio family.

In addition to being gorgeous, Carter was dangerous. He was known to be an assassin for a local mafia family, but what wasn't known to anyone beyond a select few, was that he was out. He'd bought his way out, and he'd done it for me. He'd also bought *my* life back after I killed a member of a rival mafia family while trying to save my friend. Those were our secrets.

Almost a year later, when my choices had seemed to be die or run for my life, I went to Carter: my brother's best friend from childhood, the guy I knew because he'd slept on our couch for so many nights. This was still how I preferred to think of him, not as the man the city knew as the Cold Killer, Carter Reed. He was my soul mate.

But when I heard the low warning tone of Theresa's words, every part of me went on alert. My expression didn't change, but I mentally ran through the possibilities of who this man could be and why he might be watching.

A low buzz began around the table and then someone asked, "What do you need from us, Emma?"

I looked toward the voice, confused.

It was a secretary for one of the senior officers from The Richmond. Her eyebrows were fixed forward, bunched together, and her lips pressed in a flat line. I'd never talked to her before we sat together this evening. Six months ago, I would not have gotten this reception. People would've gossiped and judged. But now, as I surveyed the rest of the table, it seemed they wanted to help.

Then I felt a presence at my elbow and looked up. It was Thomas, the security guard Carter had appointed as my personal bodyguard. I had three of them at all times: Thomas, Mike, and Peter. They all looked the same. Tall. Imposing. Built like professional athletes, but with the skills to disappear like ghosts or stand and fight the best of the best. Carter trained all his men himself. I knew they moved with the gracefulness of a cat, appearing and disappearing when they chose, but the abrupt arrival of one of my bodyguards could still cause my breath to catch in my throat. Once again, a hush fell over the group around the table. Half of the girls recoiled from the intimidating presence, while the other half were probably trying to figure out how to take Thomas home with them.

"We should go, Miss Martins."

I shot him a look.

The corner of his mouth lifted. "Emma."

"That's better."

His hand came to my elbow and he said again, so politely and yet with authority, "We should be going, Miss Emma."

Ah. A compromise. I saw the flash of humor in his eyes and shook my head as a grin tugged at my lips. I slid off my stool and turned to Theresa. "Did you want a ride?"

She started to shake her head, then grabbed at the table for balance. With a laugh, she replied, "Yeah, maybe. I think I drank that last pitcher all by myself."

A woman laughed from across the table. "You and me, Theresa. I think we shared it."

"Yeah. Probably." Theresa gave her a slight smile, grabbing her purse and straightening her clothes as she stood. She moved close to me and gave a nod. "I'm ready to go."

Oh, yes. Theresa had forgotten to pay. Laughing softly, I reached into my purse and laid a hundred-dollar bill onto the table. It would cover the two pitchers we ordered and the pizza we shared with the rest. The group called good-bye behind us as we headed out the door, and I lifted a hand in response. Theresa bent her head forward and was already out the door, moving in front of me. When I felt the cold winter air, I grabbed the sides of my coat and pulled them tight around me, bunching my shoulders together. I mimicked the way Theresa crossed the sidewalk to the waiting car. Dashing in after her, as Thomas held the door, I heard that guy calling from farther down the sidewalk.

"Miss Nathans!"

Whoever that was, it wasn't me. He had the wrong person. I relaxed a little bit. He wasn't someone I needed to worry about. I climbed inside, and Thomas sat beside me, shutting the door.

I glanced at him, surprised. He usually shut the door and went to the front seat, but not this time. Another guard was already seated inside the limo, across from us, and he avoided my gaze. He pressed his intercom. "We're good to go."

The car moved into traffic.

Theresa groaned, folding over to pinch her forehead with her hand. "That last pitcher was too much." She lifted tormented eyes to me. "When am I going to remember I'm a wine girl? I'm getting old, Emma. Beer doesn't sit well with me anymore."

I chuckled, letting go of my unease and forcing myself to relax. Patting her on the back, I asked, "Do you want us to take you to your place or Noah's?"

She groaned again. "Not Noah's. He'll just gripe at me." Some fight returned to her tone. "He's been on this kick lately that I shouldn't go to Friday night happy hour. We had a big fight about it last week. He actually forbade me to go tonight. Can you believe that?" Her voice sharpened. "*Forbade* me? Like he could even do that, even if we were in a relationship. Forbade? Unreal. He started to tell me *you* shouldn't even go, but he stopped himself. When I pushed him on that, he said it was none of his business if you went or not. I'm allowed to see you. That was his term. *Allowed.*" She barked a bitter laugh. "As if I'm some damn submissive wife. Hasn't he learned anything over the years? Allowed. What a joke."

I frowned, keeping my thoughts to myself. Noah was CEO of The Richmond, an international chain of hotels. Theresa had grown up with him. She worked for him too, but the real status of their relationship remained complicated. Her parents had been close with his before they died, so she'd been taken in by his family. I knew Noah had good intentions when it came to Theresa, and the two bickered like an old married couple, but he was never one to be controlling.

In fact, his initial concern about our friendship had faded as quickly as he had voiced it. He'd known Theresa wasn't a fan of Carter, but as we all got to know each other, Noah and Theresa, along with Amanda—my last friend from my old life—had become like a small family to Carter and me. I owed them so much. They'd been there for me when my roommate, Mallory, was killed a year ago, and I'd been hunted by the Bartel family.

But it seemed Noah might have some reason for his current concerns. Something was going on. A man had been watching me inside, then from the street, and I'd heard him calling me, even if it was by the wrong name. Add in Thomas' change in the usual seating arrangements and that added up to...something.

I turned to study Thomas' profile, but whether he sensed my scrutiny or not, he didn't react. He remained stoic and statuesque as we drove to Theresa's building, but that wasn't new. All the guards were like this. They preferred that I pretend they didn't exist. Carter explained to me one night that this was how they'd been taught—to guard and not interact. When I interacted with them, it distracted them from doing their jobs.

When we pulled up to Theresa's ritzy building, Thomas helped her inside. She had a doorman twenty-four-seven, so Thomas didn't have to lead her far. He just took her to the elevator where a staff member of the building took over and pressed the button. Thomas returned to the car, and it wasn't long before we'd arrived at Carter's building.

Our building. He'd correct me, if he had heard my thoughts.

"This is your home, too," he'd told me many times, but it wasn't. The car drove to the basement parking, the door was opened for me, and I took the elevator to the top floor. I don't know why I did this.

Carter had renovated the entire building so it was all one home, but he'd given me the top floor when I first came to live with him. I'd been scared, excited, and in a whole different element back then, hiding for my life.

Sometimes I still enjoyed my private elevator entrance, even though I could take the stairs. I would slip into my bedroom and change my clothes before going downstairs to the kitchen and living room on the first floor. Carter's room was the third floor. As I did this tonight, I held my slippers in one hand and tiptoed down the stairs.

It was foolish to want to sneak up on Carter. He trained ghosts. He was one himself. When I'd gone through all the floors, I hadn't found him on any of them. I checked the gym last. Still no Carter, so I went back out to the basement garage. Thomas had taken his perch outside the door, and I asked, "Where is he?"

"He flew to New York today. He's on his way home now, Miss Mar—"

"I swear to god, if you utter that name one more time, I will steal your gun from you and shoot you in the leg."

"—Emma." He flashed me a rueful grin.

"Better. Remember it this time."

He nodded, and I went back inside. Well. I had no idea what to do now. Carter wasn't in the Mauricio family anymore, but he still had business dealings with them, as well as with the Bartel family now. He owned shares in The Richmond, too. Carter also had other businesses, ones he hadn't even told me about because there were too many to mention, but I'd gotten spoiled over the last year. He'd made a concerted effort to be home, flying and conducting his business during the hours when I was at work myself.

Telling myself not to worry, as Carter was a big boy, I went back to the kitchen and poured a glass of wine. Unlike Theresa, I hadn't joined in with the beer. I preferred to keep a clear head when outside the house. It was a survival tendency I'd picked up after being shot at a year ago.

I was enjoying the wine and relaxing in the tub when the bathroom door opened.

I felt him before I saw him. A small grin appeared automatically on my face, and I opened my eyes to see Carter standing there.

It was always the same. A tingle started in the base of my stomach, and it would rise, spreading out through my body, warming me as it went, until I was almost salivating for him. When I saw him, I needed to touch him. It had been like this for a year, and I never wanted it to end. I always wanted to thirst for him.

"Hi."

"Hi, yourself." He was dressed in custom-tailored pants and a black button-down shirt, which was wrinkled and untucked with the top two buttons undone. The collar looked like he'd stretched it out, and damn, with his dark blond hair cut short, his wolf-like blue eyes, and his sharp cheekbones, Carter managed to look restless, on edge, and sophisticated all at once.

He knelt at the edge of the tub. "Did you have a good night?"

"You weren't here when I came home." I hadn't meant it to sound like an accusation, but it slipped out that way.

A smile crossed his lips, and he dipped a hand into the water, stirring it in a slow motion. "I got news today, and I had to go and see for myself."

My heart paused. Bad news? It didn't sound good. "What kind of news?"

"News that…" He hesitated, the smile slipping. "…might change a lot of things."

"There's a man watching you." Theresa's words came back to me, along with the other shout. *"Miss Nathans!"* I bit down on my lip and asked, "Is it news I should know about?"

A flicker of darker emotion crossed his features before he clamped it down. Lifting his hand to my leg, he moved his fingers in a slow caress, up and down. Just that slight touch and I began to have a hard time breathing. I glanced down, mesmerized by his fingers. Water slid down my skin from his hand. When it stopped, he dipped down and lifted the water once more to my leg. I had to pull my gaze from that vision and lift it back to his face.

His eyes were tortured, but when my gaze caught his, that look vanished right away and he murmured, "You should, but I don't know if I can tell you." His eyebrows bunched, and he shook his head, becoming unreadable once again. Then he slid his hands underneath me in the tub. He stood, lifting me with him, out of the water. Instead of grabbing a towel, he walked me back into the bedroom and placed me onto the desk in one corner. I could see us in the mirror across the room.

He leaned close, his head moving to the crook of my shoulder and neck, and he held me. His shirt stretched tight over his back, outlining his broad shoulders and tapered waistline. My arms had wrapped around his neck, and I slid one down the middle of his back. He sucked in his breath under my touch.

He murmured against my skin, "Why is it that your presence can calm me? Your touch can make me alive, and one little sigh from you makes me want to sleep for days in your embrace?"

I smiled, moving to press a kiss to his ear. "Because you love me."

He pulled back, his eyes meeting mine with only a few centimeters between us. His forehead rested on mine, then one of his hands cupped the side of my face. His thumb brushed over my cheek and tucked a strand of my hair behind my ear. "I need to tell you what happened today, because it could affect us."

He was torn. I could tell.

He added, "But not yet."

Leaning back, I put my hands on his face and made sure he was looking right into my eyes. "Whatever it is, we'll be fine," I told him. And I believed that. "We've been through too goddamn much."

"I know."

I tilted my head. This wasn't the Carter I knew. He took care of everything. He had declared war for me, and I knew he'd do it again. "Should I be worried?"

That same tortured look came to his eyes, but he said, "No." Pulling me back into his arms, he nudged my legs farther apart, moving closer, and pressed his lips to the underside of my jaw. He whispered, "Never." Another kiss to the corner of my lips. "Ever." A third kiss, his lips resting atop mine and he murmured, "I promise. Nothing will ever happen to you."

"To us." My hands gripped his shoulders.

"To us," he said.

Then his lips opened, and he took over, a command in his kiss. "Forget I said anything."

With those words, he leaned me backward against the wall and kissed his way down my throat, over my chest, and all the way to my waist as his hands gripped my hips, holding me firmly on the desk. There he paused, and I arched my back, already knowing where he was going.

His tongue swept over me, and my hands went to his shoulders, holding on blindly. When he moved farther down, a deep, guttural groan came from within me.

My god.

I loved this man.

Carter

When my phone buzzed, I wasn't sleeping, only holding Emma as she did. She'd curled into me, still naked, and I looked over at my phone. I was tempted to ignore it. I knew who was on the other end.

It was Gene, my old mentor from the Mauricio family. He'd been a pain in my ass then, and I knew he would be again. Unlike most of my men and the rest of the family, Gene didn't adhere to my wishes for privacy. When he wanted to talk, he called. When he wanted a meeting, he demanded one. We had butted heads on more than one occasion, and I'd threatened him with bodily harm another time when he'd made his dislike for Emma too known.

He was calling now, and I didn't want to hear whatever he had to say. I needed to protect Emma, no matter what happened, and I pulled her tighter into my arms as that damn phone beeped again.

It would keep going. He wouldn't stop calling.

I let out a curse before I disentangled myself from her and slipped from the bed. Grabbing my phone, I pulled on some sweats and headed down to my office. Once I was there, I held the phone to my ear and went straight for the liquor cabinet.

Pouring myself some bourbon, I answered. "Gene, you are interrupting."

He grunted from the other end. "No doubt. It took me six calls to get you on the phone."

I gripped the phone tighter for a slight second. "So you heard?"

"Yeah, I heard. Everyone in the family has heard. Cole's back?"

"Yes, he's back."

"Are you going to him?"

"I already did."

"And?"

"And nothing. He says I'm out."

"Fuck, Carter. You saved his life five years ago, and now he's back. I know you. Yeah, he might say you're out, but we both know you're coming back in."

"Gene," I started.

"Don't argue with me."

"I'm staying out."

He snorted again.

"It's not me anymore."

"I know." His voice quieted. "For her, I hope you stay out, but I know you, Carter. At the first sign of trouble, you'll be coming in. Listen to me. This is why I'm calling you. Stay. Out."

"I am out."

"I mean it, Carter. Stay out. Do it for the woman you love."

"That's the plan." But even as I said those words, I gripped my glass so tightly that the side cracked. I was out. I had bought my way out for Emma. Everything was about Emma now, but...

"I know you loved him like a brother, but you love that woman more," Gene said. "Just remember those words and you'll be fine."

"Gene." He was right. Emma was everything.

"What?"

"It was the *Bartels*."

He cursed on the other end, sighing into the phone. "We've had a year of peace. That's one more year of peace than any other time. You gave that to us, Carter. Remember that and remember my words. I know you love him, but you love her more. She's the reason for you to stay out."

"I know."

"Okay. I'll let you get back to that woman now. Tell her hello for me."

I laughed into the phone. "You and I both know you give her the creeps. She always makes sure she's not around when you come for dinner."

He barked out a laugh, a real one. "I know, but that's good. Your woman has good instincts. Keep telling herself to trust her gut. She's a strong one."

"I know." And I did.

Sitting behind my desk, I looked up to the ceiling as if I could see through the floors to where she lay. She was above me, sleeping. She was at peace. She would remain at peace. I'd promised her brother, AJ, that when we were kids, and I had kept my promise all these years.

Gene said his good-bye and hung up, but he'd gotten one thing wrong.

I didn't want back in, but with Cole back, since the Bartel family had attacked him, I would have to wait and see. I was attached to the Mauricio family, even if I was in business with both families. But if they touched Emma, all bets were off.

Emma

A week later I was at the gun range with Theresa and Amanda. Noah was there too, as he was technically our teacher, but after he and Theresa got into a spat for the third time, she banished him to an observation box above us, behind bulletproof glass. He could watch and listen, but if we didn't hit the speaker switch from our end, we couldn't hear him. Theresa made sure all our speaker switches were turned off.

As Theresa gave the instructions, Amanda and I shared a grin. We'd been learning how to shoot for a couple of months now. It had been Theresa's idea, and these sessions had started to replace our wine nights. It had also been her idea to have Noah be our instructor. Carter was the better shot, but Theresa still liked to keep her distance from him. He still made her uneasy.

Amanda had asked her about it one night at their apartment when I'd gone to the bathroom. I stopped in the hallway when I'd overheard Theresa explain, "It's not that I don't like him. It's just… he's a killer, Amanda. He's dangerous. I know he loves her, and I know if anyone is going to protect her, it will be him, but…" She'd sighed. "I don't know. He's known as the Cold Killer. It's hard to get past that, even though I know Emma loves him so much."

Amanda had asked, "Are you worried for her?"

"No." She'd hesitated. "I mean…maybe. I'm not worried for her from him, but because of him. He's with the mafia."

"She said he's out."

"Yeah, well, is anyone really out?"

Amanda had replied, "She wasn't in trouble before because of him. Emma and I did that all on our own."

"I know. I really do, and I feel bad, but I'm just on edge with the guy. He's deadly. Can't you see it in his eyes?" Theresa got up for the kitchen. "I need a refill. You?"

I had melted backward, back into the bathroom. When she'd crossed the hallway, the bathroom door was shut.

Glancing over at her now, I remembered how her smiles had seemed more forced that night, her laughter a little louder, and the secretive looks she'd sent Amanda's way. They were roommates. They were going to talk about me. That was obvious, but I'd been hurt, though I knew I shouldn't have been.

Theresa worried about me. I tried to keep telling myself it was as simple as that, but a slight wedge had found its way between us. Amanda and I were fine. We were still family, always would be. Really we were all still our little family, but there was a small distance between Theresa and myself now. I don't think she ever felt it from her end, but it was there. And I knew Amanda had noticed. I often saw a question in her eyes as she watched Theresa and me together. I felt her concern and understood it, but nothing was going to change. I still loved Theresa. I would remain close with them. The unit wasn't going to disburse. But since no one had brought it up when I *wasn't* in the bathroom, we didn't talk about it.

And again, Theresa didn't seem to think there was anything to talk about. She was currently most concerned about the date that had failed because of an explosion the night before, literally.

She growled now, aiming her gun at the target. "I shouldn't be pissed, but when that bird exploded in the oven, I'd had it. That's his idea of being romantic. Putting a sparkler in the turkey. He lit it, then stuffed it in there to hide it from me. He was going to bring it out as some grand gesture, but he forgot the sparkler was still going. My kitchen reeks of torched bird. And you know what he said afterward? He asked if I had more wine. He thought that was so funny. I swear. More wine, my ass."

She thumbed off three shots, one right after the other, then looked up to the observation box. "Yeah, it wasn't funny. Or romantic."

Noah stuffed his hands back into his pockets. A glower formed on his face.

Amanda raised her gun and aimed. "How about this? Why don't you and Noah go out tonight to one of Carter's restaurants. Emma and I will clean the entire kitchen. We'll get that smell out, too. You'll never know it even happened."

Carter's restaurants. Hearing those words, I tensed. Would Theresa go to one of his establishments? She had never resisted before, and she still enjoyed going to Octave, the nightclub, but I worried, knowing her true feelings. What would happen if she started to shun Carter's businesses?

Her eyes lit up. "That sounds like a great plan." Twisting around, she hollered up as she reached over to turn on her speaker switch. "You game for that?"

"Sure." Noah sounded resigned.

Amanda and I shared a grin at his short growl.

Theresa didn't seem to mind. She turned her speaker back off, but said up to him, "And you're bringing the wine this time."

He nodded, unable to talk back once more.

Then she turned to me. "Is that okay with you, Emma? Would you ask Carter what restaurant he would recommend?"

"Yeah, but I'm sure he'll recommend The Favre. And I'm pretty certain Carter won't even need to call. You guys are always on the list to get a table."

And other benefits. No one from Carter's inner circle ever paid, and they always left with an expensive bottle of wine to open at home.

Looking past Theresa's shoulder to Amanda, I laughed. She clapped her hands together silently, jumping up and down.

Time alone for Amanda and me was rare. We used to do Friday lunches, but she'd been promoted to upper management of a bakery across town. This enabled her to leave her side job at the diner next to The Richmond, and her new position left her without as much free time. Tonight, with Theresa and Noah on their date, was a gift for us as much as it was for Theresa. I knew Amanda would have wine chilling for us while we cleaned the place, and we could talk openly and honestly. We had a special bond. I loved her as a sister. We were the only two to make it out of our run-in with the Bartel family alive. Losing Mallory—and even Ben in an odd way—would always keep us connected.

Plus, Amanda had been pretty silent the last month or so, and that meant something was going on. I had plans to do an interrogation, twenty questions-style, to find out what—or who, if she'd started dating someone.

Theresa sent off another round of shots, and when her clip was done, she put it down. "I'm out."

"Me, too." Amanda winked at us before emptying her clip as well.

I still had a full clip.

"Emma?" Theresa had started for the door.

"Go ahead. I'll be right out."

Amanda followed her, but she whispered to me as she passed by. "You and me tonight! I'm excited. I have so much to tell you."

So my gut had been right. I grinned at her and waited until both of them were outside of the door. It wasn't that I wanted to shoot in secret or anything. I just wanted privacy. I wanted it to be me and the gun, just us for a moment. No bickering. No gossip. No heated undertones.

Learning how to shoot was really more for her and Amanda. I knew how to shoot. I had two bodies to prove it, but they were done from close range, not at a distance. And learning how to be better at what I already knew was never a bad idea.

As I held the gun, alone now, some of the old memories came back to me. But they were never very far away.

I had killed two men.

"Jeremy."

My voice had been soft when I called to him. He'd been raping my roommate, and he was going to kill her. I had no choice. When he turned around and saw the gun in my hand, I shot him. The bullet hit the center of his forehead.

I swallowed now, remembering Mallory as she had watched me, pinned to the wall by his hands. Her eyes had been so lifeless. They were the opposite of Ben's. He'd been pleading for his life, but minutes earlier he'd been planning to kill Amanda, then me. My stomach churned, remembering that he was going to take me to Franco. He wanted to barter, trade me in for more money, more drugs.

He was the one who killed Mallory, but the Bartel family set all of it in motion.

I drew in a ragged breath, cradling the gun in my hands like a precious baby. This little piece of metal had caused so much havoc in my life, and it was Carter's weapon of choice. He'd killed plenty with it when he worked for the Mauricio family.

Somehow, I knew this weapon would have a place in our lives again. I didn't want it to, but I knew it would. And with that last thought, my hand closed over it, and I raised my arms, aiming with my feet apart, my shoulders rolled back. I shot, one after another, until my clip was done.

All except one hit the bullseye. The other one, the outlier, was just outside the inner circle on the target.

I'd have to get better.

"Emma." There was a knock on the door, and Amanda waved from the other side. She yelled through it, her voice muffled. "Are you coming?"

I nodded. Putting my gear away, I stepped into the hallway. Amanda held my bag, and I put my gun inside the holding container with the ammunition beside it. Then I locked it and put it back into my bag. "Ready."

She looked up and down the hallway. We were alone. "They've been fighting a lot, but he's trying. I think Theresa's actually scared because he's trying."

"What do you mean?"

"He asked her to move in."

We had started for the front door, but I stopped. "What?" I hadn't known they were officially a couple. "They're so on and off all the time."

Amanda grinned, ducking her head. "I know, but I overheard it. They're more 'on' than they let anyone know. He asked her—gave her a key and everything."

"She said no?"

She shook her head. "Theresa didn't say a word. She went on a cleaning frenzy last weekend, after it happened."

"And the turkey exploding—"

"She's not really worked up about the bird. It wasn't that big of a mess either. I think she's scared of what else he had planned with that romantic dinner."

"Wow." Theresa moving in with Noah. "That's great."

"She cries in the bathroom. I can hear her."

"Really?"

Amanda nodded. "Every morning. She lost her family. I think she's scared of losing him."

I nodded slowly, and we started for the front door again. "Yeah, that makes sense." Amanda and I shared a look. We had lost people, too. Mallory. Mallory's baby.

"So tonight…"

"Yeah." I pushed open the door, and we stepped through. I could see the driver behind the wheel, and the car was running, so I assumed Noah and Theresa were inside waiting for us.

Amanda walked beside me. "I have to tell you something."

"Okay."

Her head bobbed up and down. Some strands of her light blond hair fell free from her ponytail. She tucked them behind her ear in a distracted manner. Biting down on her lip, Amanda looked agitated.

"Is everything okay?" I asked.

"Yeah." She nodded again, but it was more to herself, like she was reassuring herself of something. "It is. It will be. I'm excited for tonight. I'm glad you're coming over."

"Me, too." I grinned at her and reached over to squeeze her hand. She squeezed right back.

The door opened, and Theresa asked from inside, "Where did you gu—"

Then another shout drowned her out. *"Miss Nathans!"*

My head snapped up to see the same man from outside Joe's. He waved his arm in the air and hurried across the road.

Suddenly three things happened at once:

One of my guards materialized out of nowhere and stopped the man. He literally blocked him, towering over the guy.

Another of the guards appeared behind me and cupped my elbow in his hand. As he directed me to a different car, he said to Amanda, "Please, get inside. Emma will be coming with us."

Then I was hurried into another vehicle, and we sped off—even before Theresa and Noah's car. I turned around to find Thomas inside, along with the driver. I hadn't even known they were around. Only Michael had accompanied us to the range, and I thought they trusted my security to be adequate with him and Noah, but I'd been wrong.

Before we turned the corner, I saw a second car speed toward the guy who'd yelled, and more of Carter's guards got out. I relaxed, knowing my guard wasn't alone, but then I focused on the guy. This was the second time and second place he'd appeared. This was no coincidence. He was there for me, and apparently, I was Miss Nathans.

Before I could get a good look at him, we turned, so I turned to Thomas. "Who is that man?"

He didn't answer at first, but then said, "We'll find out."

"Where's Carter?" He'd been gone this morning, but he'd been disappearing every night and for longer hours than normal. I hadn't been questioning it, but that time was done. I needed to know what was going on.

"He's in New York again."

"Will he be there all night?"

He hesitated again. "I believe so. He's supposed to be calling you about it."

Fine. I'd have my night with Amanda, and then tomorrow I'd hunt Carter down whether he wanted it or not. "I am going to Amanda's tonight," I said, to make sure there was no confusion. "I don't care who that guy is. I'm going."

He nodded. "Of course, Emma."

I grinned. "You're just saying my name so I don't make your night hell and demand to go to Carter, aren't you?"

"Maybe." A flicker of a grin appeared, then vanished, and Thomas went back to being his stoic, statue-like self.

I relaxed back against my seat. Little did he know, I was going to be that nightmare tomorrow. He could have peace for one night.

CHAPTER 3

Emma

"Who was that guy?"

That was Amanda's first question when I walked through the door after going home to change. Instead of answering, I took my coat off and put my purse on the counter.

Glancing around, I asked, "Is Theresa already gone?"

Amanda's head was deep inside the oven as she answered. "Yeah. Did you call Carter about the restaurant?"

I hadn't, but I'd called the restaurant myself. Spying a bottle of wine and two empty glasses beside it, I started to pour. "They'll be taken care of."

"Oh, good." She emerged and gave me a lopsided grin, brushing her arm over her forehead as some hair covered her eyes. "Hey, you look nice."

I glanced down. I'd swapped the sweatshirt and jeans I wore at the gun range for a sweater and pair of pants. It wasn't much, but they were nicer quality than the clothes I would've been wearing a little over a year ago. "Thanks." Handing her glass of wine, I asked, "So what's the news?"

"Oh, jeez. You get right to it, don't you?"

I nodded, taking a sip. "I'm waiting."

She groaned and finished her entire glass in one swallow.

I lifted an eyebrow. That wasn't typical Amanda. She was nervous...or excited. Yes. Her cheeks were pink, and her face flushed. She brushed her hair back. She was excited, which had me more intrigued.

"I met a guy."

I felt my face light up. It was time. Amanda had been there during Mallory's dating escapades and while I went to Carter. She'd turned someone down because of me, because of Carter's mafia connections. So she deserved this.

"Who? When? Where? Does Theresa know?" I asked in a rush.

She shook her head, but she was bursting from happiness. Squealing, she motioned for more wine, and I made sure to fill her glass all the way to the top. Giving it back, I added, "Spill, woman. I want to know."

"He asked me to move in with him."

My eyes got huge. For Theresa to move in with Noah was big, but for Amanda...I fanned myself and joked, "About to pass out here. I need to know everything about this guy."

And that was when she grew quiet.

Oh, no.

My gut churned. Amanda had been giddy two seconds earlier, and now she looked in pain. My mind started backpedaling. I remembered the last time she'd spoken of a guy—back when she worked at the diner beside The Richmond, almost a year ago.

"*He's a cop,*" she'd said. She'd pushed off his advances because of me, because of Carter, because of what happened after Mallory... Amanda had been the one to tell me to kill Ben.

"*Make him pay. I don't care if he was our friend. He killed her. You make him pay, Emma,*" she'd said as she was dragged out of the apartment. I did what she said, but I didn't have to. All the guilt was on me. I'd pulled the trigger. She hadn't.

"Oh." I put my wine down. The celebratory mood was gone. "I see."

She hugged herself and turned away. "He kept coming back to the diner. I couldn't...it was hard, Emma. But I've never said a word. I promise. I haven't."

But she would. She was in love. I could see that much.

I let out a sigh. "Amanda."

I didn't know what to say. This was bad, really bad. If Carter found out...I didn't want to go there. I couldn't. Amanda was family. She was from my old life. I felt sliced through the stomach, gutted.

She whispered, looking at me with begging eyes, "I love him, Emma."

"He's a cop." There was no way around it.

She looked down, and said again, her voice hoarse, "I love him."

I couldn't be there. I knew that much. I couldn't be anywhere around her. Dumping my wine, I went to grab my purse. Amanda beat me there. She clamped a hand over it and said, "I won't say anything to him. I promise."

I shook my head. She didn't get it. "Amanda—" I started. I was dying, going to lose my last original family member. "He's going to be *it* for you. You're going to move in with him. He's going to be your teammate. He's going to be the other half, and eventually, it's going to be only him. Your allegiance will be to him."

Like mine was to Carter.

I loved her, but it was Carter first. Why couldn't she see this? My hand curled over hers as it still held my purse. "He's a cop," I said again. He was the other side. "I've killed."

What was she thinking? She hadn't been, but even as I thought that, a voice whispered in my head that I still would've gone to Carter—even if I hadn't needed him. Sometimes the heart decides. I would've gone, and I still would've loved him, no matter what.

"So have I," she countered, breaking me out of my thoughts.

"No." I shook my head. "You didn't pull the trigger. I did."

"You saved Mallory."

I nodded. The first time had been about saving her, saving me, but the second time… I couldn't stretch the truth with Ben. I'd killed him because I wanted to. That was the truth. If I hadn't done it, I knew Carter would. Either way, Ben was going to die. I pulled the trigger because I wanted to be the one.

She saw the look on my face and shook her head. "Stop, Emma. Stop it. I told you to. I mean, Ben's death is on me, too. I couldn't ever…" A haunted look came over her.

I felt it, too. It was Mallory. She was in the room with us.

I closed my fingers over hers and held on to her. I loved her. Amanda was a sister to me, and this was my good-bye. But I wanted to not think about it. "I love you," I broke out, as a tear slipped from my eye.

"I love you, too." She held my hand as tears fell down her face, too. "So much. I'll never say anything."

She would. She was the only one not admitting it.

My heart split in half. I tried to smile at her. "I know. We're sisters."

She nodded. "We are. I wanted you to know. I couldn't keep dating him and not tell anyone. I wanted to share this with you. You're family."

I nodded. A surreal feeling came over me. She'd been living with Theresa for a year, but I understood what she meant. We had a bond. We were special. We both loved Mallory. I got it. I did. I couldn't stop the tears anymore. "I shouldn't know. I shouldn't be the one you told. He's a *cop*, Amanda."

She flinched as if I'd struck her and took her hand back. "I know." Her head sank, almost pressing to the tops of her arms as she hugged herself.

"I should go."

"Stay. Please."

"Amanda."

"Please." She lifted her head. The plea in her eyes stopped me, and I sighed. She wanted to talk about him. She wanted to gush about him. I could see all of that in her gaze. She was a woman in love, and she just wanted to tell someone close to her.

This was going to make it harder. I already knew that, but I heard myself saying, "For a little while."

Relief washed over her. Her eyes brightened, her cheeks pinked, and she bit down on her lip to keep from smiling too much. Her hand brushed away a tear as she said, "Thank you."

I nodded. It was wrong, but we went to the couch and she told me about him. His name was Brian. He wasn't just a cop. He was a detective, and he'd kept going to the diner where she worked. He'd kept ordering the same bagel and coffee, and he'd made sure to go when she worked. She found out from a coworker that he was friends with the manager, so he knew her work hours. Their first date was an accident. She'd been closing the store when he came in. She'd been exhausted and hadn't stopped him when he began helping her clean. He swept the floor while she counted the money.

Their second date had been the same, except he walked her to her car. He wanted to make sure she was safe. It had escalated from there. By the third week of 'dates,' she would sit with him when they'd finished, both having a cup of coffee.

He kissed her after the second month, and they went to dinner the next night. That was their first 'official' date.

She now told me about the first time she'd spent the night at his place. It was a funny story, you see. They'd gotten caught in the rain. His place was closer, so they'd sprinted there, holding hands. She took a shower, and he made her hot chocolate. They'd cuddled on the couch, watched a movie, and ordered a pizza.

They made love that night. It was their first time.

She was so giddy as she told me everything. She deserved to find love. She was an impeccable friend. The love emanated from her. She was so happy.

But a cop. I pulled a blanket over my lap and tried hard not to rip it to shreds. He was a fucking cop.

I couldn't get around that. So I stopped listening to her as she kept going on about him. I could almost hear Carter's voice. "Leave." He wouldn't have sat here, hearing all the details about Brian that made him human. He wouldn't have listened to how his friend had fallen in love and started to feel happy for her. No. Carter would've walked out and dealt with it later.

I had to go. There was no way around it. So I stood up.

"Where are you going?" Amanda stopped mid-sentence in a story about when they'd gone to a carnival.

Maybe he was a dirty cop? But even as I thought it, I knew Amanda wouldn't fall in love with someone like that. He'd be honorable. He'd be genuine. He'd be an amazing person, and that would extend to his job. That was the kind of person she was, so that was the type of person she would love.

"I have to go."

"But—" She stood with me, her hands twisting around each other. "Emma."

I put my glass of wine back onto the counter. It was still as full as when I poured it. I grabbed my purse and went to the door.

"Emma, please."

I whipped around. "What do you want? You know who Carter is—"

"He's out."

"You know what I did!" *Me.* This was about me, too. "Ben. You *know*, Amanda."

The pink in her cheeks fled, and she turned pale, so pale. "I swear I'm not going to say anything to him. I can't. I told you to kill him. Me. I did that. I told you, Emma."

"What are you going to say to Theresa?"

Theresa had never been okay with Ben's murder. We'd all been concerned about her loyalty, but Noah kept her in check. She hadn't said a word, but with Amanda going to the legal side of the law...I wasn't sure what Theresa would do.

"Nothing. She has no idea. The few times I've slept at Brian's have been when she was at Noah's. I've always been back when she gets home. She doesn't know."

"Amanda." There'd be a night when Theresa would come home early and find Amanda gone, even if she did eventually agree to move in with Noah. She'd find out. "She's going to know, at some point. You're not going to keep it a secret. What then?" My voice cracked as I realized I couldn't trust either of the two friends I still had in my life. "Do I worry about her encouraging you to come clean? About throwing me under the bus?"

"What?" She sounded horrified. "No. My god, no, Emma. How could you—how could you think that of me?"

Because that was where this road was going. How could I be the only one to see it? "It doesn't matter. It's done. You love him, and I can see that you really do. I..." *had to go.* Without saying another word, I took my purse and left.

The hallway was so quiet. The building was quiet. It had never bothered me before, but I had never felt so alone as when I walked to the elevator and out the door. When I stepped outside, I remembered I hadn't called ahead for the car.

Thomas materialized at my side.

It didn't matter. They were already there anyway, and he opened the back door for me. I slid in, and when he started to get in beside me, I stopped him. "Please. Can I be alone?"

He pulled back, a flicker of surprise in his eyes, but he nodded and shut the door. The front passenger door opened a moment later and I envisioned the three grown men squashed together on the other side of the barrier—the driver and the two guards together.

Another time, I would've grinned at that image, but not tonight.

I wasn't paying attention to the drive, so when the car stopped and my door opened, I was surprised to find we weren't in Carter's basement garage. I stared at a private plane, the stairs already extended and waiting. I looked to Thomas. "What's going on?"

"Carter called. He'd like for you to join him in New York."

"Oh." For a moment, I thought he might be coming down those stairs, and I'd be in his arms in a matter of seconds. Sweeping that disappointment aside, I nodded and started forward. "Okay. My clothes?"

"He'll have clothes there for you."

Of course. He provided for me. Everywhere. Always. I never needed to question that. I walked up the stairs, ducked inside the plane, and went to the back. As I curled into the bed, Thomas and another three guards took their seats. I didn't question where the other guard had come from. They always appeared, but I had a feeling that Thomas had called Carter. He could tell I was upset. And instead of coming to me, Carter was having me flown to him.

It didn't matter, however it came to be. I lay in the bed and closed my eyes, knowing I'd soon be in his arms. That was where I needed to be.

But I wasn't going to tell him about Amanda. I couldn't. I felt too scared of what he would do. Not yet. I promised myself that. Not yet. And as the plane started down the runway, I was able to sleep.

When I woke, Carter was sliding his arms underneath me and picking me up. He cradled me against his chest as he carried me from the plane and into the back of another car. Burrowing my head to his shoulder, I let the sleep overtake me, and it wasn't long until I woke once more in an elevator. Then we were in a room, and he slid into bed behind me.

He pulled me once more to his chest.

"I love you," I murmured.

He pressed a kiss to my forehead and said, "I love you, too. Sleep, Emma."

I did.

Emma

When I woke, Carter was gone and the whole night felt like a strange dream—or nightmare. It was daylight now, and I had to figure out what to do. But first, coffee.

Padding barefoot down the hallway, I let my nose lead me to a dining room large enough to fit a pool. It was grand. Carter had nice things, but this place was the definition of extravagance. I glanced through the floor-to-ceiling windows and decided this was an apartment, probably a penthouse. I also noticed we were in the heart of Manhattan and forgot the coffee for a moment. Going to the window, I stood and basked in the view. It was so much. I'd been to New York for work, but never like this.

"Remarkable, isn't it?"

I turned and found myself staring at the second-most gorgeous man I'd ever seen in person. Carter was first, always first. This guy was almost his opposite in some ways. He had sleek dark hair, cut short, dark, almond eyes, and a lean face like Carter's. He also had a model's chiseled features and a physique Theresa would've pretended to faint over. He was similar in height to Carter—over six feet with broad shoulders and a lean waist. Actually, he was slightly leaner than Carter. As he moved toward me, I was surprised. He moved like Carter, like a ghost.

I knew without a doubt that this man was why Carter had been in New York so much.

"The view?" I remembered his question.

He handed me a cup of coffee and backed away, leaning against the counter and folding his arms over his chest. I knew what he was doing—trying to diminish his presence so I wouldn't be so intimidated. I grinned, but didn't comment. He could think I was easily swayed by a simple body posture. Instead, I took a whiff of that coffee and almost climaxed. It was heaven.

He laughed, tilting his head to the side. "Carter said you liked coffee. I didn't realize how much."

I grunted. "I'd marry it if I could."

He barked out another laugh. "Well, I don't think Carter would stand for that."

"He'd adjust."

Grinning, he looked down at the floor and shook his head. "Carter said you were quick-witted. I see he spoke the truth."

"Funny. He didn't say anything about you."

His eyebrow went up and he unfolded so he wasn't slouching anymore, which lent a feeling of authority to his presence. He wasn't as dangerous as Carter. I didn't feel that from him, but he was someone, and he could be lethal.

"Because until last week, I was no one."

"That's hard to believe."

"Emma." My name drifted in from the hallway. It came as a caress, and Carter approached me with a gentle smile. He was dressed the same as his friend, in dress pants and a button-down shirt. As he came to me and kissed my cheek, he tugged at his collar, unbuttoning the top two buttons. Lingering for a moment, his lips remained on my cheek, and he whispered, "Are you okay?"

I was suddenly exhausted, so I shook my head. "I don't know." I spoke the truth.

He pulled away enough to see my face and narrowed his eyes. His hand came to rest on my arm.

Oh god. What had I just done with those three words? He would push me later, and even if I didn't say anything, he would know I'd been with Amanda earlier. He would figure it out himself. That's what he did.

"If I ask you to leave it alone, would you?" I had to try.

He turned from concerned to questioning. "As loving you, my job is to help with whatever's wrong. I can't do that."

My hands curled around my mug. Feeling the weight of his friend's gaze behind us, I shrugged a shoulder and whispered, "I'll tell you later. I just...can't right now."

He nodded and moved to kiss my lips. Hovering over them, he murmured again, "I'm sorry I didn't wake you and explain where we are. You shouldn't have woken in a stranger's home. That's my fault."

He held the side of my face as he gave me the slightest of kisses, enough to make me yearn for an afternoon for just the two of us. I wanted to bury my head in his chest and feel his arms as I had when he'd carried me and held me hours earlier. I wanted to feel only his touch. Nothing else. No outside world interrupting us, leaving me cold and hurt.

"I love you," I whispered to him.

"I love you." Then he stepped back, his hand still touching the side of my face for a moment, before falling away. Regret flashed over his features for a split second before it vanished, and he became the Carter who spoke to the guards—or even Noah. This was a different side of him. He'd slipped back into his persona: business-like, professional, and with an air of power clinging to him. He gestured behind him, and his friend came forward. "Emma, this is Cole Mauricio."

Cole smiled. "Refill?"

My cup was almost empty, so I nodded, handing it over.

As Cole went to refill it, Carter continued, "Cole's been away for the last few years—"

"I'm back now."

"—and he's returned to take over the Mauricio family holdings." Carter's tone dropped.

A shiver wound its way up my spine. Carter was trying to tell me something. I shoved all emotion aside and checked back in. *Take over," he'd said.*

Cole returned with my cup. He'd added a touch of creamer and sugar. How he knew I enjoyed it that way, I didn't want to know, but I said, "Thank you," as I took it and stirred it a few more times. I kept stirring, mulling over Carter's words.

Then it hit me.

Cole Mauricio was the head of the family. He had come back. Whatever brought him back was the reason behind Carter's words, a week ago: *"I need to tell you what happened today, because it could affect us."* It was this guy.

"Nice to formally meet you, Emma." Cole gave me a half-grin.

I saw it then. My gut had told me he was dangerous earlier, and I was right. Even now, he leaned back against the counter, but he leaned the way Carter did at times: his back to the wall, his arms open, always close to a weapon if it's needed. And his eyes darted to the door—to an exit.

I nodded again to him. "And you. Carter doesn't introduce me to many people from the Mauricio family."

"Cole." Carter stood.

He excused us with that one word, and Cole nodded, giving him a grin. "I'll be in my office."

Carter took the coffee from my hand. As Cole went down the hallway, Carter led me back to our bedroom. Once inside, he grasped my face and pulled me to him. An intensity took over, and he backed me to the wall. His lips were on mine, insistent, demanding.

"I need you," he whispered, his lips commanding. "You were hurting last night. I wasn't there to stop it."

But he had. He had in so many ways he'd never know.

I tried to shake my head, to reassure him, but his hand raised my shirt. My body plastered against his as my back arched, keeping my shoulders and hips against the door. I wanted to feel him cup my breasts, tease my nipples, but he opened his mouth to kiss me more deeply. I felt him wanting to claim me, getting as close as possible.

I needed him, too. Right now. Right here. I needed the touch of my man. I needed to feel exposed to him, my soul displayed so we could connect on the deepest level. After last night's feeling of impending doom, I needed to be reminded who I belonged to and whose soul belonged to me: Carter.

My mind turned off. I would let him do anything he wanted, as long as he was with me, always with me.

He held me, still pressed against the door, and my legs wound around his waist. My hands sank into his hair, and I gasped once for breath, then I kissed him again. I needed him. Opening my mouth, his tongue swept inside. It wasn't enough. I needed even more. My hand fell to his pants, unbuckling them. He shifted so one of his hands was free and pulled down my pants. At the same time, my hand closed over him. He was hard and ready, and then he was at my entrance. He didn't hold back. It was rough, hungry, and primal. I gasped, lifting my head for air as I closed my eyes. I wanted to savor this, the feeling of him inside me, but he didn't let me. He pulled out and went right back in. He continued thrusting, holding me suspended against the door. His hips rolled against mine.

His finger touched my chin, and I opened my eyes. He stared at me with earnestness in their depths. He yearned for me as much as I did for him. I saw the same desperation and holding his face in my hands, I used my hips to thrust down over him, matching his rhythm. As I did, he closed his eyes.

"*No!*" I insisted.

His eyes flew back open. I needed to see him. I needed to watch him. When I did, I knew what was going on inside him.

He nodded slowly, thrusting harder, rougher, understanding what I needed.

We neared the climax. I felt mine coming. Carter scooped me against him and went to the bed. As I lay beneath him, he pounded into me. I soared over the edge, but I kept my legs wound around his waist, urging him to go as hard and as deep as he wanted.

He went deeper.

He went harder.

Then, as a guttural groan left him, I felt his release. He collapsed on top of me, his full weight bearing down on me, but he wasn't heavy. He was mine.

After we could breathe again, he shifted to the side and pulled me against his chest. "I'm sorry you woke up alone."

I nodded. He'd said it earlier. "I know. It's fine."

He held me tighter to him. "Thomas called, but I couldn't come to you. Then you were sleeping so soundly on the plane. He called again and offered to just bring you here, but I didn't want anyone else to hold you. So I met the plane and brought you myself. We're in Cole's home. He owns this building, and it's very private, but there are five other residents who live here."

"Why are you telling me this?"

"You have to understand. While we're here, you can't leave Cole's home. He lives on the top three floors of the building, but the other floors have people living there. If you go anywhere, you have to have the men with you."

"Of course." He was so insistent. I frowned. What was really going on? "Like always."

"No, not like always. You usually have men with you and others trailing you, but this time, I want all of them surrounding you. I mean it, Emma. If I'm not with you, you don't go anywhere. Cole won't listen to me. I told him his home should be private and isolated, but he refuses. He won't kick the other tenants out."

"It's okay. I'll be fine. But…" I bit my lip.

"What?"

"How long am I going to be here?"

He shrugged. "As long as necessary."

"My job. I can't stop going."

"I called Noah. He said there's work you can do here for him. There's an account you can take over and manage from home, if needed."

"Carter, you can't keep interfering with my job."

"I will," he barked, then immediately softened his tone. "If I have to—if it means you'll be safe. Any other time, I wouldn't, but right now you have to be safe."

Something was happening. Something was changing. I knew, though Carter wouldn't tell me the details. Whatever was going on, it was here, very present with us. Fear like I hadn't felt in a long time began to well up in me, filling my body. *Trust Carter.* That's what I had to do. But then I heard his next question, and the fear crept back up again.

"What happened last night?"

I shook my head. Not yet. "Who is Cole Mauricio?"

"You're not going to tell me?"

"Are you?" I asked right back.

He grinned, his eyes searching my face in a loving way. I felt sheltered and protected. "Cole was like a brother to me," he said.

I don't know what I expected, but it wasn't those words from him. He and my brother AJ had been like brothers. Hearing someone else referred to the same way, a twinge of jealousy pierced my chest, though it was unreasonable.

"After AJ died and I went into the Mauricio family, Cole and I became close," he continued. "His immediate family were the head of the entire organization. His dad. His brothers. Him. The rest are elders, like his uncles, or people like me who aren't related by blood, but are still considered family. For a long time, with the Mauricios, the true leaders were only one family: his. All of that ended a few years ago. The Bartel family started a war and killed every single member in his family. His dad went one week. His mom was the next. Every week, they found another member of Cole's family and executed them. They were hiding, but the Bartel family always found them. His three brothers. Then his older sister. Cole had two little sisters, twins, and both of them were murdered too, until he was the last one left."

I swallowed. Another nightmare had unfolded in someone else's life.

Carter grew quiet for a moment. Then said, "I was assigned to protect him. Cole's a year younger, but with everything I had done, I felt like I was ten years his senior. He was like a little brother to me. They found us one night and almost killed us, but I got us out. I went against the family protocol. Instead of taking him to a Mauricio safe house, I took Cole away."

"Away?"

He nodded, turning over to stare straight up at the ceiling. He was back there, back in his memories. "I cut off all communication with the family and took him away. I trained him, taught him how to be a killer, how to fight."

It began to click into place, why Cole moved like Carter.

"He'd been off the radar for five years until two weeks ago. The Bartel family found him and tried to kill him. They killed two of his friends, but Cole got away. He killed them instead."

Carter had said something happened, something that would change things for us. My blood grew cold as I connected the dots. "The Bartel family moved against him?"

Carter nodded, his eyes hooded.

"And now he's back?" *What did that mean?*

"He's resumed his place in the family." Carter's voice was somber with the gravity of what he said.

"Why are you telling me all of this?" I asked.

"Because you need to understand. It's time you know more. You're mine, Emma. My first allegiance is to you." *But Cole was family, too.* He didn't say the words, but I heard them anyway. Then he added, "Things are going to happen now, and I can't control them. The Mauricio family has always followed me. I saved their leader. Even if Cole wasn't with the family, he was still alive. His uncles and cousins have followed me and allowed me to do whatever I needed. They helped me save you."

Suddenly I realized—he was going back in. A tear formed in my eye, and I ignored it. This was what he was telling me. I swallowed over a lump. "What happens now?"

He didn't answer at first. Then he let out a soft breath of air and turned, his eyes pained. He said one word: "War."

Carter

Cole had slacked with his training over the years. I adjusted, leaning forward, and he didn't catch the movement. Five years ago, he would've been alert and reacting the same instant. He'd grown soft.

His eyes narrowed, and he twisted back on his leg, sweeping out with the other one.

I dodged the kick, but saw his hit later than I would've liked. I evaded both, blocking his arm and knocking him back a step. I should've countered with a hit of my own, but I didn't. Maybe I'd grown soft, too?

No. I smirked at my own question. I wasn't soft. Cole was.

A wicked grin appeared on his face, and he shook his head, falling back a couple of steps and putting distance between us as we sparred.

The room was dark. A single light bulb hung over our heads. Us—no weapons, no audience, and nothing to distract us. Hardcore training. We fought, and we got better. This was how I'd taught him so long ago. I called it night-style fighting. Most times an enemy doesn't make their presence known. They use the darkness to conceal their approach, so a person needed to "feel" them coming before they arrived.

It's what gave my men the "ghost" feel Emma always talked about. It was true. Be a ghost. Fight like a ghost. Disappear like one. That was the best way to ensure you lived.

"Like old times, huh?" Cole flashed a smile, but he watched my feet warily.

I didn't respond. I waited for his eyes to glance away, and when they did, I swept my leg out, tripping him so he fell to the mat. He recovered before he even touched down and shot his hand up. I dodged it, grabbing his wrist, and I fell to the floor as well, but rolled him over with me. I kicked at his hip and flipped him to the side, then wrapped my other arm around his neck. I had him in a paralyzing hold.

Apply pressure and he'd fall asleep. That's all I had to do, but Cole tapped out, so I let him go.

"Shit," he exclaimed, recoiling from me.

I was the one to flash him a grin this time.

As we stood, he shook his head. "I forgot how fast you are."

I shook my head. My quickness needed work. "I heard about the car accident. You thought fast on your feet there." But he'd need to go more quickly. He knew it. I knew it. This training session was for both of us.

He grimaced. "Well, when the car hit the tree, that was a good indicator that I needed to do something." He looked away. "They murdered two of my friends." Then he swung back to look at me, and I saw their memory in him. "You know me. I didn't get to have a lot of friends where I was."

"Did you have others?"

"One other."

"Do you need to bring them in?" Would the Bartel family find them and kill them?

He shook his head as his hands closed into fists. "Nah. It was an old woman. No one special."

"You don't get attached. If you make friends, be ready to say good-bye at a moment's notice. You will get them killed." That was one of the last things I'd said to him before I returned to the Mauricio family and told them Cole would remain hidden, from everyone.

He'd been away for five years. Three friends in five years. I had no doubt that "old woman" was someone special, and for his sake, I hoped the Bartel family wouldn't track her down.

The Bartel family. Cole and I hadn't discussed them yet. First priority had been bringing him back into the family. Then we'd finalize a plan of retaliation. There'd been a few hiccups, making the process of extracting him longer.

Cole asked me now, as if following the same train of thought, "How'd the meeting go this morning with the elders?"

I shrugged. "They'll accept your leadership."

Cole gave a sharp laugh. "I saw a few of them, remember? Before you got here and carted me away. I know some of them aren't happy I'm back. Have you been leading them?" Cole went to the wall and bent down to grab a towel and water bottle. He wiped the back of his neck, waiting for my answer.

"No."

"But they'll follow you?"

I didn't grab a towel. I didn't grab a water bottle. I didn't stretch. I stood there and waited for him to come back. Whether he realized it or not, our session wasn't done. "It doesn't matter what I say. You're the official head of the family now. They'll follow you whether they want to or not. That's how it is. Your bloodline is the true leadership. You'll do well for them."

"Really?"

He was still a child there, needing approval, needing to be reassured that he hadn't been forgotten. He was still a Mauricio. Even if he hadn't been living as one for the last few years, he had been hunted down because he was. Cole wasn't stupid. He knew his return would cause resistance from some of his relatives who had enjoyed their power.

I dipped my head in a nod. "They'll fall in line, Cole. There are too many who respect the old way."

"And you support me."

"That won't matter. I'm out."

His mouth formed a mocking grin. "Could've fooled me."

"I am."

"For your woman?"

"I'm in business with the Bartels."

"And with us, right? That was the deal. You continue to make both families rich so your woman can live with no retaliation."

"Yes."

"And if anyone violates that deal?"

They already had. They'd gone after Cole, and one family couldn't move against the other. But Cole had technically been living outside of the family. They would argue that, saying they hadn't broken the agreement because he'd been in isolation. It was a game now between the two families, each watching the other to see who would make the next move.

I motioned to the middle of the room. "We can discuss this later. Let's keep fighting."

"So you can keep kicking my ass?" Cole tossed his water to the ground, along with his towel, and came forward. Rolling his shoulders back, he raised his hands in a fighting stance.

I held back a smile. When would he learn I didn't fight like that? But instead of saying so, I batted his hands down, swept a leg around his waist and lifted myself in the air. Flipping backward, I used the leverage of my leg around him to pull him over me and threw him against a far wall. I went with him. We were out of the light. He would need to sense my attack.

He didn't.

With one swift punch, I knocked him out.

Emma

You're gone next week too?

My phone buzzed as I got the text from Theresa. I'd been in New York for one week and had remained inside Cole's home the whole time. Carter spent every morning and every evening in the gym with Cole. If he was out late, for whatever reason, that just meant the hour of training got pushed back until he returned. I figured out they were training the second day when Cole appeared with a black eye and swollen jaw. Carter sometimes returned with a swollen lip and a few bruises on his jawline, but that was it.

He would spend the rest of the day out while Cole remained behind. I never asked what was going on, but I overheard Cole asking him one night in the kitchen, "Salba still refuses?"

Carter's voice was quiet, but sneaking closer, I heard him say, "—matter. We move forward as planned. You'll be initiated Sunday."

"And you?"

"Me?"

"Will you remain here?"

Carter's voice was muffled so I couldn't hear his reply, and Cole didn't respond.

Feeling guilty about spying, I snuck back to the room. I had just gotten under the covers when Carter came in. He stopped, shook his head, and closed the door behind him.

"What?" I asked.

"Did you get the answer you wanted?"

"What are you talking about?"

A faint smirk teased at the corners of his mouth, but he sighed and tossed a file onto the bed. With one motion, he pulled his shirt over his head, and my mouth dropped. His face had remained relatively clean after the sparring sessions, but not his chest. Carter had avoided showering with me or undressing in my presence all week, I now realized. His chest was full of cuts and bruises. There were welts over his ribs, too.

"Oh my god." Scooting toward him to the edge of the bed, I stopped right before touching one of the cuts. "Carter."

He looked down, surveying his chest. "They're mostly superficial wounds." He bent and pressed a kiss to the top of my head. "No need to worry about me."

As he went into the bathroom, I followed him. He turned on the shower, and I perched on the counter.

"Is that why you've not undressed around me this week?" I asked over the water. He'd slid into bed late at night, after an hour in the gym with Cole and showering. He kept the lights off so as not to wake me, and he was gone when I woke. When he returned to shower and change, I was working in the office. My eyes roamed over his body, and I ached for him, but not in the usual way. Some of those cuts looked nasty.

He stepped inside, but left the door open and angled his head so he could still see me. His eyes found mine. "It wasn't on purpose."

I tucked my hands under my legs. "Did you get them checked out, to make sure you haven't broken anything? None of those cuts are infected, right?" I eyed one in particular. A red circle had formed around it.

"I'm fine." His eyes slid down my body, lingering where my shirt fell low, revealing some cleavage. "I'm definitely okay enough for you to join me."

I smiled, but stayed where I was. "Maybe later." With him on the bed, me on top, I knew he wouldn't be hurting...too much.

His eyes darkened, but he ducked underneath the water, wetting his hair. I waited until he finished showering, and when he was done,

I waited some more while he dried himself before going back into the bedroom. As he went to the closet, I spied the folder he'd thrown onto the bed earlier. I picked it up and asked, "What's this—" as I began to flip through it. My words died as I saw the first picture.

It was my baby picture.

"What *is* this?"

Carter finished pulling on a shirt and sweats. Both clung to his form in a way that would've distracted me thirty seconds earlier. He said, so gently, "The men told me about that man."

I heard the shout again in my head. *"Miss Nathans!"*

"Oh." I was six months old in the picture. I recognized it because AJ had given me a similar one. Only the backdrop was different. This picture had a tree and flowers in the background instead of a plain white wall. But it was me. Same dark eyes. I had light blond hair then. Some of it curled upward, like it was standing on top of my head, and my cheeks were plump and red.

I'd been happy in that picture. Tracing the image, I murmured, "AJ and I never really talked about our parents. He didn't like to, so I never asked. The few times I did, he got really upset."

Carter sat beside me and he took the picture, examining it for himself. "He never talked to me about them either."

"Really?"

He nodded, handing the picture back. My breath caught at the look in his eye. It wasn't...he rarely looked at me like that, but it was regret and sadness.

"That picture's not of you, Emma," he said.

I frowned. "What?"

He turned it over and showed me the back. Someone had written 1988.

"What?" I was born in 1986. "That doesn't make sense."

"Emma, listen to me..."

I pulled out the other pictures—my old home, a smiling woman holding me—no, I double checked that picture, too. It was me, but dated 1989. I kept going. More pictures. All of me as I grew up. I shook my head. This wasn't happening. AJ had had similar pictures of me, but I wore different clothes. His pictures had been of him and me, different times, different places.

Not these.

Then I came to one and froze. It was a woman. She was older—maybe early twenties—and she was standing with the man who had called my name twice as I got into the car, or at least the man I thought I'd seen. Biting down on my lip, I tried to remember. I hadn't looked when he called *"Miss Nathans"* outside of Joe's, and I hadn't gotten a good enough look outside the gun range. The guard shielded him from my view. I held the picture up for Carter. "Who is that?"

"It's the man trying to talk to you."

On the back of the picture was written Andrea Nathans and Kevin Thorne. That couldn't be, but...I turned it back around and stared hard at the woman. She had my eyes, my cheeks, my lips. She had my face and even stood how I did with her head tilted to the side and her chin up, just slightly. But her hair was lighter than mine, and her eyes were warm, friendly.

Mine were sad. It was a thing I'd noticed as I looked at my own pictures growing up. I'd been sad until...I glanced up at Carter—until now.

Lonely. That's what I'd been.

This woman wasn't lonely, but she had my face. Feeling so many knots in my stomach, I asked, "Who is she?"

Carter didn't answer that question. Instead he said, "Kevin Thorne is a lawyer, and he hired a private detective to find you."

I didn't give a shit about Kevin Thorne. I raised the picture higher. "Who is *she*?" Carter's eyes held mine over the photograph. They were understanding and sympathetic. I didn't want to see his sympathy. I wanted answers. "Carter."

"I've been in contact with the private detective. He's the one who supplied us with these pictures."

But they weren't of me.

"Who. Is. She?"

"He said Mr. Thorne reached out to him years ago. He wanted him to find you, but he never could. He said there were no trails, no paperwork. He didn't understand it until—"

Until Carter. Until my face became a permanent fixture with his in the media.

"—he was able to determine where you worked and also certain patterns. That's how Kevin Thorne knew to wait for you outside of Joe's and the gun range." He hesitated for a beat. "Emma, I had my own guy check everything out. I had your hair sent in with a piece of hers for DNA testing. They tested everything."

"Carter." It was a soft warning, but I was gritting my teeth. If I didn't get answers soon… My eyes flashed. "Cut the bullshit. Who is the woman?"

"Your sister."

I had a sister.

They'd tested, and Carter had said it. I had a sister. I couldn't…

I felt myself becoming numb. "Who is she? Are you sure?" *I had a sister…*

He nodded. "It was a match." His hand cupped the side of my face. "I met you and AJ when we were little. AJ didn't go to school, and I never thought about it. Hell, it wasn't my place to question it. My own dad didn't care, as long as I was out of his hair, but AJ made you go. I remember that now. There was a day you two were fighting about it. You wanted to stay home and play. He wanted you to go. He called you Ally that day."

Ally.

"How old was I?"

He shook his head. "I don't know. You don't remember?"

It was my turn to shake my head. "My memories are jumbled. I remember you coming over and sleeping on the couch. I remember getting excited when you were there and being worried if you didn't come. I didn't even care if you talked to me when you were there. You were there. You were safe. That's what I remember. I hated when you left."

He called me Ally. I couldn't remember.

"You have information?" I asked. "We can get a hold of this Kevin person?" I didn't push about her. I wasn't sure anymore, what I wanted.

Carter nodded, watching me steadily. "Is that what you want?"

"I…" I was going to say it was, but now that I was given the option…I didn't know.

"You can take your time, Emma."

AJ called me Ally.

I asked, my throat constricted, "Did he call me Ally only that one time?"

"I don't know. It was the only time I remember." He paused, frowning. "He called you Alley Cat a few times. I think I did too, once."

"You did?"

He nodded. "I thought it was a nickname, but it felt wrong. I stopped and only called you Emma after that."

"Oh."

Ally. Alley Cat. Now this woman, Andrea. What else had AJ kept from me? "He loved me," I murmured, not wanting to think about why I'd been separated from these people. "He was a good brother."

"He was." Carter covered my hand with his. "He died for you, Emma."

"He fed me. He got me clothes—maybe not the best, but we had clothes. We had a place. I went to school. He was a good brother.

He let me watch television, no matter if he was watching something else. Well—" I flashed a rueful grin. "—most of the time, he let me. He never brought a girlfriend home."

Carter laughed. "He had them, but yeah, he always said they couldn't go to his place. They always went to their place. He loved you, Emma. Don't question that."

My eyes fell back to the picture. She had my smile, with a twinkle in her eye. "Does she love this man?"

"I don't know. The private detective didn't say. Do you want to know?"

Did I? Should I open this door? "I don't think I can *not* know."

"Okay." He stood and bent down to press another kiss to my forehead. "I'll send the word and have my own guy look into this. He'll find out everything."

I nodded.

I had a sister.

Andrea.

I was fully numb. This information had come out of nowhere, and I didn't feel prepared to take it in and digest it. Carter started for the door, but I caught his hand as he went, feeling a desperation I didn't want to admit to. "Where are you going?" I asked, my voice hoarse.

He looked down, his eyes warm with love, and turned on the lamp. Going back toward the door, he locked it and turned the overhead lights off instead of leaving as I had feared. The feel of the room changed drastically. It was instantly warm, intimate, and cozy. A safe haven. He returned to the bed, but instead of sliding under the covers, he knelt and slid one arm underneath my legs. His other arm went around my back and he picked me up, but only to lay me down again in the middle of the bed.

I had a sister.

Carter pulled me into his arms, and as I lay there, for some reason, AJ's voice came back to me.

"Hey there, Alley Cat."

CHAPTER 6

Emma

I found it somewhat ironic that the first time I left Cole's building was because Carter was unwilling to let Theresa inside. He was still protective of our space.

Amanda had been to our building back home once. Noah had come over a few times, but Theresa still hadn't been inside. I knew it bothered her, but it wasn't my call. Carter had his reasons, and they were pretty obvious. He didn't trust her. The rest of us respected his decision, even Theresa, but when I got a phone call from her the next day in New York, we were faced with the same dilemma.

"You never texted me back!"

I cringed, holding the phone away as Theresa yelled from the other end. "I'm sorry."

"Sorry? Sorry? If you were sorry, you would've texted me back. I have problems. I have issues that need talking about, and you're part of the triad. I need the triad. I need the gun range or a really big night at The Octave where I'm going to get wasted. That's what I need."

"What about Amanda?"

"She's only part of the triad. You're the other part. I've decided. We're coming to New York."

When I'd relayed the impending arrival to Carter, Cole offered one of the floors in his building that was open and fully furnished. Carter responded with a firm no.

"Not here. I do not want them to mix with you." He'd been talking to Cole as he said those words, but a deep, ominous feeling passed over me. For some reason, I felt like he was talking to me. I still couldn't shake the uneasy feeling in my gut.

"Okay."

The two looked to me and then Carter nodded once, with authority and finality. "She'll want to see you, but I don't want you traveling back and forth. Noah has a place here. You can stay with them, and I will call in more guards to secure his building."

"What about you?"

"I'll come for the nights."

So I would still have him at night. Relief swept through me. I'd been scared for a moment that he would pull back, spend all his time with Cole, and I would be alone. "Okay. That'll work. Theresa will want to spend the days together, anyway."

"I'm sure Noah is hoping to get work done at the New York Richmond."

"I'm sure."

"You will not go in with him." His eyes flashed in warning.

So I was officially hiding? It wasn't just for this week. "Carter." I moved closer, making my voice quiet. This question wasn't for Cole to hear.

Cole stood, giving me a polite smile, before he gestured to the door. "I think that's my cue. It was nice having you here, Emma. I'd like for us to have dinner before you go back home." He glanced at Carter, at me, and gave another smile. "The three of us."

I reached for Carter's hand as Cole left. "Is the war already happening? Is that why I'm hiding?" Déjà vu washed over me. Like with Mallory, but this was worse. I saw the fear in Carter. It was shimmering just under the surface, and it had him on edge.

"I…" He stopped, then drew me onto his lap. Pulling me so I was straddling him, he rested his hands on my hips and didn't look me in the eyes for a moment. His gaze was downcast. He leaned forward, resting his head into my chest. A deep shuddering sigh left him, and I blinked back tears. I felt his fear then. It was in me, too. Closing my eyes, I wrapped my arms around him and held him. No matter what he said, this war was real. If it wasn't full-blown now, it would be. Carter knew it, and I trusted him.

"Carter," I whispered.

He tipped his head back, looking up at me.

I framed his face with my hands and vowed, with every inch of me, "I will stay alive. No matter what happens, I will."

His Adam's apple jerked up and down. I could tell he wanted to believe me, but that was the fear. "I can't lose you."

"You won't."

"They could come for you."

I shook my head. "You're not in, right? You're making money for them. Why would they want to hurt you?"

His hands rested over mine. "Because it's not about money. It's about power. They didn't kill you before. I handed them a solution on a silver platter, but Cole is back. His presence changes everything. They thought he was dead. It's a matter of time before they find out I'm the one who saved him."

Carter was to blame. That's what he thought. I frowned. "You think this war will be because of you?"

He shook his head, slightly. "No. If the war happens, it's because the Bartel family wants the Mauricio land and assets. That's all, but this isn't like last time. I didn't have anyone to lose." His hand touched the corner of my lip, resting there. "No one knew about you."

They did now. Now he had me to lose.

Oh god. I started to feel a different form of terror. He had to think clearly. He had to be ruthless. He couldn't hesitate. I knew that much. If you wanted to survive, you fought back.

"If something happens, you don't hesitate," I told him fiercely. "For any reason. I will fight back. I will stay alive. I will, but so will you. Got that?"

He gave me a half-grin. "When are Theresa and Noah coming?"

"In three hours."

"Good." He stood, holding me against his chest, and walked to our bedroom. "That gives us plenty of time."

I wrapped my arms around his neck, and my mouth found his. He laid me down on the bed and as he slid inside me moments later, I sighed from contentment. I loved this man. He was scared of losing me, but it went the other way, too. No one would take him away from me.

I wouldn't allow it.

That's how I had come to be sitting in a limousine outside of JFK, waiting for Theresa and Noah with my own bag packed in the trunk. The door to the limo opened, and I shifted down in my seat, unsure who all was coming with them. Theresa burst inside first. She looked haggard, though her hair was pulled to the top of her head in a bun and she had on a trendy black coat. She plopped down and let out a deep breath. "I hate traveling."

"I thought you came in a private plane?"

"We did, and I'm thankful for that, but I'm still exhausted." Pressing a hand to her stomach, her lips pressed together. "I feel a little nauseous."

Noah had been climbing inside as she said those words and, hearing them, he switched to the seat opposite from where she sat. "I'll take this one. Thank you." He grinned at me. "Hey, Emma. Is Carter around?"

No. Carter was where he always spent his time during the day: in meetings with the elder board of a very powerful mafia family, but I couldn't say that. I didn't know what he'd shared with Noah, but I knew Theresa couldn't know. So I just shrugged. "He's got some business to handle. He'll come tonight, though."

The car door was still open, and I waited, wondering if Amanda had come with them. But just as I was about to ask, the driver closed the door and returned to the front.

"Amanda didn't come," Theresa said. "She couldn't get off work, but she might fly out next weekend if we're still here."

"You're going to be here that long?" I asked Noah.

He nodded. "It works. When Theresa mentioned coming to see you, I had something coming down the pipeline with The Richmond, so instead of coming here later, which I would've anyway, I pushed everything ahead."

Theresa beamed at me. "And I get to help you with your account."

"Really?"

She nodded, and just like that, she'd slipped back into the professional Theresa I'd met first and worked with on the bourbon project. She touched Noah's hand before her eyes widened and she retracted it. "He said you're updating the records for a new launch, right?"

"Yeah. I've worked through half the file."

"I'll help with the rest. Once we're done, Noah's promised a full day of shopping." She winked at him. "On him."

He stared at her like a stranger was talking. If he'd been one to show his emotions, I knew his mouth would've been hanging open. Instead, he only blinked at her, his face an impassive wall, but he couldn't look away.

Noticing this, Theresa rolled her eyes. "What? I might be snippy because of our personal life, but I'm still a damn good worker."

"No, I know. I didn't—" He stopped himself. "I...you were very adamant about this being a week of vacation for you and Emma. The two of you were going to be shopping every day and to hell with your work ethic for one week. Your time, not my time. Right? Was that how it went?"

She flushed, folding her arms over her chest. "I was mad. I said things I didn't mean, but I'm a good worker. Emma and I can get it all done, and then we'll have a fun day. Besides, I'll be spending time with her. That's why I came." She turned to me again. "And we'll have Amanda fly out, whether she wants to or not. A fun weekend in New York will be the ultimate girl's trip."

Amanda and the secret boyfriend who could ruin Carter's life, or mine. Yes, that would be lovely. "Just Amanda?"

Theresa cocked her head to the side. "What do you mean?"

She still didn't know. That was the answer I needed. "Only the triad?" I teased. "Just making sure we're enough for you."

Theresa just smiled.

By the time we got to Noah's home, I had shoved Amanda to the back of my mind. I followed Theresa inside and to the part of the house where Carter and I would sleep. We had our own entrance even. That'd be helpful for Carter and his need to slip in and out.

Later, after the bags had been put away, Theresa poured wine for us and said, "I'm surprised Carter doesn't have a place here."

"I am, too."

Noah came in and reached for The Richmond's bourbon. "He does, but he said it's under construction."

Theresa whirled to look at me. I hadn't known. That was the realization she'd just come to. I lifted a shoulder to answer her silent question. Her lips pressed together, and she held her wine in front of her, seeming so casual. But her eyes were sharp and alert. "Really?" she asked.

Noah poured himself some bourbon. He didn't seem to notice Theresa's hidden agenda. "Yeah. To be honest, I thought that was why he was here—so he could oversee it and you know..." He gestured with a hand in my direction, putting the bottle away.

"That's why he wanted Emma here, too. He asked for a few months off for her."

I straightened. This new information, coupled with Carter having his own place, had my stomach churning. A few months? He had his own place? Why wouldn't he want us there? Was it because of Cole? I knew he wanted to keep an eye on Cole, but that didn't feel right. Carter wouldn't have had me there too, if that was the reason... No, it was more than that. He didn't want me at his place—and then I got it.

His place. The family knew it was his. I would bet money they didn't know where Cole lived—not yet—and that meant the Bartel family didn't know. But the Bartels might know where Carter lived...where I would've been. This was Noah's place. I heard myself asking, "Your name is on the deed for this building?"

Theresa turned to study me. She'd been watching Noah with narrowed eyes.

He looked over too, a slight frown marring his face. "No, actually. This building belonged to a great aunt. I inherited it from her. How'd you know that?"

I shrugged. "Lucky guess."

I was still in hiding. If Carter was willing to let me stay here, he didn't think The Bartel family knew of this place.

"You okay?" Theresa had migrated closer. She asked so Noah wouldn't hear.

I nodded, my head moving up and down in a jerky motion. This really was like last year, except it wasn't by my hands. I wasn't hiding because of what I had done, but because of Carter. Last time, I had pulled him in. This time, I was the one being pulled.

Carter

Gene had called for a meeting at one of the warehouses the Mauricio family used for storage. Cole was back at his place, waiting. The initiation was set to happen in twenty-four hours. No matter what went down, Cole would take his place as the head of the Mauricio family. It'd been years since there had been one, but it was set to go. All the elders had been talked with. Their concerns were answered and managed. It was going to happen. But when Gene called for this meeting, I knew he wouldn't be bringing good news.

Too many loose ends right now. I wanted Cole back in so I could tend to the others. Emma had a sister and a man trying to get a hold of her. I'd sent my best to find answers, and I'd thought this last phone call would be him, not Gene.

Now Noah and Theresa were here in the city. That was another loose end I wanted tied up. Even though Emma had been quiet, I knew Theresa was someone she worried about. I'd kept surveillance on her over the last year, listened to her calls. She never met with any press or anyone in the government. Only Noah knew she was being watched. He understood the concern and had agreed, but I knew he was growing tired of the secret. It was one of the reasons he wanted her to move in with him. He wanted to protect her from me, shield her as much as he could, but she was fighting him.

When he'd first told me of their argument, I wanted to laugh. He looked distraught, but dumbstruck. He was in love. I understood. Hell, I grinned to myself now. I hadn't given Emma a chance to think about it. I told her she had to move in, but I'd been worried that after everything was done she would want to get her own place. She hadn't. She seemed content to remain with me, which I was continuously thankful for. But now this long-lost sister was a future concern of mine. Who was she? What was the real story? They'd found Emma because of me. It wasn't a stretch to consider that they might be trying to use her to get to me, or that they were working for the government somehow…

"He's here."

I'd brought Michael with me, and his voice now alerted me to the headlights coming toward us. When the car drew to a halt and Gene got out, I nodded. Michael opened our door and led the way. Another guard came behind me, but when Gene motioned that he wanted privacy, I stopped both of them and kept going.

After another ten feet, my mentor came to a stop and scanned the warehouses around us with a wary eye. He stroked his jaw before he said, "I don't like this feeling."

I knew what he meant. "Until they make a move, we have to be cautious," I said. The Bartels could strike again—against anyone, at any moment. We were all playing the waiting game.

"And Cole?"

"What about him?"

"You've pushed for his place to be reinstated. If he makes the first move—"

I narrowed my eyes. "Which he can. They killed two of his friends. He has the right." And the power. That's what everyone was reluctant to give up. They'd enjoyed having their power, but now it was mostly Cole's. His decisions—unless overthrown by a majority vote—would be the fate of the Mauricio family now.

"I know. We get it. We do, but everyone's nervous."

This was why he'd called. "We've been talking this over for weeks," I told him. "It's time." Too much more time and our family might be dead. "You're moving too slow. Decisions have to be made in an instant. This is the right move."

"He's been gone for too long."

"He's been learning in those years."

"I don't like it. No one does."

It was done. "The time to complain is over."

Gene shook his head. "They sent me to appeal to you one last time. Stop this, Carter. If anyone should lead, it should be you."

"No." *I'm out.* "My job is done. Cole will take over tomorrow."

"You're the go-between. No one trusts him. They trust you."

"I'm out, Gene." My voice rose. This wasn't a point of discussion. "Everyone knows this."

"And if they attack you?"

"Well..." My voice lowered, and I'm sure my eyes grew cold. "Then things will change. But unless that happens, I'm out. For her."

He nodded. "I know, I know." He pinched the bridge of his nose. "People are antsy, that's all. They're concerned. What if he's a bad leader? What if he makes the wrong decisions and gets all of us killed? We all have family—"

"No one understands the value of family more than Cole." *Did I need to remind him?* "His father was one week. His mother the next. Each of his three brothers. Then his eldest sister. His two little sisters. One after another, Gene. It would do the elders good to remember that their own brother was murdered."

"I know." His voice was laden with regret. "I do. I loved William. He was my brother, too."

"And Cole's your nephew."

"I know." His shoulders rolled back as he continued to nod to himself. "I know. I forget. There are others in the family who are..." He hesitated. "They're forgetting, like I am. He's our blood."

I was the outsider, yet they treated me as if I were Cole. *"He's your blood." Not me.*

Sensing the unspoken sentiment, Gene shook his head. "Don't think that. You're just as much blood as him, more even. This family would follow you anywhere, and we have, but you're giving someone a lot of power, someone who's been outside the family for five years."

"I know, but I trained Cole before I left him. It's time for him to return to the fold."

"Yeah. Okay."

"Is this really why you wanted to meet tonight?"

"Yeah. Well, I talked with Anthony. He's concerned there's another traitor in the family. I know we caught the other one, but how'd they find Cole?"

"No." I was the only one who knew where Cole had been. "It wasn't from the family. They found him another way."

"Are you sure?"

"Yes." I didn't want to think about another traitor. I'd almost lost Emma because of the last one. "But if there is one, he'll die." I would kill him myself.

Gene grew silent. He turned to look around us again; the wariness had never left him. "This life, Carter, it gets to you."

I knew, maybe more than he thought. I understood. "I've been watching Cole."

"You have?"

I nodded. "He's ready."

"I trust you." *Not him*, I knew he added silently.

I patted Gene on the shoulder. "You'll trust him, too."

If not—I didn't want to think of the consequences. Cole was supposed to lead the family. The elders would remember this, eventually.

Emma

"Can we talk about the elephant in the room?"

It was the next evening, and Theresa had decided our wine night needed to take place at a nightclub. Noah had intervened, vetoing the club idea, so we were at a five-star restaurant instead.

My guards had walked us to the door, and we were seated immediately in a back corner. Not only did we have privacy, our view was spectacular, looking out over an indoor waterfall. Based on the friendliness of the staff and the fact that they hadn't batted an eye when Thomas walked in first, I suspected that Carter owned this restaurant. But I didn't want to tell Theresa that. My answer would come at the end of the night when I saw whether we got a bill or not.

"What elephant?" I asked, looking around. I didn't know why it was starting to bother me, but I wanted to know where the guards were when they took their cover. I was safe—that wasn't the concern—but their invisible presence unnerved me. But I couldn't see any of them, so I refocused on Theresa.

She was saying, "…you and Amanda."

Okay, what? "Say again."

"You and Amanda." She leaned forward, her eyes sparking with interest. "Did you two have a fight? She was weird the next day after you guys cleaned the oven and had your night, and then you suddenly decide to go to New York. Come on, Emma, like I didn't notice how tense you were in the limo, wondering if she was coming. I saw how you kept looking at the door." She shook her head. "And you were so relieved when she wasn't there."

I frowned. "I thought the elephant was you and Noah."

"Me and Noah?" She'd been leaning forward, but she recoiled now like she'd been smacked. "What are you talking about?"

"He asked you to live with him."

She sucked in her breath. "How do you know that?" Real panic flashed in her eyes.

"Amanda overheard. She told me about it that night."

Her forehead wrinkled. "Wait, is this what that's about—the you and Amanda thing? You talked about me, and that's why Amanda was weird? Did she say anything bad?"

I shook my head. "Just that he'd asked you to move in and you freaked." Like she was doing now. As I talked, her face grew redder and redder. "What's going on? You look ready to flee."

"Oh my god." Letting out a rush of breath, she bent forward and covered her face with both hands. "Oh my god."

This wasn't normal. Carter told me to move in, and I jumped at the chance. The circumstances were different, but I didn't understand the almost-paralyzing effect the offer looked to be having on her.

"Theresa, he loves you. What's the problem?"

I waited. Nothing.

When her hands finally fell away, I saw tears brimming. She sniffled and wiped at her eyes. One tear fell, which she ignored it as it trailed down her cheek. She was thinking about something else.

"Theresa." I reached over and grabbed her hand. "Tell me what's wrong."

"I can't lose him," she whispered. She looked away, but I still heard the words. She moved her head back and forth before glancing to me. "I lose everybody, Emma. Everyone. I was engaged once. Did I tell you about him?"

"What?"

She nodded, a glazed look coming over her eyes. "He died, too. Everyone who loves me dies. Everyone in my family. Jeffrey. I can't love Noah because he'll die, too."

I felt my mouth drop open. She believed this. I saw the fear, and I scooted close, wrapping an arm around her shoulder. "No, no, no. Noah won't die."

She turned into me, but kept shaking her head. "I know it's dumb. I know it's a superstition, but it's how I feel. I'm afraid of being happy with him and letting myself love him, but I do." More tears swam in her eyes. "I love him so much, but I can't lose him. I can't lose anyone. If he went, it would destroy me."

I wasn't sure what was more shocking—her belief that if she loved someone, she would lose them or the fact that she'd had a fiancé. She'd never said a word, but seeing her tears, I could only imagine the love she must've had for him. She looked broken, a side to Theresa I had never witnessed. So many emotions swept through me—sorrow, pain, tears. I wiped my own away and pulled back. "Theresa, you won't lose him."

"I'm terrified."

She was terrified of losing the man she loved. I couldn't help but sit back and reflect on my own situation. Carter was still a part of the mafia, even though he was technically out. He wasn't. He was still in, no matter how he and I were trying to delude ourselves. He was here. He was hiding things, or keeping things from me. He was still *in*. I should have been terrified—Carter had a better chance of being killed than Noah. But I wasn't.

What did that say about me? Was I numb to it now? Or was I really not worried?

Theresa wiped more tears away and sat back, trying to compose herself. I sat and pondered my own love.

Was something wrong with me? Or had I gotten comfortable with the constant fear? I glanced around again and this time, I found where Thomas stood. I caught sight of him behind a post across from us. I didn't know why I hadn't seen him before. Maybe he allowed it this time, like he knew something was wrong. I didn't know, but I looked around again. There was Michael. Peter. Thomas 2, as I called him. My guards. They gave me a sense of security, but I realized that security was an illusion. They were protecting me for a reason, protecting me from a real threat.

I should have been terrified too, but I wasn't.

An unsettled sensation rested on my shoulders.

I swallowed over a knot in my throat. I shouldn't feel secure. That wasn't the truth of my life and sitting here, hearing Theresa's very real fear, chipped away at my reality. I couldn't stop it.

Carter's face flashed to my mind. He was scared. I'd seen it that night when he came to tell me about all this.

"I need to tell you what happened today, because it could affect us… Things are going to happen now."

My hand reached for Theresa's again. Swallowing my memories and the terror I should have been feeling, I said, "If you love Noah, don't waste time."

I had asked Carter later, *"What happens now?"*

I wouldn't let Theresa go. "You don't know how long you might have."

His eyes had been in so much pain as he said, "War."

"Live with him and love him," I told her, leaving off the *as long as you can.* I kept that from leaving my tongue.

Her eyes clung to mine. This wasn't a normal exchange for us. Theresa was my superior at work and a friend, a sister at times. She was professional, spunky, and liked to have fun. But she didn't enjoy facing the world head-on. She liked to stick her head in the sand.

I understood it now. Living life that way, denying the truths and harsh realities, could make you feel secure and sheltered. She looked at life as black or white, wrong or right. This was why she didn't like Carter. He was in the gray area. She couldn't proclaim him as bad and stand in judgment, putting her head back in the sand, because I loved him and Noah considered him like a brother. Noah was Carter's "right" brother—in the world he wanted to go to, not from the world he wanted to leave.

Cole was the "wrong" brother, the other one. His mere existence was pulling Carter back to the wrong way of life.

"Emma?"

"Mmm?" Focusing on her pulled me from my thoughts. My unsettled sensation was still there, and even as I concentrated on my friend, my wine night with her, I couldn't shake the edgy feeling.

"You okay?"

"Yeah." I forced a grin. "Why?"

"Because I'm losing circulation in my hand." She lifted it, and I saw my death grip on her.

I immediately let go. "I'm so sorry. I was just…" *Realizing my own truths.* "My mind wandered."

"You think I should get over it?" Her smile slipped a tiny bit. "Live with the fear of losing him, as long as I can love him while I have him?"

I nodded. "I do."

"Okay." She reached for her wine and downed the rest of it. "Can I get drunk first, though?"

"Yes, please." I laughed and scanned the restaurant for a server. Both of our glasses were empty. A waiter appeared and filled them back up, and continued to do this as we stayed there for another two hours.

I didn't know if it was the wine or the bonding I had experienced with Theresa, but I let go of all her wariness about Carter. It had become a wedge between us, whether she realized it or not, but now I felt the old kinship we'd had when we first began working together. I'd missed this time with her. Theresa was once again my sister, which made me think about my real sister.

Her name was Andrea. And she was waiting to meet me, whenever I made that decision. *Live with him and love him as long as you can.* I had shared this sentiment with Theresa; maybe I needed to follow my own advice.

After no bill came to us, confirming my suspicions, we left the restaurant. I wanted to tell Carter as soon as I saw him. I wanted to say thank you, again, for every time he took care of us at his businesses, but also talk to him about my sister. In a way, it was because of him that she found me.

Riding home in the limousine, I couldn't stop thinking about Andrea. She looked like me in the pictures. She would have memories of our mother and maybe an explanation of what had separated AJ and myself from her. The more I thought about her and considered our first meeting, the more excited I grew.

When we got to Noah's place, I called Carter. I wanted him to come home. I wanted to feel him hold me, and I wanted to share everything I had figured out that night, too.

He didn't answer my call. And after I texted him, he didn't reply. There was no response an hour later, so I went to bed without him. I didn't sleep well. I was waiting for him. I wanted to wake up and talk to him, but he didn't come home that night.

Carter

Late that night, Cole's initiation was final. He was now the head of the Mauricio family. My job was done. I had trained with him twice a day, every day, over these last few weeks. I didn't know if he was ready, but it was done. Glancing down at my phone, I saw that Emma had called and texted, but I didn't call her back. I couldn't, not yet.

"Sir."

I looked up. The door was open, and I got out of the car, heading toward the private plane waiting for me. Once inside, I sat down, and as I clipped my seatbelt into place, I glanced at the man beside me.

"This was your idea, but you didn't need to come with me," I told him. "I assure you that I'll be back as soon as everything is set." Gene had been the one to advise me to return home, make it safe and ready for the coming war.

Gene didn't smile. He only nodded and ran a hand over the scar on his face. He did that when he was uneasy. He didn't know he did it, and I wasn't going to give away one of the only tells I had on him.

"I'm the one talking you into leaving your woman's side," he said with a grunt. "It's common courtesy. I'll go back with you, help as much as I can. Besides, if shit goes down, I want to be at your side."

Gene had been a mentor and in an odd way, he was like my own bodyguard. I knew he hadn't approved when Emma first came back into my life. I hadn't cared then, and I didn't now. I would do as I pleased. She was most important, and Gene knew this was how I felt. That's why he'd been around so much before we concluded the deal with the Bartel family.

I was glad to have him back at my side. He felt like home. Grinning, I shook my head. Gene was not like home. He was large, cold, mean, and distant. Emma was home, but still, I looked over at him. He cared. That's why he was here, and why I allowed him to be here.

"You mean if shit's going to go down, you want to be around the person who will probably keep you alive?" I murmured.

"Don't be a fucker." He faced forward, his jaw clenching.

I chuckled, turning in my seat as well, as the engines were starting up.

Then he added, "Maybe."

"Don't worry. I'll keep you safe."

"Shut it."

I wanted to laugh, but I didn't. Gene was with me because he was concerned for me. Neither of us were dumb. If the Bartel family war was going to commence, I would make a good example. I'd brokered the truce, and I could end it. If they killed me, the war was officially on.

My gut had been telling me the Bartels knew about Cole. They knew he was being prepped to take over, and they'd just been waiting. If the war was going to happen, it would be soon. Either that, or we'd wait for what Cole decided the family would do, whether he would launch his own attack.

"They killed his two friends, but he killed four of theirs." Gene looked back to me.

He'd been having the same thoughts. I nodded. "One of them was Stephen Bartel."

"The last battle was because of Dunvan, but this is closer to the core of each family."

"A Bartel and a Mauricio," I said. Ours had walked away. "We have to wait and see now."

"I don't like it. I don't like any of it."

Neither did I. "We follow Cole now."

He grunted again and shot back, "*I* follow Cole now. You're out, remember?"

I nodded. "You know what I mean."

"You scare me, Carter."

Those words threw me. I wasn't prepared for them, and I didn't respond. I waited. I wasn't surprised at what he said, just at the timing of this statement. I had been teasing him moments earlier.

"A year ago you had your hand at my throat because I disagreed with you," he added.

That was about Emma. I narrowed my eyes. "That was different. It wasn't family business."

"Everything you do is about family business." His eyes were hard. "Whether you realize that or not. You're not out, Carter. You're not even trying to talk like it anymore. Just now you said, 'We follow Cole.' You're still in. You were never out."

My jaw clenched. "Get to the point."

"You're a man in between. You're in one world, but you're trying to live in another. Living like that will make you sloppy, and that makes you dangerous to anyone around you. If you're out, you're out. If you're not, you're not. Choose." He gestured to me, his hand moving in a sharp, savage motion. "You would've killed me last year because of her, but you're the one who's going to get her killed. Make a definite choice. If we're going to war, you need to start preparing for it."

"I am," I growled.

"You're not. I made a few calls. Your woman was drinking wine at one of your restaurants."

My blood ran cold. I saw where he was going.

"She was laughing with her friend. If they weren't drunk, they were tipsy. They drank three of our bottles. And now, where are we going?"

My eyes narrowed. "Stop, Gene."

He didn't. "I know about this sister of hers that's appeared. I can make phone calls, too, and I know that's where you're going right now. You're going to check out this person yourself. You want to make sure she's the real deal before letting your woman anywhere near her. You're running an errand for your lady when you should be stopping all of it."

He was right. My blood turned from cold to boiling. He was right, and I hated that he was the one to call me on it. I should've made these decisions long ago, when I first heard about Cole's attack. I hadn't. I'd wanted Emma to keep living in freedom, as much as she could, but he was right.

"Send her away. She'll be safe. Stop this fool's errand right now. You want her to be safe, but she's not because you've grown lazy."

Goddamn, he was right. "Stop." I closed my eyes. The need to protect her was right there, lying just under the surface. It was right next to the Cold Killer. I was best at assassinating my enemies. He'd been kept in check, shoved down, but as Gene kept talking, I felt him crawling back up inside me.

Gene was right. Emma had to go away. As we flew from New York, I decided I would allow Emma to have a few more days while I got organized. The war was coming. We all felt it. And there were things I needed to do to prepare for it. When I was done, I would call for her, and she would go into hiding. Once she went, I had no idea how long it would be until I could be with her again.

A few days. I would give her a few days.

CHAPTER 8

Emma

When I woke the next day, there was a message from Carter. He needed to fly home to take care of business. I didn't like it. He'd kept his New York home from me, and now he wasn't telling me what was going on. Cole had been initiated, so I knew that portion of business was done, but this was Carter. There was so much I still didn't know, and sometimes, when I was honest with myself, I wasn't sure I wanted to learn all of it.

"Okay!" Theresa came into my room, clapping her hands. "I talked Amanda into flying here. Noah sent the jet for her, so she really didn't have much of a choice."

"It's Wednesday."

"And tomorrow is Thursday. She said she could do work on the plane and then take tomorrow off." Theresa's smile stretched from ear to ear. "We're going to have the triad. I need you, ladies. And you know what this means?"

"We're going to the gun range?"

"Oh." She perked up. "No, but we should do that, too…after we go dancing. Noah told me Carter has a friend who owns a nightclub here, so guess where we're going Thursday night?" She snapped her fingers twice in my face. "Turn that frown upside down and get your dancing face on, because that's what we're doing. Drinking.

Dancing. And....being divas." She laughed. "I had to think of another D word, but it fits."

"It fits you," I told her.

Theresa turned back for the door and waved at me over her shoulder. "I'll take it. I already knew I was the diva in the group."

We were nearing our thirties, but we were going dancing, we were going to drink, and we were throwing the word *diva* around. As I lay back down in my bed, I couldn't stop smiling. I wouldn't have it any other way.

However, when Amanda arrived the next night, my smile had disappeared. I hadn't been thinking about her since I got to New York. My thoughts had been focused on Carter, my sister, and the impending war. Since he'd gone, my thoughts had been only on Carter and his absence, but now Amanda was coming up the elevator, and I kept remembering she had a cop boyfriend.

The elevator pinged its arrival, and Theresa squealed as she went to meet it in the private entrance. I stood and followed at a more sedate pace, as did Noah. Theresa waved her hands in the air in excitement. Noah and I shared a look. Only Theresa.

Then the doors opened, and Amanda came inside pulling a piece of luggage beside her and carrying another large bag slung over her shoulder, along with her purse. Her eyes were wide as she took us all in. She choked out a laugh as Theresa flung herself forward, wrapping her arms around her in a tight hug.

"You're here. You're in New York. The triad is together again." Theresa kept holding her, rocking her back and forth.

Amanda laughed again and stepped back. Frowning, she reached up to shake some of the snow from her hair. "I am, and it's snowing outside. Are we really going dancing? It's crazy out there."

"We are. Damn the snow, I say," Theresa announced.

She finally let Amanda loose so she could give Noah and me a hug. Things felt a little awkward with both of us, though Amanda made all the needed motions so the hugs seemed normal. She searched my face and gave me a small, tight grin before moving back. Theresa linked elbows with her and began pulling her to the bedroom she was going to use. As they went down the hallway, Theresa explained, "Going out is not a chore. You and Emma act the same way lately…"

As her voice faded, Noah shook his head. "She doesn't give a damn about dancing tonight. She's just avoiding me."

I stiffened. My boss wasn't one to share things with me. But I could see the pain Theresa was putting him through on his face. We had never discussed their relationship, but maybe now was the time. "She's scared of losing you," I said. "That's all it's about."

He cursed under his breath, raking a hand over his jaw. "I'm getting damn tired of it. If she doesn't want to move in, she doesn't have to. What does she think will happen? That I'll die?"

"Yes."

He looked taken aback. His eyebrow raised. "Are you serious?"

I nodded. "She lost her family. She lost her fiancé."

Another soft curse came from him. "She told you about him? She doesn't talk about him ever."

"She brought it up, but didn't say much about him."

"He was a wanker. He died in a bar fight. That was the tragedy of it. He didn't die from a car accident or cancer. He got pissed drunk and started the fight."

I frowned. "Does Theresa know he started it?"

He nodded, turning to look in the direction she'd gone. "Yeah, but I get it. He died. Her family died. I get it." He looked at me for a moment. "She's terrified of losing you too, you know. Our association with Carter worries her. She doesn't say anything anymore, and she knows Carter will protect us both, but I know it bothers her."

My eyes got big as I processed that. This made more sense. I patted Noah on the arm, heading for the bedrooms. "Just move her in one day. It's the only way she'll go, and she won't leave. She'll be panicked until it happens, but when it does, she'll settle down."

He barked out a laugh. "My luck, she'll quit her job and move to Bali if I do that."

I chuckled, moving down the hallway to where I could hear Theresa and Amanda talking. He was probably right. I could see Theresa doing that, but she'd come back. I had a feeling Theresa would always go back to Noah. He was her anchor.

Knocking softly on the door, I pushed it open and met Amanda's gaze in the mirror. Theresa held a dress up in front of her, and Amanda had one hand holding her hair up behind her neck. She faced the mirror, and in that moment, pain sliced through me. In a way, Amanda had been an anchor for me too, especially during the mess of what happened with Mallory.

She bit her lip and looked away as Theresa twisted around to me. "What do you think?"

The dress was black, form fitting, and would stop mid-thigh. I spoke the truth. "Sexy as hell, Amanda."

Her cheeks grew pink, and she let her hair fall back down. "Thanks. That's what I go for, sexy as hell on a daily basis."

I perched on a chair in the corner. Theresa grabbed a different dress from the closet and held it in front of Amanda again. "This one?"

It was pink and lacy. Amanda's eyebrows shot up. She paled for a quick second before shaking her head and grabbing the black one instead. "I'll wear this one. I'm good with it."

"Really? You're sure?" Theresa frowned at the pink dress. "Maybe I'll wear this one then?" She glanced at me. "Emma?"

Cue my retreat. I stood. "Oh, no. I'll find something in my room." Making a hasty escape, I heard Amanda's soft laugh, and I paused out in the hallway. A different pain filled my chest. I missed her.

I would miss her.

No. Squeezing my eyelids shut, I told myself I wouldn't think like that. I couldn't. We'd have to figure out the cop boyfriend, somehow. She was another sister to me. At that thought, a yearning washed through me. I wanted to talk to Amanda about Andrea, fill her in on everything, but that meant more questions and more answers that I couldn't give her anymore.

"You okay?"

I looked up. Noah frowned at me, now dressed in a black sweater and jeans. I blinked a few times. Noah was my boss and Carter's friend. He was big and usually grumbling in the background, especially with Theresa, but right now he looked like he'd stepped off the cover of a fashion magazine. I grinned at him. "Theresa is going to go nuts when she sees you."

"Why?" He cocked his head to the side.

"In a good way. You look good, Noah. She's not going to be able to keep away from you tonight, especially if she has a few shots."

"Really?" He mulled that over. "Yeah. Okay. She likes my cologne. I'll put some of that on, too." Decision made, he gestured to me again. "You okay, though?"

I looked at the closed door to Amanda's bedroom. *No*, but I said, "Yeah. I'm fine."

"Carter's coming back."

"What?" I looked at him again.

"Carter. I know he took off this week, but he's dealing with stuff. You know him. He'll be back," Noah reassured me. "Whatever it is, it must've been important."

Carter hadn't called me since he left that message telling me where he was. There'd been a few text messages, but hearing those words, a floodgate opened. Blinking back sudden tears, I nodded quickly and turned away. "Yeah. I know." But I missed him. I wanted him here. He was *my* anchor.

"Emma?"

I turned my back to Noah and closed the distance to my room. "I'm good. Promise." Forcing a cheerful sound to my voice, I hurried inside. I knew I wasn't convincing, but I didn't care. Pressing back against the door, another tear slipped free, and I held my hands to my stomach. It was churning, doing somersaults inside.

I couldn't even think about Carter and what was going on. Noah had no clue. None of them did, and I realized something: Tonight might be the last night I got to spend with my friends. Carter would send for me. Whatever he was doing, he was doing it to make things safe, and then he would call for me. I'd go to him, and everything would be all right again.

I could feel a raging headache starting. It rose from the base of my head, and I pinched at my temples, rubbing in a circling motion. *Amanda's cop boyfriend. My unknown sister. Carter. The impending war.* Maybe drinking tonight would be a good time—my last hoorah. I laughed at that thought. *Fuck it.* I was going to forget everything for a night, just one night.

I nodded to myself, feeling my stomach settle down with the decision. I would have fun. I would, or I would try.

When we left for the club a little later, it felt like everyone had come to the same conclusion. Theresa was flirting with Noah—no surprise. Amanda and I shared an amused look as Theresa's hand rested on Noah's stomach.

She murmured under her breath to me, "What's the saying? She can't keep her hands off her guy? Literally this time."

I nodded in agreement. Theresa was pressed to his side, and her hand rubbed his stomach. He leaned down, bending his head to hear when she murmured something, and locked them in a private moment.

Amanda chuckled. "I have a feeling we won't be seeing much of Theresa tonight."

I grinned. "Good for them, though."

She nodded. "Yeah. She really loves him."

"I can hear you two." Theresa looked at us, pulling away from Noah just slightly. She sent us an accusing look. "We're not deaf, you know."

Amanda waved her away as she teased, "Get back to canoodling with your man. Whisper sweet nothings to him."

Theresa laughed. Her cheeks were red and flushed, and her lips puckered together, as if she was holding herself back from kissing Noah right then and there. Her free hand came to rest on his arm as he turned sideways to face her, placing his own hand on the side of her hip.

Amanda leaned closer to me. "Why do I get the feeling this is the image we're going to be seeing all night?"

I laughed. "Because they're in love, and they're happy."

"Finally."

"Finally."

We shared another grin. It felt right to be on the same page.

"Again," Theresa groaned. "Shut up, you two. I could do without your commentary."

"Then don't canoodle in front of us." Amanda gestured at the two of them. "Look at you. This is prime entertainment. How can we not watch? Our men aren't here—" She bit off her words and looked at me, panicked. Her face paled.

"Wait. What?" Theresa untangled herself from Noah. "Your men? As in both of you?"

Amanda sent me a pleading look, biting down hard on her lip.

"She meant Carter." I leaned forward, blocking Amanda from their view and patting her arm. "She's being nice, trying to distract us all by saying that. And see, it's working." I gestured to Theresa. "This would've lasted the whole drive to the club." I turned back to Amanda. "You don't have to distract me, though. Watching the lovesick couple isn't making me miss Carter," except that it was. I patted her hand again. "Thanks for trying to distract me, though."

"Oh." Theresa frowned, her voice softening.

Amanda closed her eyes and let out a silent breath of relief. She mouthed the words, *thank you* to me before shifting back in her seat and looking once again to Theresa and Noah. "Sorry. I didn't mean for you two to stop cuddling. Keep going. Emma and I will keep up the commentary." She whispered loudly to me, "Do you see that? His hand is shifting, and he's going for the lay-up."

Noah froze.

Theresa frowned.

I laughed. "Two points if he makes the basket."

"Oh!" Amanda snapped her fingers. "He just got the rim. So close."

"What the fuck?" Noah rolled his eyes.

Theresa relaxed and shook her head. "They're making fun of us. Don't worry. It's not really a play-by-play of us having sex."

"What?" he asked again. "What the hell is going on here?"

"So when's the move-in date?" Amanda asked.

I sucked in my breath. Theresa's mouth fell open, and Noah's forehead wrinkled into a scowl.

"Damn, Amanda." Theresa closed her mouth, shaking her head as if to clear her mind. "Way to just dig right in."

Amanda shrugged. "My question stands."

I shot her a sideways look. Where was this coming from? But I caught the swift rise and pause of her chest as she held her breath. I frowned. Was this still about distracting from her slip before? I had covered it. Theresa took the bait—hook, line, and sinker. We'd just been laughing, and now a sudden tension filled the car.

No one said a word.

Theresa shifted and looked out the side of the car. Noah glanced at her, his scowl deepening, then he sighed and leaned back in his own seat. He turned to look out the other side of the car, so now it was just Amanda watching them, and me wondering what the hell was going on.

Those two had checked out, but the car was slowing to a stop, and it wasn't long before the door was opened for us. Thomas and Michael stood outside. They waited as Noah let Theresa out first. He moved behind her, placing his hand at the small of her back. Amanda was next, and she held back for me. As I got out, I shot her a look. "What the hell was that about in there?"

Her face was stony, and she jerked a shoulder up. "It was nothing."

"That wasn't nothing. You seemed fine with them being like that. We were joking even."

"Leave it alone, Emma." The wall slid away, and a haunted expression flickered across her face. The sides of her mouth curved down slightly, and she pressed a hand to the corner of her eye. Her eyelid had started to twitch. "I'm sorry. I—I'm sorry." She started forward, ahead of me.

"Miss Emma."

Thomas held his hand out, and I started forward. The car door shut behind me, and I was soon flanked by two guards, and Thomas and Michael behind me.

Everyone else had gone ahead toward the front door of the club. A line had formed on both sides of the sidewalk with large bouncers keeping people back. There was no rope, but it was evident that people couldn't enter freely. As Noah and Theresa walked through, a protest rose from the crowd.

"Who are they?" yelled a voice. "What the hell, man?!"

The bouncers ignored them.

Amanda was allowed in next and then as I approached, I felt the wave of attention turning my way. I swallowed tightly. I could be recognized any moment, but I held my breath and hoped no one would notice me without Carter. As I walked past the front of the lines, I didn't hear any other protests. Once inside, my shoulders dropped from relief.

I hadn't been recognized, and I'd never thought to look at the name of the club either.

CHAPTER 9

Emma

One shot.

Two shots.

Three shots.

By the fourth shot, Amanda was toasting by herself. Theresa had dragged Noah to the dance floor, and we could watch them from our private box. Amanda took her phone out and texted someone, but then left it forgotten to the side.

When she signaled for a fifth shot, I knew it was time. I'd been waiting since we got inside to confront her again. Theresa had stuck close to Noah, and I wasn't sure if that was why Amanda was pushing the drinks or if she would've been anyway. I sat back and shook my head when she offered me a shot, too.

"Suit yourself." Amanda tipped back her head, downing the drink, as soon as the server left. She practically tossed the shot glass back on the table and turned, her frown becoming a scowl as she went right back to watching Theresa and Noah.

I had covered for her earlier, pretending I'd been missing Carter as I watched the two, but now, my eyes narrowed. Maybe it was her. She was missing her boyfriend. Then I thought, *fuck it* for the second time that night and prepared to go in.

"You're still seeing him?" I began.

She leveled her eyes on me. "What?"

"You know what I'm talking about." I raised my chin and squared my shoulders. This was going to be talked about, whether she wanted to or not. "You're still seeing him?"

"Was I supposed to break up with him?"

I ignored that. "You haven't told Theresa?" I knew she hadn't.

Her eyes narrowed. "Where is this going?"

"You're not a nasty bitch."

Her head reared back slightly.

"But you're acting like one right now," I added, holding steady.

Her mouth fell open, just a little bit. "Excuse me?"

"What's your problem? And don't lie to me. You might be living with Theresa, but I know you better, and I know you're not like this. What's going on?"

"Who do you think you are—"

I cut her off, shooting forward so I was halfway across the table and almost in her face. "Your friend. Your family. That's who I am."

"And you? What about you?" she countered.

I sat back, frowning. "What about me?"

"We're all in this mess because of your guy. He's in the mafia—"

"No, he's not." *He was.*

She rolled her eyes. "Stop, Emma. He still is. You're the only one trying to fool yourself into believing he's out. Theresa's so scared that something will happen to you because of him."

"I went to him. *I* did. Because of Mallory. Because of what I had done. Me. He didn't pull me into this life. Remember that."

"But you're still in, because of him, and where is he? You two hardly go a night without seeing each other, and Theresa told me he hasn't been around since they got here five days ago. Where is he, Emma?"

I couldn't answer that. All I could do was shake my head. "This wasn't a problem before."

"No," she sighed, losing some of her fight. "That's the thing. You're not leaving him. No matter what, we all know that's the bottom line. You're tied to that life, and that means we're tied to it, too."

"Noah is friends with Carter, too—"

"But he would pull away. For Theresa, he would pull away. It's one of the reasons she's scared to move in with him, because of his connection to Carter."

I stopped. Amanda's response was so quick. She was so certain, and there was truth in that statement. I saw it on her face. She wasn't looking away. *They've talked about it.* I sat back, blinking a few times. It made sense. Theresa had confided in me about Noah. Amanda confided about her new boyfriend. I shouldn't have been surprised that they'd confided in each other about me.

"Theresa didn't tell me that," I murmured.

Amanda shrugged. "There are other reasons, I'm sure, but I know that's one of them."

"Noah said that?"

She nodded. "He said that to her one time, and she told me. He's already pulled away from Carter. Haven't you noticed?"

I hadn't. Carter had been so busy with Cole and the Mauricio family. "Their friendship is none of our business. They still train together."

"Not for a month. Noah stopped going in the mornings. He said Carter's been gone, and since we're all in New York, I thought he'd be here. Where is he, Emma?"

I laughed, and the sound was bitter. "What is this? A Carter intervention?"

"Maybe it should be," she shot back, but then let out an exasperated sound and looked away. As she did, she wiped away a tear. Her fight was completely gone now, and instead, she just looked sad.

"Is that what you want? You want me to leave him?" I asked.

She didn't look at me. She glanced down at her lap and shook her head. "No. I know that's not fair. I know everything you said is right. Carter wasn't in your life until you needed him, and it's not fair. Now that you love him, you can't leave him. I'm sorry. I just—I blame him sometimes."

"Why?"

"Because…" Another tear fell. "Because if there was no Carter, I could be with Brian."

New understanding dawned. This was about her and her boyfriend. None of this was about Theresa and Noah, but about Carter and me. And her and Brian. My hand fell from the table to my lap. It hit with a thud, and that's how I was feeling—a bus had hit me.

"Are you thinking of leaving him?" I had considered pulling away from her, but never that she would leave him.

"I have to, don't I?" Her eyes raised to mine. The pain in there was like a second swift punch. I hadn't seen her like this since she'd found out Mallory was dead.

"Amanda," I sighed.

She shook her head. "Stop. I've gone over this, over and over in my head, and that's the only thing I can see as an out. I knew about your relationship with Carter before I fell in love with Brian. I knew it was wrong. I tried to stop it, but I let it happen anyway. This is on me. I should've banned him from the store, but, Emma…" Her voice dropped, and I could barely hear her. "I was so lonely and he was so…" She sucked in a breath of air and used both hands to wipe her face. "It's the only way out. I have to leave him. I have to do it now before…" Another statement she couldn't finish, but I didn't blame her. She asked me, "You haven't said anything to Carter?"

I shook my head. "No. I haven't had the heart."

"Good." She sounded relieved. "Good. I haven't said anything to Brian, and I'll break it off. I'll do it when I get home."

"Now." I said that word, but it wasn't me speaking. It was a different Emma, someone I didn't recognize. She was cold and firm while I was comforting and soothing, or that's how I should've been. Amanda's eyes widened, but I had to say it again. "You should do it now. Get it done. You're here with us. Maybe you could take some time off next week. We could all stay here and help you."

She stiffened at my words. "Theresa doesn't know."

"*I* know, and I'm here." God, I was a heartless friend. I was wrong. I was the nasty bitch, not her, but this wasn't the life we lived anymore. That was the truth about our situation. I couldn't be the friend to her that I would've been before Mallory, before Franco Dunvan. "If you're really going to do it, do it now." I reached over the table and slid her phone so it was right in front of her.

She took her phone. Her eyes didn't leave mine.

"It'll be better this way," I said. My heart was ripping, though. Chills went down my back from the sound of my own voice. I was so hard right now.

"Okay." She held the phone to her chest and slid out from her end of the booth. As she passed by me, she paused and said, "I'm going to need you after this."

I was going to hell. Grasping her arm, I squeezed it before letting my hand fall away. Pushing someone I considered family to end her relationship, that wasn't right. She loved him, I could tell, and she'd never told Theresa. She'd be mourning in silence.

I was a shitty person.

Then my phone buzzed with a text from Carter: **I love you. I'm coming back tonight. I'm sorry for leaving without seeing you first, but I'll explain everything. It took a day longer, but it was necessary. How are you?**

I replied, **Fine. It'll be good to see you. I love you.** As I put my phone away, a tear fell onto the back of my hand. I hadn't even known I was crying.

Two songs later, Theresa returned to the box. Smiling and sweating, she ran a hand through her hair, fluffing it up as she slid next to me. "Where's Amanda?"

"She's on the phone."

"Oh." A small frown and then a shrug. "I hope she stays on it for a while."

"She's not normally like that."

"I know." Theresa cast me another frown as she picked up her drink and sucked from the straw. "Something's up her crack, but I know it wasn't me. She's the one who wants me to move in with Noah. Maybe that's what it's about? You think she's jealous?"

I tensed. "Jealous?"

"Of me and Noah. She's alone. I mean, I don't know why. She's beautiful. I know she's had offers, but she never dates. Is that what it's about? She's worried about when I'll move in with him." Her eyes got big and her hand flung up to cover her mouth. "Oh, no. I can't believe I said that."

"When?!" I teased. "When? So it's happening?"

"Oh god. I just admitted it, didn't I? I said it out loud."

"You did."

She leaned back against the seat and gripped her drink. She shook her head. "I can't take it back. I mean, I'm doing it. I can't believe I'm doing it."

"Speaking of doing it. Where's Noah?" Sending her a knowing look, I asked, "Are you supposed to meet up with him in a private room somewhere?"

She giggled. "No. But, damn, that'd be nice, huh? No, he got a phone call, and I think he was looking for an excuse not to come back here. Amanda's usually quiet, you know?"

I knew.

"And she's usually friendly, always kinda in the background. I don't think he knows how to handle her when she's like this." She scratched her forehead. "Come to think of it, I don't either. Did you fix it?"

"Fix it?"

"Fix Amanda. Did you send her off to get a new attitude before she comes back?"

My heart broke a little more for my friend. She was off ending a relationship and was going to walk back into this? *"If there was no Carter, there'd be no dilemma."* Amanda's words came back to me. Hearing how tormented she'd been, I hadn't known what to say. She'd said Noah would pull away, but maybe it was me. Maybe I needed to do what I'd considered doing before—pulling away from Amanda. I turned with new eyes toward Theresa. Would she be better off without me?

Yes.

The answer resounded in my head. They all would be. That was the right thing to do. Seeing Amanda so grief-stricken, I knew this was the right thing to do. She could still be with Brian, but the phone call—"Let me out."

"What?"

"Let me out, Theresa!" I hadn't meant to shout, but it got her going. She scooted out, and I was right behind her.

"Where are you going?"

"To stop a phone call," I yelled over my shoulder as I ran from the private box.

"What?"

I heard Theresa behind me, but I kept going. Within seconds, as I knew they would be, the guards were around me. The new one who had shown up this afternoon was bigger than the rest, and he moved in front of me, clearing the way. I didn't know his name.

They needed to know where I was going, so I turned to Thomas. "I need to find Amanda."

He nodded and pressed a hand to his ear, speaking into his other hand at the same time. The new guard nodded and headed down a separate hallway. When we went past the exit door, I figured he knew where to go, so I kept following until we got to a back area. The music had faded, and there were fewer people in the hallway. The farther we went, the hallways grew lighter and lighter until I couldn't hear the music at all anymore. Only two staff people passed us going the opposite way, and they frowned at us, but didn't say a word. One girl had a black shirt tied in a knot underneath her breasts. The guy with her had a matching shirt on, and as I looked back, I could see the word *SECURITY* on the back of it.

"Here."

The new security guard was at a door, but Thomas stepped in front of me, holding me back. The other guards went outside, shutting the door behind them. We waited for a moment until a soft tap sounded on the door, followed by a succession of three more taps.

"She's outside, Miss Emma." Thomas moved to stand guard against the door.

"You're not coming out?"

He shook his head, pressing his hand to his ear again. "She's coming out. Mitchell, come back inside."

I heard a soft voice from his ear saying, "Coming." Then the door opened, and Mitchell waited for me to step through.

This was normal protocol. I don't know why I was surprised. As I stepped outside into a back alley, I found Amanda with her jaw hanging down. She leaned against the wall with her phone still in her hand.

I looked around at the guys. They'd positioned themselves ten feet from us at both ends of the alley, and Michael took point at the door. They were all going to be able to hear, which meant this would be reported to Carter—*which you should've done yourself by now*, an inner voice reminded me.

"Is something going on?" Amanda asked me, straightening from the wall.

"I came out to talk to you." *And not with them.* I studied the guards. The conversation I needed to have—it couldn't happen. Plan B. "Don't say what you were going to say to the person on the other end of that phone."

"What?" She looked at her phone, her forehead wrinkling.

"The phone call you left to make—don't do it."

She showed me her phone, and I read the name, Shelly, on the screen. "To her?"

"No. Is that who you've been talking to this whole time?"

She grew sheepish, glancing down at the ground and biting the inside of her cheek. "I chickened out."

"Oh."

"I will. I promise—"

"No, don't. I…" What could I say here? "Don't."

"But…" She gave the guards a meaningful look.

"I know. I'll fix it. I'll make it work somehow." *By leaving you,* but I couldn't say that. That wouldn't be a topic of discussion. It was just going to happen, and by the time they realized it, I'd be gone. It would be done. I'd need help with Carter, but that was for another day. "I promise. I'll make it right," I told her.

"How?"

I shook my head. "Who's Shelly?"

"My coworker. I was asking if she could take over some of my workload for next week."

"Oh." I felt a tiny bit foolish. "Okay."

She skirted between me and the door, then asked, "You hurried out here to tell me that?"

I nodded, feeling my throat tighten. I rasped out, "Yeah."

"Do you mean it?"

"I do." A little hole had formed in my chest, and I felt it growing as this conversation continued.

"Thank you, Emma."

I couldn't talk. I knew what this meant, what I was saying. Even if I changed my mind, she might not be willing to end it with Brian. Love was powerful. I had been given a blessing. Amanda had felt a moment of weakness, but it wouldn't come back. I could see the relief in her eyes. It was so strong. She loved this guy with everything in her, and Amanda had never loved a guy before. She'd dated a couple, but that had been it. There'd been no mention of love. My soul mate couldn't be the reason she had to give hers up, and I hoped, right now, that he'd be that to her—her soul mate.

I was giving my family up for him. He'd better goddamn well be.

"Theresa and Noah are still inside?" she asked.

I nodded. "We should go back."

Amanda grabbed my arm. "I mean it, Emma. Thank you." She pulled me in for a hug and murmured, "I really love him, a lot."

I hugged her back. "I know you do. I can see it."

And then the ground shook underneath us, and a force hit us, throwing us to the ground. I looked up, my ears ringing, and saw one of the guards standing over me. I couldn't hear anything. I couldn't feel anything either. Everything was numb at first, and I tried to look for Amanda, but then the pain hit me.

I sat up, coughing as more and more pain sliced through me. It felt like a thousand knives were trying to cut their way out of me. Feeling wetness on my hand, I held it up and saw blood. Then the ringing almost doubled.

But I heard one shout, one word, come through it: *Bomb.*

Emma

The pain didn't subside. It felt like I'd been lying there for hours before Thomas reached down and picked me up. He started running somewhere with me, but where was Amanda? I tried to look around for her. When I couldn't see her, I tried hitting Thomas' chest to get his attention. He ignored me and kept running. With each step he took, pain jackknifed all through me. I kept coughing up blood. I needed Carter.

"Amanda," I whispered. But my lips couldn't move. They hurt. Every inch of me hurt. Then Thomas turned the corner, and I saw that a crowd had formed across the road. People were backed up against the building. All were pale. Tears in their eyes. Hands covering their mouths. One girl ran from behind us to their side and was swept up by another girl. Both were crying, but their relief was evident. They were happy to have found each other.

"Car," Thomas barked to someone, careening past the crowd at a breakneck speed.

My friends. They had to get my friends.

Then he stopped and bent down. There were shouts all around us. A swarm of others surrounded the car. Were we under attack? I tried to look, but the men who had rushed to us had their backs to us. They were acting as a human shield, but I could see someone coming to us. I could see him through the human wall. They moved aside for him. He wore a black sweatshirt with the hood pulled up and black pants. His eyes were fierce and his jaw clenched. He was cold and livid at the same time. A sliver of recognition went through me, but this wasn't Carter. It was Cole.

Thomas waited for him, but my friends—Amanda. Noah. Theresa—where were they? I tried to lift up so I could see. They might already be inside the car, but I had to see—as I moved, a scream tore from me. I didn't recognize it as mine, but I knew it came from me. It sounded like a wounded animal.

"No, Miss Emma."

Thomas tried to urge me back down, but I refused. I shook my head, knowing fresh blood and fresh tears streamed down my face. As I wrapped my arms around his neck, I brushed against his face, and I tried to bite down on my lip to keep from crying out again. I failed. I couldn't stop another guttural cry, but then I looked past the men. *My friends.* Where were they? I couldn't see them. It was just the men, so I looked past to the crowd and froze.

Every part of me held still; my pain was forgotten for a moment.

It was me. Standing across the road, pressed against the wall with terror in her eyes. It was me.

I lifted my head higher, confused. Was I over there? Was this an out of body experience? I needed to see more. Her eyes locked to mine. They were full of tears, and she pressed her hands against her mouth. Then she began shaking her head, and someone cradled her shoulders. She turned toward the man next to her, and his hand lifted to support the back of her head as he held her to his chest. After a moment, she turned so she could peer over his shoulder at me.

But then Cole blocked my view as he stood before me with his hand raised in the air.

He was scared. There was nothing to indicate this, but I sensed it, because it was in me too. I was scared.

I needed Carter.

Cole's hand touched the back of my head, and Thomas got into the car. Cole was protecting me, so my head wouldn't hit the car, and then we were inside.

"Are you coming?" Thomas asked him.

Cole shook his head. "I'll be there later. I'm needed here now."

"My friends," I gasped out, finally able to form the words. "My friends." Even as I spoke, I strained to see across the road. I couldn't see her now, but I needed to. It was me, but it wasn't. That made no sense.

"We'll find your friends." Cole stepped back and shut the door.

"No." I pushed up from Thomas' chest. But I couldn't. I was too weak. Instead, I lay down and looked up at him, pleading. "My friends, Thomas. Are they okay?"

"Amanda's already in another car."

Oh, good. Relief swept through me, calming me a little. "Theresa and Noah?"

"Cole will find them. He'll take care of them."

The car sped away then. It wouldn't be until later that I wondered why Cole was even there. In those moments, so much didn't make sense. That woman—I couldn't get her out of my head. She lingered with me, in the back of my mind, as I was taken to a private clinic. Amanda was already there, and a doctor had taken care of her by the time I limped inside. When she saw me, she choked on a sob and rushed over.

"No, Miss Amanda." Thomas swung his arm out, keeping her back.

"I won't hurt her," she rasped.

"Place her here," the doctor said, and after that, everything was cold and pure agony. He poked and prodded me thoroughly to assess my wounds before cleaning them up. Amanda stayed with me the whole time, holding my hand. She didn't say a word. Neither did I. No one spoke except for the doctor, who asked me questions as he checked me over.

When his assessment was done, he'd determined I had a few sprains from the impact and a significant cut inside my mouth, which is why I'd been coughing up blood. But the cut had stopped bleeding now, so nothing more was needed. He bandaged me, gave me a painkiller, and wrapped a clean blanket around my shoulders before Thomas helped me to the car. Amanda never let go of my hand.

Back in the vehicle, I kept a death-grip on her hand and asked Thomas, "Where are we going?"

"Back to your friends' place."

Amanda squeezed my hand. "Are they okay?"

"They're there. They're fine."

"Thank god," she whispered. More tears slipped from her eyes.

I wanted to reach up and wipe them away, but my other arm was wrapped in the blanket, and the medication made me so sleepy.

Then she asked, "And Carter?"

"He's coming," Thomas said after a moment.

"Good," she said, anger clouding her face. "Good. Whoever did that, they need to be found." She looked Thomas in the eye, and a dark message passed between them.

I pulled on her hand, needing to get her attention. A thought had occurred to me. When she glanced down, I said, "Don't call your boyfriend." *He couldn't come. He couldn't know.*

She nodded. "I know. I know, Emma." She looked back to Thomas. "I mean it. Find who did this."

"We will."

When we arrived at Noah's place, I limped up the stairs. Noah and Theresa waited for us just inside the door.

"Oh my god," Theresa cried. "Is she okay?" She looked at Amanda. "What happened?"

Amanda shook her head. "Not yet. Questions can be answered later. Thomas, help her to the bedroom."

I shook my head. The painkillers had fully kicked in, but I wanted answers, just like all of them. I needed to know what happened. "No, no."

He helped me down to the bed, and I sat up.

"Lay down, Emma." Amanda was beside me. Her hand went to my shoulder, but she jerked it back before it touched me. It formed a fist, trembling, then she forced her fingers open again. Her palm barely grazed me. She was scared to touch me. "You need to rest."

I wasn't Mallory. I wanted to growl at her, but a mewling sound came out. I shook my head. Thomas placed a blanket over me, but I threw it back. I wouldn't sit there like a victim. I wasn't helpless.

"Emma!" Amanda stood, panicked. "Stop. Please."

I kept shaking my head, pushing myself to the edge of the bed. "It's a few sprains and a cut. I'm fine."

"You haven't seen yourself, Emma." Theresa spoke up from the doorway. "You look like you *were* the bomb. Trust me. She's not overreacting."

I was fine. The doctor had said so, and I shoved myself upright. I shouldn't walk on my own, but I would if I had to. "I need answers."

Theresa sighed. "Fine. We can all talk in the living room. Can you help her to one of the couches?"

He looked back down at me, torn, but he did. When I sat down, Amanda sat next to me.

Theresa stood back, wringing her hands. "I need to do something." She looked at Amanda. "I have no idea what to do. What do I do?"

Amanda leaned forward and tucked a strand of my hair behind my ear. "Do you have broth or tea without caffeine? I think you could heat some up for her. That would help."

"Good idea. I'll do that."

Suddenly, Thomas pressed a hand to his ear, listening to something. It was so quick. His hand fell almost as soon as he'd touched his ear, and he turned to the guard closest to the door. "Open the door. Let them in."

Theresa had turned, starting for the kitchen. Now she froze.

"What?" Noah called, craning his neck to see.

"What's going on?" Amanda scooted to the edge of the couch.

Thomas ignored everyone. The guard yanked open the door, and another wave of security guards came in. They spilled out into the living room and kitchen, continuing on to every room. After a moment they began to return, barking out, "Clear." Echoing calls came from the other rooms. All the same word. They were dressed like my own guards, in black clothing, but their guns were held upright, ready to shoot if needed.

"What the hell?!" Noah's voice was sharp. "What the fuck is going on? Who are these people?" he tried to ask Thomas, who continued to ignore him.

Thomas waited until the last guard had returned to the room. Then they filtered back outside until only two remained. One took point in the living room, standing between our room and the kitchen. The other went to the door, standing beside the wall, and then the door opened again.

Cole came in.

His hooded sweatshirt was gone. Instead, he wore a black long-sleeved shirt, but it was bulky, and I could tell as he came toward me that he wore a bulletproof vest, too. When he stopped in front of me, no one said a word. Theresa and Amanda's eyes were glued to him, while Noah glanced from Cole to me to Thomas and back again. His hand kept clenching, unclenching, and forming a fist again. He clearly didn't know what to do, but he kept quiet, and I knew why.

It was clear that my guards knew this man, and that meant he was someone important.

Looking back at Cole, I realized he was waiting for me. Gone was the cold and livid look he'd had earlier. Now his anger lurked under the surface. Like Carter, a lethal aura emanated from him. But this wasn't Carter.

Where was Carter?

I closed my eyes as a wave of longing came over me. Forgetting everyone in the room, everything that had happened, even the woman who looked like me—in that moment I wanted him so badly I tasted him. I could feel him. I remembered the feeling of being held in his arms, hearing his voice as he whispered he loved me.

I wanted him there, no matter what.

"Okay." Theresa broke the silence. "Who the fuck are you?"

"Theresa," Noah said. He held a soft warning in his tone.

"What?" She gestured to Cole. "He stormed in here, and now he's not saying a word. What the *hell* is going on?!"

"They all know him. Connect the dots."

She stopped, readying another retort, but looked around the room instead. "Oh."

"Are you okay?" Cole asked me.

Thomas moved to my side. "You shouldn't be here," he said. "Carter wouldn't want you here."

Cole met his gaze. "The woman he loves was hurt at my club tonight. Nothing would keep me from making sure she was all right. She's in my city. She's my responsibility."

"So you know Carter?" Amanda asked, more to herself. She had been watching the exchange, but looked back down at her lap.

"I'm fine," I said. My voice was firmer this time. It didn't come out as a weird squeak. "Carter's coming back anyway, but I'm fine. What happened?"

"Wait a minute. That was your club?" Noah stepped forward. He loomed over Cole, or he should have. He was taller and larger, but Cole's complete stillness somehow outmatched Noah instead.

"It's my family's club, but mine now." Cole narrowed his eyes. "Did you not know the name?"

"The name…" Noah trailed off. "Fuck me."

Amanda looked at Theresa. "I didn't pay attention. What was the name?"

Theresa's shoulders dropped as she realized it, too. "Mauricio. That's the name of the club. We didn't—I didn't even put two and two together."

"Carter said he knew who owned it, but I never considered." Noah shook his head. "We wouldn't have gone there if we'd known."

I tuned them all out. I didn't care whose club it was. "Was I the target, or was the club the target?" I asked Cole.

"The bomb went off in the back of the club. If you'd been closer to the door, you would've been killed." He glanced at Thomas.

My gaze jerked over to him, too. There had been guards on the other side of the door, at least two. "Thomas…"

He looked at the floor, shifting away from me slightly. I got my answer.

Those men were gone. We'd lost two of our men. I gasped, a new pain filling me. Those men had died because of me, for me. "I'm so sorry, Thomas." Looking at Michael, I repeated, "I'm so sorry."

"What? What's happening?" Theresa's head swiveled around. "What happened?"

"Theresa," Noah murmured. "They lost some of their men."

"Oh!" Her hand flew to her mouth. "Oh my god."

Amanda gripped my hand again, flicking a tear from her eye with the other one. "I'm sorry, Emma," she whispered.

They were Carter's men, and they were all like brothers. I didn't know the ins and outs of their operation, but I knew Carter would be wounded when he found out. He trusted his life and mine to them. I nodded, but it hurt to move. The numbness was going away. Suddenly it hurt to breathe again.

I didn't want to be there. It was too much. I patted Amanda's arm, as tears swam in my eyes, blurring my vision. People had died because of me. It hurt to be there.

"Emma?" she asked.

"Bed. I just want to go to bed."

She nodded, looking at Thomas, who came over to help me down the hall.

Once I was underneath the bedcovers, Amanda helped the rest of the way. She waved Thomas off, saying, "I'll help her. This is what we do."

He nodded and headed back outside, but before the door closed, Theresa came in with a cup in her hand. She placed it onto the bed stand and asked Amanda, "What can I do?"

Amanda slid into the bed next to me. "Listen to them out there. Get all the information you can. Emma will want to know later. She's in mourning right now."

"Okay. I can do that."

I closed my eyes, but I could feel her gaze on me.

"I'm so sorry, Emma," Theresa whispered.

A tear slid down my face.

"She needs Carter," Amanda said. "I'll stay with her until he comes."

"Okay." Theresa moved away, then murmured from the door, "Love you guys."

"Love you, too."

The door closed, and Amanda asked, "Do you want the light off or on?"

"On." There was no question about it. Definitely on.

"Okay." She lay down and held my hand.

I just hurt. That's all I knew then. I might've slept, but I had no idea. I just hurt.

Carter

Though every phone on the plane seemed to ring at once, it was Gene who told me about the bombing. I knew something was wrong, and when I picked up my phone I expected Thomas, but before I could speak into it, Gene thrust out his hand, an unspoken command to wait. So I did.

When he hung up, he wasted no time. "There was a bombing at the Mauricio."

I knew then. The family's nightclub. Theresa was in New York. The question about Emma was forefront, but I searched my mentor's gaze. He hid nothing. He looked back at me, gazing steadily, and there were no shadows in his depths. I would've been able to see it if anything had happened to her. But still I asked, "She was hurt?"

He didn't answer. He couldn't.

My phone rang again, and I answered this time. "Is she hurt?"

Cole hesitated the briefest of seconds. "From what I've been told, only a few sprains, and she had a cut in her mouth."

Okay.

She was fine.

The storm brewing inside me didn't rage, but it was there. It simmered.

I asked my second question. "Was she the target?"

"God help us," Gene muttered beside me.

I ignored him, waiting for Cole's answer

"We don't know. The bomb was left in a bag at the back of the club. She was outside talking with a friend. If she was the target, that was the closest they could get to her. If she wasn't the target, it might've been left as a warning to us? They might've been hoping not to kill as many as they did." He sounded wary. "We can't know for sure."

"She was outside?"

"In the alley."

I knew the layout. My men would've positioned themselves all around her, which meant some of those men were close to the blast. I didn't say anything about them to Cole. He was family, but he wasn't in that family. Those men were mine and Emma's. They would be avenged. I didn't need to think about that vow, I just breathed it.

The storm kicked up to a low boil.

"Where is she?"

"At the friends' that you told me about. I went and checked on her."

He'd made himself known to them. Noah, Theresa, and Amanda now knew about another player in my life. I gripped the phone tighter, but kept my voice even. No reaction. "She was fine?"

"She was. Her friends were taking care of her."

I knew why Cole had gone. Emma was my life. She'd been left behind in his city. He felt an allegiance to me and needed to see for himself that she was fine. I understood it, but I wasn't happy about it.

"Cole," I murmured.

"Yes?"

"Do not ever go near those friends again."

There was silence for a beat. "Carter?"

"If my men are with her, she is fine."

"I went to see for my own eyes—"

I cut him off, holding the phone so damn tightly now, "I know. That's not needed."

He grew quiet. "I owe you my life. This is my city—"

Another interruption. "You don't owe me anything. You owe the family everything now. I am not your priority. They are."

I saw Gene turn his head to look at me. I'd cut Cole off, but what I said was true. His first priority was to the Mauricio family, not my family. It pained me to say this, but Emma wasn't and shouldn't have been his focus. He should've checked on her the next day.

He was silent on his end of the phone, which was fine. I expected nothing else. "Am I right to assume the bomb came from the Bartel family?"

"Carter."

He didn't answer my question. "You need to make sure it was from the Bartel family."

"Carter."

"What?"

"I will never apologize for checking on your woman, and I *will* do it again."

I closed my eyes. I shouldn't have wanted to hear that, but I was proud of him anyway. "You need to plan your next move," I told him.

"I already have." He paused a moment. "Was your trip home worthwhile?"

"Yes." I glanced to Gene, who didn't hide that he'd been listening to the conversation. He lifted an eyebrow, and I said, "Very."

"Good. Now go home to your woman, Carter. She needs you. And no, this family does not."

Not yet.

I heard the hesitation from Cole's end, and felt a slight grin inside. Cole had been outside of the family before, when the Bartels first attacked. He was now back in the family, and they dropped a bomb in the nightclub. Whether Emma was the target or not, it had happened in a family business. I knew what Cole's message was. I was still out. But despite what he wanted, it wouldn't last. I knew this. Gene knew it. We'd gone home to take steps for when I was pulled in. Now I flew back. I had to take care of Emma now.

"I'll talk to you later."

Cole chuckled from the other end. "I'll be seeing you. You're a lucky man, Carter."

As I hung up, I turned to Gene. "Your nephew will be a good leader."

He laughed. "He put you in your place, that's for sure."

We both wore a grin, but it wasn't a laughing matter. Once our plane landed, Gene went to his family and I went to mine.

When I entered Noah's home, the lights were off, except for a few lamps in the corners, and I heard a murmur of conversation from the master bedroom. Noah and Theresa must've still been up. But I went straight to the bedroom Noah had told me he would put her in, and when I opened the door, there she was.

My world righted itself once again.

She lay a bit awkwardly on her back with her head turned to the side. She must have chosen her position based on her injuries. Her hand rested on top of the covers, her fingers entwined with Amanda's, who lay next to her.

I stood and watched. I wanted to pull her into my arms, take her from Amanda's side, and protect her from the world. That's where I should've been instead of leaving her. My jaw clenched, and the storm began inside me again.

I should've been here.

It should've been me holding her hand the entire time, not Amanda, though I was grateful for her presence.

Then Amanda's eyes opened. She didn't start when she saw me, just smiled slowly and sat up. Untangling her hand, she whispered,

"She'll be okay. She's just missing you."

I nodded. I didn't trust myself to speak. I shouldn't have gone away. "Thank you," I finally managed.

She slid out from the covers. Coming to me, she asked, "Can I talk to you? Outside?"

No. Inside I raged against the idea of leaving Emma again, but I nodded and followed her back to the hallway. With the door shut, she said, "Do we need to be worried about her?"

I didn't ask what she meant. Amanda and Theresa were smart. They both knew something was going on. Instead, I nodded. "Yes."

She sucked in her breath. "I didn't think you would admit it."

"Would you rather I lie? I can do that." I didn't bat an eye.

"No, no." She shook her head, folding her arms over her chest and hugging herself. "I...What are you going to do?"

"Never leave her side."

She searched my eyes, but that was the truth. Emma was hurt. It was my fault.

"Thank you for being here with her," I said.

She grimaced, looking pained. "Has she said anything to you about me? About my relationship?"

Ah. So Emma knew. I shook my head. "No, but I wasn't aware that she knew."

Her eyes got big. "You know?"

"Brian Camden is a good cop. Yes, Amanda. I have taken extraordinary measures to protect Emma, and that includes watching you and whose bed you share."

She sucked in her breath, pressing a hand to the side of her face. "My god. Hearing you say it like that—I love him."

"I know."

She wiped her hand over her eyes. "I was going to break up with him tonight, but Emma stopped me. That's why she was in the alley with me. She ran out there to stop me. I couldn't go through with it. I love him too much. Do I…" She turned away, but I heard her anguish. "Are you…"

"Am I going to kill him? Is that what you're trying to ask?"

She nodded, jerking her head up and down. She couldn't say the words.

The irony that a woman who had comforted my soul mate was asking if I was going to rip hers apart wasn't lost on me. And I told the truth, "No."

Her shoulders had lifted, tensing, but they dropped at my answer.

I added, "But I will if he starts investigating me or Emma. I won't hesitate."

She didn't answer. She couldn't look at me, and I was sure she couldn't respond to that. It wasn't a threat. It was fact. I would have it done, if needed. Sometimes I was a cold bastard, but I wasn't heartless, not unless I needed to be, and with that, I gentled my tone. "Thank you again, Amanda."

She looked at me now. I had no bags, and I still had my coat on. She glanced back to the main entrance and saw Thomas waiting. "You're taking her with you, aren't you? You're leaving tonight."

All the men were downstairs, waiting in their cars. "Right now."

Thomas started forward, but I held a hand up. I would get her. I would carry her. That was my job. He nodded, stepping back, and I went back into the bedroom. I lifted her from the bed, bedcovers and all, and walked through the door as he held it open.

I'd sent word to have her bags packed and ready, and Thomas had messaged me, even before our plane touched the ground, that everything was cleared to go. They had only been waiting for my arrival.

Emma didn't move. But once she was in my arms, I felt her body relax. She remained asleep during the car ride to my place, and when we arrived, I lifted her again and carried her into our room.

Before I went to bed with her, I checked my entire home—every window. Every door. Every inch of my house. And my men checked the land around it. Then I went to my office and opened the back closet. A wall slid away, revealing an entire closet of guns and ammunition.

I took out a 9mm and silencer, then pocketed two boxes of bullets and closed it all back up. Going to bed, I placed the gun onto the nightstand and turned to pull Emma into my side.

I held her for the rest of the night.

Emma

I knew he was there, even before I opened my eyes. It was his smell, the feel of his body beside me, the way his arm held me to him. I smiled, feeling a rush of excitement surge through me. He was home, and I turned, savoring what was next.

There he was. Nestled next to me, his eyes closed and his breathing even, he was asleep. His hair was a little messed, flattened from the pillow, but he was adorable. That wasn't a word I would usually use to describe Carter. He was gorgeous. He was stunning. He was lethal. But not adorable, and that's why I relished this moment. His walls were gone, and it was just him, the real him at his most vulnerable.

I let out a silent breath.

I loved him so much. I wanted to wake him, but I also didn't at the same time. He looked like a little boy, all his guardedness gone. His eyelids were soft, the lines around them a little smudgy from sleep. I knew all that would go away when he woke. He'd become alert and ready to take on the world. He would become a predator.

But not yet. For now, he was just mine.

Then, after a moment, his eyes opened, and my heart skipped a beat. It was cheesy, but it was real. And I laughed because of it.

"Hey, you," he murmured, lifting a hand to tuck some of my hair behind my ear. His hand lingered on my cheek, and his thumb brushed back and forth.

It was such a loving gesture. I felt warmth fill my body, all the way to my toes. This. I loved this about him, along with so much else.

"How are you feeling?"

I shook my head. "Nope. I'm not answering that because I haven't moved. If I don't move, I won't feel any pain, right? Then I can just stay here and look at you, and everything's okay."

He laughed softly, then sighed as his hand fell away from my face. "I love you."

"I love you, too." And I wasn't going to cry. I'd done enough of that. "Where were you?"

He sighed again. "I had things to do, but I'm back. I'm so sorry I wasn't there."

"Nope. We're not talking about it. Not moving. Not talking about it. Just staying here in bed all day." I sent him a blinding smile. I knew it was ridiculous. It wasn't going to happen, but of all days to hide away from the world, this was the day. And he was finally back.

"I really am sorry." His voice deepened, and I heard the emotion there. "I had to get things ready, for this war." He hesitated before adding, "For your sister."

My sister. My mouth fell open. Why hadn't I considered that before? "I saw her."

"What?"

"Outside the club last night. She was there. She saw me." She'd been crying. "I think she felt bad. She was across the street, part of the crowd watching everything."

"What?" He sat up, staring down at me now. "She was there?"

I nodded, and fuck—that hurt. "Yeah. Carter, she looks just like me. I thought it was me for a second. I was confused, but now—it was her. I know it." I thought for a moment. "I might've been recognized when I went in. Maybe? It's not that long of a trip from home. One hour on plane. Maybe..." But that felt odd. She was crying. I couldn't get that out of my head. "Carter, she looks just like me."

I couldn't get her out of my head.

Then I noticed the wall—it was gray. The walls at Noah's place were tan. I kept looking around. A closet. A fireplace across from our bed with a television mounted on the wall and a desk built in. There was a door that I assumed led to a bathroom or a closet, or both. I didn't know, but I turned back to Carter. "Where are we?"

"My place."

"*Your* place?" The one he'd kept a secret.

He nodded, hesitating for a moment. "I brought you here to be safer."

"I wasn't aware you had a place," I lied.

He grinned. "Yeah, you were. I'm sorry I didn't say anything before. I meant to, but I was renovating it. Better security measures."

"Better security measures?"

He nodded.

Someone knocked on the door. "You have a phone call, Mr. Reed."

"I have to go."

I rolled my eyes. "I thought we were going to have passionate mad sex here."

The amusement fled from his face. He grew somber. "Are you okay?"

I swallowed a burst of emotion, hearing the tenderness from him. "I'll be fine. I want to know what happened, but I'll be fine for now."

"Okay." Carefully so he wouldn't hurt me, he pressed his lips to my forehead. The entire thing was so tender, so gentle, that I felt like crying again.

"I have to go," he said. "It started last night. I have to make sure everything will be okay, for us."

War.

He didn't say the word, but that's what it was. I knew what a bomb in Cole's nightclub meant.

Carter slipped from the bed, going through the door I'd wondered about into the bathroom. I watched him, taking in his trim waist and the way the muscles in his back moved, gliding seamlessly under his skin. He was beautiful to look at, from behind as well as from the front. And he was all mine.

But I was terrified.

The war had started.

Carter

When I walked into the Mauricios' house, the conversations grew silent. I knew Cole had moved his base of operations here, taking the library as his office. Ignoring looks from the men and a few of the women, I headed straight there. Cole had told me to stay out when we spoke last night. He was the leader, but that was the thing—if I wasn't in the family any longer, he wasn't my leader.

Shavon met me outside the closed doors. A serene smile on her face, Cole's cousin looked sultry and dangerous all at the same time. "Carter, Carter, Carter."

I narrowed my eyes. I'd been coming to this same house, smoothing over Cole's initiation, almost every day for the last month and today she met me like I was a long-lost stranger? "Don't press me, Shavon."

A smooth chuckle came from her. She cocked her head to the side, studying me. Her smile never slipped from her face. "Press you? Why? You're more family than he is."

I got it then. She wasn't doing Cole's bidding. She was going against him. I shook my head. "I'm not interested in that."

As I moved around her, she stepped with me and blocked me. "Come on, Carter. Can you hear me out?" Her hand rested on her slim hip. Moving closer to me, she trailed a finger down my chest.

"You used to have all the time in the world for me. Remember those days?"

Pre-Emma and never again. "Back up, Shavon. I'm not in the back-stabbing business." My eyes flashed a warning, and this time, I physically held her in place so I could go around with no problems. I ignored her swift intake of breath and walked inside, thrusting both doors open. Not waiting for them to close, I announced, "Just so you know..." Cole looked up from the desk, as did the three other men in front of him. "Your cousin is plotting your demise."

"Carter!" Shavon gasped from behind.

The doors slammed shut, and I didn't need to look to know she was scurrying out of the house.

Cole grinned, standing up from his chair. "Did you just take care of a problem for me?"

"Knowing Shavon, she'll be on the plane for Florida in the next thirty minutes, and she'll be there for the next six months."

"Well, then." Cole's gaze slid to one of the men and lingered there. "I hope your daughter doesn't play with knives, Leo."

Shavon's father chuckled, shaking his head. "My daughter, well, what can you do about her? She does what she does."

Cole narrowed his eyes, but didn't say a word.

I did. "If your daughter is moving against the family's leader, I'll be paying her a visit one day." I let that hang in the air. I'd been their Cold Killer before.

"Well then." Cole cleared his throat. He gestured to the man on the far right. "Carter, this is Police Chief Smith. He's been bringing us up to date about the bombing at the club."

The police? He was on the payroll?

Cole nodded, seeing my unspoken questions, and I leaned against the wall. Folding my arms over my chest, I tucked my head down. I was content to wait, but I wanted to hear everything this man had to say.

He gave me a nervous look. Holding a baseball cap in his lap, his hands fidgeted with the strap, and his Adam's apple bobbed up and down.

Cole said, "Ignore him, Jack. Carter's woman was at the club. No, he's not with us, but he wants to know everything so he doesn't worry about her any more than he needs to."

"Oh." He kept looking at me. He didn't look appeased.

I didn't care. Sending Cole a slight nod, I signaled for him to continue their meeting. "So, Jack. You were saying the results were…"

"Uh." He sent another skirting glance to me before swinging back to Cole. "Yes. We think the backpack had been left there when the club wasn't open. It was in a back locker, and when we checked to see what employee used it, there was no one. It was an empty locker."

"Prints?"

He shook his head, but glanced at me once more. I stared him down. This cop was dirty. I shouldn't look down on him, but I did. I'd killed. I had blood on my hands, but I was loyal to those I loved. If I had taken an oath to serve and protect, I would've followed that allegiance to my death, no matter what. But this man, he was here, sweating and wiping his hands on his legs. He was betraying his family for a paycheck. A lot of people told us things, did things for us, because we paid the best and the Mauricio name was honorable. But this man wasn't worthy. He got a paycheck because of his job. That was it.

"You're not in the family." A voice in my head reminded me. *"If you're in, you're in. Stop saying you're out when your actions show you're in."*

"Without video surveillance of your club, we won't be able to find out who put the bag there. If we had that—" He swallowed again. "We could rule out a lot of scenarios."

He wanted eyes inside. He was lying.

Cole rounded the desk. His eyes met mine for a second and flashed their own warning. He wanted me to back off. I got it, but I'd do what I wanted. And even though there was no visible reaction from me, Cole got that message, too. A slight grin flickered over his features before he turned to face the police chief, his face wiped clean of all emotion.

A mask stared down at the man, who clutched his cap in a death grip. His knuckles were turning white.

"Jack, I know there was evidence collected. I know there are little things, things telling you how the bomb was put together, maybe where those pieces were purchased. Bombs have their own signatures. I know this, and you're sitting here telling me you found nothing except that it was in a locker?"

"Sir—"

Cole shook his head, cutting him off. He leaned down, resting his hands on his legs until he was right in the police chief's face. "I know you're feeding me a line of bullshit. I don't know what other family members you've worked with, but that won't work with me. I'm smarter, and I'm less patient. Give me the name of the person behind that bomb by tomorrow, or you'll find out I'm not as nice as whoever you were dealing with before."

The man's sweating had dampened the collar of his shirt. He bobbed his head up and down. "I will. I'll find out and bring it to you tonight. I will."

Cole's eyes were still narrowed, but he leaned back, allowing the police chief to stand. "Thank you, Police Chief Smith. I'll be waiting for you tonight."

"Yes. Yes, sir."

Cole flicked a hand to Leo. "Escort him out, please."

Leo and the police chief left the room, leaving one other family member still with Cole: Gene. He shook his head, leaning back in his chair and resting his ankle across the knee of his other leg. He looked at me. "You think he's working for the Bartels?"

I didn't say anything. I waited for Cole to speak.

Cole ran a hand down his face as he went to his desk chair. "Has he worked with us before?"

"He was with Leo," Gene said.

"And Shavon?" Cole asked me. "Was that the truth, what you said before?"

I shrugged. "I don't know. She tried to prevent me from coming in here. One guess is that Leo is running his own agenda, and he wanted to see if you'd buy what the cop was saying. Maybe. Maybe not."

"Or he is working with the Bartels and wanted the last bit of evidence we might have on them, the cameras?" Gene asked.

Cole shook his head, frowning. "Either way, I can't trust some of my own family, or I can't trust who each of them has in their pockets."

"We have family politics, just like every other family."

Cole shot Gene a look. "I'm not an idiot, and I know I came in and took over. I knew my place as the leader wouldn't be met with smiles and thumbs-up, but that was complete bullshit. They have evidence."

"Wait and see what he shows you," I murmured.

He shook his head, rubbing at his jaw. "I have to order surveillance on all the elders, don't I?"

Gene glanced at me. The question hadn't been directed to me, but I answered it anyway. "It wouldn't be a dumb idea."

I'd thought the takeover was fine. I'd thought the initiation was successful. I was wrong, and I knew I'd been too quick to hope this change would be smooth. I'd hoped because I'd wanted everything to be handled and dealt with so none of it would affect Emma.

"I can't trust anyone except you two," Cole murmured, his voice deep and low.

I started to shake my head, and he looked right at me. "I need your help, Carter."

"I came here for information. I needed to know if Emma had been the target."

"I know, and I know you're technically out, but I'm telling you—I need you *in*. I need you to help me." He looked to Gene. "Because of you, I know I can trust my uncle here."

Gene stiffened. I knew he was remembering his doubts about his own nephew, but he nodded. "You can trust me. I'll take care of the surveillance with the rest of the family. I'll handle it."

His gaze met mine, and I knew he was doing that to help me. I was here to protect Emma; that was all. And I nodded, thanking him. That was one item off the list Cole would need help handling.

"Thank you, Gene," Cole said.

Gene nodded, then glanced at me. I nodded as well. He was leaving, letting me have my time with Cole.

We waited until he closed the door, then I started. "You're bringing the police chief in here? To see your face? To see mine?"

Cole tensed, frowning. "What—"

"That's reckless. You meet with dirty cops, dirty politicians, whoever, outside of the house. *Never* in the house."

"What, you're the All Mighty Trainer? Do you have a rulebook? *How to be a Mafia Leader for Dummies?*"

"Cole."

"What?" His eyes flashed a warning. "You trained me to fight and to kill. This stuff I have to learn on my own."

"Trust Gene."

Cole scoffed. "Right, because my uncle isn't judging every mistake I make, huh? Because he really thinks I deserve this chair."

Well, fuck. He'd sensed Gene's reservations. "He means well."

Cole waved me off. "My father was the head of the family. I just—" His hands fell to his desk, and he held onto it for a second. "This was his. This whole house. This chair. I have so many memories of watching him in here, and now it's me and…" Shadows flitted across his face. "There are a lot of ghosts in here, Carter. More than I thought there were going to be."

His father, mother, brothers, sisters—and he would've been another. I softened my tone. "I'll help you, with what I can."

"Oh, gee." His lips curved in a mocking grin. "Thanks so much for that."

"Don't be an ass," I growled.

I kept getting pulled in. Granted, I had come myself, but I needed to know for sure. "Who do you think was the target?"

Cole sighed. "I have no idea. I really don't. How's she doing?"

She'd been sleeping when I left. "Bruised, sore, resting." I needed to get back to her.

"You're at your place?"

I nodded.

"Are you going to be training tonight?"

I raised my eyebrows. "Always."

"I'm going to come over."

Despite all the complications, at a basic level, it felt good having him back. We'd fallen into our old routine. When AJ died, Cole had replaced him as my brother. I hadn't been looking for another best friend, but we were alike, and when I took him away from the family to hide and train, we became even more alike. Neither of us had blood family. I had been in the shadows, watching over Emma, and he was in the shadows, just surviving.

I stood by what I'd said to Gene on the plane. Cole would be a good leader, but he had to find his own way. Only he could be the leader. I couldn't do that for him. However, training him, making him the best fighter he could be, I could do that.

"Carter."

"Hmm?" I'd been distracted by my thoughts. "Yeah?"

"This is different for me." He hesitated. "I've been out in the cold, you know, and I'm coming back in. It's just…different."

I didn't comment. I don't think he expected me to. As I left, my hand curled around the air, and I could almost feel the weight of my gun. It was coming back to me.

Emma

I heard the dull thunk from the top of the stairs. The closer I got to the basement, the more the sound grew. Carter was in the gym. Even before I rounded to the doorway and saw him, I knew what I heard.

I found him hitting a punching bag, wearing a sleeveless sweatshirt with the hood pulled over his head. His feet danced lightly as he struck again and again. His hands were wrapped in white tape, but it had become smudged black and worn out.

I must've made a sound because Carter stopped and looked over. "Hey." His voice was so soft. My heart melted.

"Hey, yourself." He was sweating, his muscles glistening. I wanted to drag him up to bed. Instead, I said, "Teach me."

"Teach you?"

I gestured to the punching bag. "How to fight. I want to know."

He stepped back and unzipped his sweatshirt. A shine of sweat covered his chest as it heaved for air. He rested an arm on the bag, watching me. "You want to fight?"

I've killed two men. "It wouldn't hurt."

"No."

I hadn't been expecting that. "Excuse me?"

"I said no."

He started to turn for the bag again, but I caught his arm. "Why not?"

Instead of looking me in the eye, his gaze went past my shoulder. "Because you shouldn't have to fight. That's my job," he answered, with his mouth stretched tight.

"Hey." I reached up, took his chin, and forced him to look at me. "Fighting is both our jobs. Dunvan. Ben. I killed those men. My hands are already bloody, and I'm in this fight. Whatever it is—I'm here. I'm at your side. If the woman you love doesn't know how to fight, she shouldn't be there."

A stricken look came over him, and the corners of his mouth softened. "Emma." He reached for my hand.

I moved back, my hand falling away from him. "No. I'm by your side, Carter. This is our life now. A bomb went off. You can't protect me all the time. I know you try. I know the guards are there, but if anything happened—I have to know, too." My throat constricted. "And if something happened to you, god forbid, I'm going to be there, trying to protect you, too. I'll do it whether I know how to fight or not."

"Emma." His voice was so quiet.

I swallowed over a lump. I was right, and he knew it. "Look, I understand. You love me. You don't want me to deal with this life, but I'm here, and it's happening. Teach me to fight, and maybe I can help, in some small way."

He touched the side of my face. "If anything happened to you…" He hesitated.

I rested my hand over his. "Something already did." My voice grew firm. "It's time, Carter. I'm not innocent. Stop treating me like I am."

"It's because I love you—"

"And I love you. Equip me with the best skills to be the woman at your side. It's the smart thing to do."

He closed his eyes. He nodded and let out a deep sigh. "I know. You're right."

He was the man I loved, but I had gone to him in the beginning because he was the Cold Killer. He was going to be pulled into that world, no matter what he did, because he still loved those people.

I could understand his pain. He didn't want me to be affected any more than I already was. Giving me the tools to fight might cause me to tread somewhere I wouldn't have gone otherwise. Maybe. But if he was in danger, my friends were in danger—I would defend them no matter what.

"Trust me," I urged him.

"I do." His eyes searched mine, and I saw the struggle there. "You shouldn't have to be somewhere and worry about a bomb going off—or even worry about having to protect someone," he said. "That's my life, and I hate that it's affected you like this."

"I know, but it has. I pulled you in before. Now you're pulling me in. That's how it is. That's what you do for someone you love." I grabbed the ends of his sweatshirt and pulled him close. "You go where they go. You walk their same path. What happens to them, happens to you. It's the burden of loving someone. You deal with it because that person is there when you need them. You helped me; now let me help you. Give me the skills to help you, too."

He caught the back of my neck and pulled me to him. He smiled. "No matter what, I'm proud you're at my side." Then his lips fused with mine, and he murmured against them, "Once you're healed, I'll train you. I promise."

I was going to hold him to that.

CHAPTER 13

Emma

It was the middle of the night when I woke to find Carter slipping from the bed. I sat up, groggy, and looked at the clock. 3 am. Then I heard the knocking.

"Who is that?"

Carter looked back at me, pulling a shirt on. "There was no warning. I'm assuming it's one of the guards." But after he pulled some pants on and reached for his gun, I knew there was a question to that statement. He gripped the weapon in one hand and bent down to press his lips to my forehead. "I suppose you're not going to go back to sleep."

As he straightened, I threw off the covers and clambered for my own clothes. I snorted. "Are you kidding me?"

His eyes darkened in disapproval. "You stay back. I mean it, Emma."

I threw him a quick frown, hopping on one leg as I struggled to pull my jeans up. Sleepiness, a sore body, and jeans were a deadly combination, but I was going.

"I mean it, Emma. You stay back, no matter who it is."

When they knocked again and he didn't leave to answer, I knew he wouldn't until I agreed. So I did so, reluctantly. "Okay, but I'm coming to listen. I'm not staying in bed."

The knocking came again. Carter looked back at the door. "Come quietly. I'm going."

"Okay."

He disappeared from the doorway, and I hurried. Grabbing the other 9mm—the one Carter didn't know I knew about—from the closet, I made sure the safety was on and headed down the hall behind him. Shoes. *Shit*. Remembering one of his rules—always be prepared to run—I went back and slipped on some sneakers. Then as quietly as I could, I went out to the living room. When I got there, Carter was talking to Thomas so I slowed to a walk, knots in my gut. They spoke in quiet, hushed tones, and as I approached, both looked at me with emotionless faces.

My pulse spiked for a second. "What is it?" Another bombing. Someone had been shot. Scenarios flashed through my mind.

"It's your sister," Carter said, and images of her—with my face—bloody and broken, replaced those other thoughts.

I reached for the wall to steady myself. "What? Is she okay?"

Thomas left, shutting the door behind him, and Carter came over to me. "She's at a club asking for you."

"Club? What club?"

"One of mine. She caused a scene, and the staff took her in when someone snapped her picture. She wouldn't stop yelling until they promised to get you." He paused a beat, skimming over my face. "It's up to you. What do you want to do?"

"I want to see her." I remembered seeing her the other night, after the bomb went off. "So it *was* her."

"Looks like."

"Oh." Okay then. This was actually happening. "I'm going to see my sister."

He nodded again, still watching me intently. "Are you sure you want to do it this way? She commands, and you show up? Do you want to control the environment?"

My sister. I couldn't get over it. "What?" It was really happening. "Huh?"

"Emma." Carter took my shoulders and bent down so his eyes were level with mine. "Focus. Your sister chose this time and place. What if it's a trap? What if the Bartels got to her?"

My hands clutched at his arms. "We have to go now, then, before they do something."

"No, you're not listening. What if she's working for them? Another attack? You could be walking into that."

I wanted to scream. He had a point...but she was my sister. She had answers about AJ and what happened to us. I took a deep breath. "Then that's a risk I'm willing to take, Carter." My fingers gripped more tightly around his arm. "I want to see her, too. She was there that night, and she looked scared for me."

"Are you sure?"

I knew where she was, and I knew it was her. A stampede of horses couldn't keep me away. "I am. I really am." Then a storm of nerves started up in my stomach. "I'm ready."

I didn't pay attention to where we were driving. As the car pulled up to a club, I focused on getting inside without looking at the surroundings at all. It was Carter's. He had so many. Right now I was barely aware of Carter himself beside me.

I glanced down for the hundredth time and smoothed my hand over my pants. I hadn't known what to wear. It was the middle of the night, so dressing up too much seemed silly. I'd changed three times, but I ended with a form-fitting black sweater and black pants. They weren't jeans, but they weren't dress pants either. They looked simple and comfortable, although I wasn't paying attention to that either. I just wanted to look presentable for her...my sister. I still couldn't believe it.

A guard opened the door, and as Carter went in, I reached for his hand, though we didn't do public displays of affection. The few times the media caught us hugging or holding hands, those images never seemed to go away. A picture from eight months ago was still being recycled on a few news channels, but I couldn't help myself tonight. I needed his touch. He settled me.

We passed the usual crowd of those who'd waited all night to get inside, but never did. They were slow to leave while celebrities were still standing around, having just been ushered out. It was the same scene I remembered from when I had stayed all night long, waiting to see Carter, at another club.

At the sight of us, people snapped to attention. "Hey! It's Carter Reed," someone hollered.

"It's Emma! Emma!" called another.

More and more people turned to look at us, and out came the phones. Flashes lit up the night.

The guards beside us held their hands up, trying to block the views. Carter lifted his arm as well, over my shoulder, and I ducked underneath, hurrying forward through the opened door. Once we were inside, Carter issued the order: "Get rid of them." A waitress came down a hallway to the right and he added, "Get rid of the staff, too. I want this building empty."

He touched the small of my back and ushered me down a hallway. We moved quickly, going all the way through the building to the back exit.

When I saw it, I started to slow down. "Carter, what—"

His hand was firm on my back. "Trust me." He guided me out the door to where another car waited for us, and as we exited, I saw Michael. He opened the back door to the car, and we got inside. One of the guards pushed in behind us. Before I could settle into my seat, the car was already shooting ahead.

"What..." The question died in my throat.

Sitting across from me was my sister.

"Oh."

She lifted a hand and ducked her head. "Hi, Emma." Then she managed to look me in the eye.

I'd been right. She had my eyes, my nose, my lips, even my chin, but her face was more round than mine. She studied me as well, lingering on my bruises with her lips pinched together. Even somewhat concerned, I could tell how lovely she was. Her hair was a lighter color than mine and pulled back into a tight bun behind her head. She had makeup on, but it wasn't much. She went the natural beauty way, but I could understand why. She was beautiful.

Realizing we were just staring at each other, her cheeks grew pink, and she looked down at her lap. Her hands fidgeted until she crossed one leg over the other and stuffed her hands between them. She glanced back up, jerked away when she saw I was still watching her, but then swallowed and looked back up once more.

Then I realized it, too. I was staring. I was rude.

I didn't care.

I couldn't stop taking in all the details of her. Her clothes were expensive. Carter had money, and even though I tried to buy my own clothes, he had someone buy clothes for me, but my style was more understated. I didn't enjoy letting people know my clothes were tailor made. My sister didn't shout money with her clothes, but I recognized a lot of the brands. They were high-end and not bought off the shelf. The toes of a black boot peeked out from her sleek, gray pants and her light cashmere sweater had zippers going from side to side. A scarf around her neck completed the look.

Whatever had happened to her, it had blessed her in the end.

She cleared her throat and nudged the guy next to her. My gaze turned to him. It was the same man I'd seen with her after the bombing.

"Miss Nathans?" I said to him.

My sister's cheeks flared bright red. She looked down at her lap.

He leaned forward in his seat, tugging his jacket's collar away from his throat. "Uh, yes."

"My name is Emma Martins."

"Uh, yes," he repeated, glancing at Carter. "I don't know why I called you that. I knew, I mean—the media referenced you as Emma Martins. I had hoped, no—I had thought…" He quieted as my sister placed her hand over his.

She leaned forward. Her chin lifted. Her shoulders went back. The red had faded quickly and, somehow, I now stared back at an elegant, sophisticated woman. "What Kevin is trying to say is that he'd hoped the name Nathans might've triggered a memory with you. You were taken so young."

Taken. Young. Triggered.

None of those words sat right with me, and I tensed, but Carter took over. He must have felt my distress and, much like she had, he now commanded the attention. "Let's keep the pleasantries to a minimum until we get to our destination."

"About that—" The man coughed into his hand, then did it again. "We had asked to meet Emma at your club. After searching us, your men didn't allow us to voice our feelings about moving the location—"

Carter spoke over him. "Because it was my call. Not yours."

Red spread up the man's neck, but he didn't respond.

My sister patted his hand. "It's okay. He's…I mean—" She gestured to Carter and myself. "We don't know you…at all…"

We were mafia. That was the meaning behind her words. They were scared of us. As soon as I realized that, laughter bubbled up my throat. But I kept my mouth shut and shoved it back down. Laughing, at this moment, wouldn't be appropriate. And if I started, I didn't think I could stop. There'd been too much tension over the last few weeks.

Instead, I sighed. "This is awkward."

My sister sputtered out a sound that was half a laugh and half a cough. She tried to cover, touching her chest. "Oh. I'm sorry. I—"

But the corners of her lips curled up, and so did mine. When she saw my smile, she looked back down, her shoulders shaking as she laughed softly.

I wasn't laughing, but I couldn't wipe the grin from my face.

"I—" She looked back up, her hand covering her mouth as another chuckle escaped from her. "I'm so sorry. This is, you're right. It's completely awkward, and Kevin's only trying to protect me." She gestured to Carter, addressing him, "As I'm sure you're doing the same with Emma…" She trailed off, her gaze going back to me and holding there. An awed expression came over her, and her hand dropped back to her lap. "I…it's just that, you're here." She sounded choked up. "We're in the same car. I never thought…" She blinked and dabbed at the corners of her eyes. "I never thought I'd find you."

I didn't know what to say. I'd never thought about her, period. It had been AJ and me. That was it, but since finding out about her… "Thank you for finding me," I said. My hand fell down between Carter and me. I held it there, pressed against him. I just needed to touch him. "There've been things going on, but I've been thinking about you, too."

She nodded, clearly trying not to cry. She kept wiping at the corners of her eyes.

This wasn't the time or place. So much had to be said, but I didn't say another word until we arrived at our destination. When the car slowed to a stop and the door opened, we were in a large, brightly lit warehouse. There was nothing inside, only an office with a window in the door. As my sister followed us out, and then her friend, our guard went to a side door. Another guard took position beside him, and another two went to the main garage-style doors. As they closed it behind us, I saw three other cars parked outside. They had formed a wall, and more men waited by each of those vehicles.

We were heavily armed and heavily protected.

"Oh my." My sister pressed a hand to her throat, taking in the scene before the doors slid to the ground.

Now it was only the four of us and the four security men inside. I was used to this, but seeing her reaction, I remembered the first time I became aware of how powerful Carter was. That's what those men did. They were physical reminders of who Carter was, of what he could do. She looked at me, her eyebrows bunched together, and she stepped closer to her friend. I wasn't sure if she was aware of doing it or not, but I understood. He was familiar. He was safe to her.

I wanted to go to her. I wanted to reassure her that I was safe too, but I felt Carter beside me. His hand touched the top of my arm as if he was reminding me. We didn't know these people. We didn't know anything about them.

I looked up, saw the concern in his wolf eyes, and nodded. The worry disappeared, and he pointed to the office. "I think Emma and Andrea might want to talk alone."

"Yes." I breathed.

My sister nodded her agreement right away. "Yes."

"Andrea—" her friend started.

She patted his arm. "I'll be fine, Kevin. We sought them out, not the other way."

"But—" He grabbed for her hand.

She evaded him. "Stop, Kevin. This is her. I want to talk to her."

"I don't think you should be alone."

"Stop." Her eyebrows lifted in warning. "I mean it, Kevin. I don't think these men will have any qualms about having you wait outside."

He glanced around him before returning to look at Andrea. The red had begun to creep up to his face again, and he lifted a hand, itching the backside of his neck. "Andrea, I…okay. I guess."

Carter went to the office and opened the door. I started to follow Andrea inside, but he held me back. "One minute, please," he said to her as he shut the door.

She frowned at him, but didn't respond.

"What?" I glanced over my shoulder. We were out of hearing distance from her friend. "What is it?"

"Stay within eyesight of me."

"What?"

"I don't trust you alone with her either. The door can't be locked, and I'm right here on the other side. If you start getting a weird feeling, scratch behind your ear. I'll come in."

"You think, what? She's going to attack me or something?"

"I don't know." He was insistent. "But I'm not willing to risk it. The Bartels killed AJ. I don't put anything past them."

"Oh." I tensed immediately. "But her…"

"Emma," he said quietly. His hand still held my arm, but he softened his hold and his thumb began rubbing back and forth. "Just be careful, okay?"

"Okay. Yeah." I pressed a kiss to his cheek. "I will."

I started to step back, but he caught the back of my head and pressed me to him again. One more kiss. One solid touch from him to me. This wasn't about passion. It wasn't even about comfort. This was a connection between us. I felt his need for me, and my own matched it, rising within me. It wasn't sexual. It was primal. It was the need for both of us to be okay. My lips pressed back against him, tasting him, and then I leaned away, gazing up into his eyes.

I saw a bleakness there and my hand lifted, reacting to it. I hated seeing that. He shouldn't feel that way, ever. I touched the side of his face to reassure him.

He nodded, but the bleakness didn't leave.

I stepped inside to talk to my sister.

Emma

It was just her and me.

With the door closed, it felt like the outside world had been cut off. The room filled with questions, but one thing rose to the top. "Our mother?" I asked.

Her eyes widened. "Oh."

I swallowed. "I mean, how is she?" *Is she alive? Is she well? Does she know about me?* So many more questions waited on the edge of my tongue, wanting to spill out. I gripped my arm and held tight, physically holding myself back.

"I—" She stopped. Her chest heaved up and down in a dramatic breath. "She's..." She looked down for a second. "Dead. A car accident."

I stepped back. I hadn't expected that.

"She died when I was little," Andrea continued. "I don't remember a lot of it." Her voice was strangled, and she dabbed at the corner of her eye again. "I was adopted when I was five—"

"You're two years younger than me." I would've been seven. I glanced at Carter. I didn't meet him until I was eleven. That didn't make sense.

"I remember you."

"You do?"

She nodded. "I remember playing together. I liked to play with dolls. You hated dolls."

"I did?" The side of my mouth lifted up.

"I think we played hide and seek in the house. You don't remember?"

I frowned, shaking my head. "My past is cloudy. I don't remember a lot."

"I'm going to get you, girly!"

I shrieked, giggling as I ran away. "No, no, Mama!"

I shook my head. AJ's face loomed over me next. *"It's dangerous."*

I focused back on Andrea. "I think I remember playing hide-and-seek with you, but then I remember AJ saying it was dangerous." At the mention of my brother, a scowl formed on her face.

"AJ." I frowned at her. "Our brother."

"He's not my brother, and he wasn't yours either. He was your kidnapper." Her eyes grew heated, and her arms crossed over her chest. "I can't listen to you talk about him like that."

My own eyes darkened. She couldn't listen to me? "You might want to leave right now then. I don't know what happened, but I remember my brother taking care of me, raising me, making sure I went to school every day. He made mistakes, but he loved me."

Her lips pressed together and she went still, standing like a statue. "Then you and I have very different memories."

This was insane. "You were young. Me, too. I don't know what happened, but I should remember you. I don't. There are lapses with both of us, but AJ did nothing except try to raise me right."

She shook her head, blinking rapidly. "I know. I…" She let out a resigned breath. "I'm sorry. I…maybe we're getting into too much too quickly? Maybe we should scale back. I mean—" A rueful laugh slipped out, and she gestured to Carter. "I never would've known about you if it weren't for him. Carter Reed. You're with Carter Reed. I saw you on television and fell off the couch."

A ball of tension started to loosen inside me. She started to laugh, and I wanted to laugh with her. The DNA tests were done. This was my sister, no matter what. Whatever had happened in the past, whatever she felt about AJ, this was still my family.

As she continued talking, saying how she couldn't believe it was me and had Kevin, her family friend, reach out to a private investigator, I realized I really did want to get to know her. She was different than me—I knew there were differences between us, but I felt a connection, too. She was like me in some ways. I wanted to find out all of them. I wanted to know everything.

"So…" She was trickling to a stop. "Carter Reed, huh?"

I nodded. "Yeah."

"He's, uh…" She waved a hand toward him. "He's got the whole mysterious and deadly attractive thing going for him. Kevin picked that club tonight to meet you. We were up all night, and I got myself worked into a frenzy. I declared it was now or never." She laughed. "I can be a little dramatic, but Kevin read in a magazine that it was the safest of all his nightclubs." She laughed to herself. "When they searched us and told us we had to come with them, I think he almost peed himself. He's still out there, quaking in his boots."

She was fond of him, but there were no romantic undertones.

"Who is Kevin to you?" I asked. "You said he was a family friend?" I moved closer, my arms falling to my sides. Who had adopted her? Were they good people? Was she loved? I looked at her hand. There was a ring on her finger. That meant she was married?

"He is. He's, um…" She began fiddling with her ring. "He grew up with me. When I was adopted, I moved to Hillcrest. It's an uppity town, and my family was wealthy. Kevin's family was, too. There's a whole scene there. I guess you could call me a socialite. This—you and who you're with—has everyone salivating back home. They couldn't get over it. Half of the girls I know wanted to come with us. Then our PI told us you were in New York, and we hopped another plane to come here. I…anyways, I'm digressing. Kevin. You asked about how we know each other."

Her head bobbed up and down. She kept playing with her ring. "Kevin was friends with Jamis." She laughed again, but it sounded nervous. She wiggled her fingers in the air, pointing at the ring. "Jamis is my husband—no, *was* my husband. We divorced a year ago. He cheated on me. Like, with thirty women, so Kevin chose my friendship over his."

She wasn't looking at me anymore. She was staring at the ground with a distant expression on her face. I saw the pain there. I heard it and felt it. My own pain recognized it immediately, and I wanted to go to her, hug her, and comfort her.

I didn't. I held back and reminded myself that I didn't know this woman. She had my face, but she had a whole other life.

"I'm sorry," I murmured.

"Yeah," her voice was hoarse. "Anyways, maybe—I mean—can we shelf this?" A tear slid down her cheek, and she brushed it away with the back of her hand. The entire movement was very graceful. She was sophisticated and elegant. After a moment she smiled at me, her eyes warming. "It's obvious that you're loved very much. Is there a way we could get to know each other? Maybe even meet for a glass of wine one night? I'll leave Nervous Kevin behind."

Carter

Emma had a sister. Wonderful.

Truly, wonderful. That had been my first response. She missed AJ. She could talk to this woman, get more information, and maybe get more closure on AJ's death. Those had been my initial thoughts about this new chapter in Emma's life.

But that had been then. That was when the woman was far away. Emma didn't know her. She wasn't in our lives. This was now.

Emma had a sister—I hated it. We needed to move. Emma needed to be hidden, but instead, we were in a warehouse while she chatted about the past with this stranger. And her man looked ready to bolt or mess himself. My men had taken their phones away, but if they hadn't, I had no doubt this man would've called the police just because he was scared.

He wasn't worth our time. Neither was this reunion. It was only endangering Emma further. The longer we stayed in town, the more chances it gave the Bartels to hurt her. A growl formed in the pit of my throat. It wanted to be unleashed, but I forced it back down. I forced myself to stand there, letting Emma spend this time with her sister, when I wanted to rip open the door, haul her out, and keep her safe.

I couldn't do that either.

She needed this time. I needed her to be safe. Two goals at odds with each other.

Stand. Be on guard. Wait. Those were my only options.

"Sir?" Thomas approached with a phone in his hand. "It's…" He glanced toward the man and didn't finish his statement. As I took the phone, he murmured under his breath, "It's Cole, sir."

I looked at Emma.

"I'll watch her, sir."

I couldn't take the call with that man in here. I shook my head and pointed at the man. "No, I'll stay. Take him out."

"What?" Kevin asked suddenly.

Thomas gestured to two of the guards and ordered, "Take him outside. Stay with him."

As they left their positions, Kevin began to back up. He looked all around him, but there was nowhere to hide. "What's going on? I don't like this. I didn't agree to any of this—"

The men grabbed his arms and started to guide him toward the door. He went limp, so they dragged him. When they lifted him in the air instead, he started to kick at them.

"Help! Andrea—" he yelled.

"Shut. Up." I held the phone against my chest. "It's a phone call. Your woman is safe. You came to us. Not the other way around."

Sweat covered his forehead and damp circles radiated from under his arms. He kept looking between the two guards who were holding him. "I—"

I didn't care and waved them on outside. The men continued on their path and shut the door behind them. Kevin continued to yell, and I fought the urge to go out there and silence him myself. That would've been uncivilized. He was the weaker one here. This was my territory. I understood his panic, given everything he'd heard about me in the media, but there was a way to deal with fear. He was like a frightened little boy. I didn't have time for men like that.

"Carter!"

Hearing Cole shouting from the phone, I lifted it to my ear. "This is not the best time."

"You're still in town?"

"And how do you know that?"

"I asked your men."

Hearing a smugness in his voice, I clutched the phone tighter. "I will make sure to give my men explicit instructions on keeping my location quiet, to *everyone*."

He laughed. "You sound like a grizzly bear waiting to attack. What's got you worked up? It couldn't be the police chief?"

I looked up, making sure Emma was safe. "Nothing. We ran into a small obstacle, that's all. Why are you calling me, Cole?"

"To give you the heads-up. I called a meeting with the elders."

I was quiet for a moment. There were things he wasn't saying. He'd said earlier that he needed to watch the elders. Now he was meeting with them? He was doing something else, playing a game with the elders.

"Did you need my help?" I asked.

"No, no. I'm just letting you know, in case there's fallout. I thought you'd be long gone by now." He sounded casual, happy even. "Are you sticking around town because of this small obstacle?"

Emma had her back to me, but I saw the compassion in her body language. Her eyes had lit up when I told her who was waiting for us at my club. She wanted to know this sister, and she didn't want the information handed to her in a folder. She wanted to foster this relationship. Even if she came out and denied that desire, I knew she would be lying to me.

She wanted a family. I couldn't deny her that, but this war... My hand tightened around the phone, and I forced myself to loosen my hold. I was going to break the thing. "Unfortunately, I think so."

"Well, consider yourself warned then."

Emma came out of the office as I hung up, with her sister behind her. Both had shed a few tears. What had they talked about in there? Emma reached for my arm, and as if she'd heard my unspoken question, she murmured, "I'll tell you later. Do you think a car can take Andrea and Kevin to their hotel?"

"Of course." I gestured to Thomas, who opened the side door on command.

Emma's sister looked around the warehouse, a small line forming in her forehead. "Where's Kevin?"

"He had to step outside for a moment. Thomas will help you to the car."

"Oh. Okay." She reached for Emma and squeezed her arm. "I'll see you later then?"

"Yes." Emma grabbed her hand for a moment. "I'm looking forward to it." She choked up on the last word, and I leaned forward to study her. Her other hand reached toward her sister, but she caught herself and lowered it back to her side.

"Okay. Good night or good morning, whatever it is." Emma's sister gave her another beaming smile before hurrying through the door. It wasn't long before a car door shut, and we heard their vehicle pull away.

Emma didn't waste any time. She turned to me, both her hands grabbing my arm. "I know you want to leave. I know there's a war going on, but I want to stay." She glanced over her shoulder in the direction her sister had gone. "I want to know more about what happened, Carter." She pressed against me, her eyes turning sad. "She doesn't remember AJ. She hates him. Kidnapper. That's what she said. I have to know. I need to understand what happened. I…" She faltered, closing her eyes a moment. "I don't have memories before I was with AJ, and according to her, it was just us with our mother. I need to know what happened."

"I can hire someone to look into it. Their private investigator's already given us most of what he has on them. I can do that." I needed to try, but she shook her head, as I knew she would.

"I need to remember. Me. Reading about it won't do the same thing. I remembered a little bit when I was with her. If we can spend more time together, maybe I'll know for myself what happened."

"This isn't just for you, is it?"

She shook her head. "AJ wasn't my kidnapper. He was my savior."

"I know."

"We'll stay?" Her chest lifted and held. Her eyes were so hopeful. As I nodded, she let out her breath. "Thank you." Touching my cheek, she lifted up and kissed the corner of my mouth. "Thank you so much," she whispered. "I love you."

"Emma." She started to pull away, but I caught her and held her there. "We're here, but it's like we're not. That means no Theresa, no Amanda, and no Noah even. None of them can know. I want us hidden as much as possible."

"I know. I understand, but I'd like a few nights to spend time with her."

I wasn't happy about it, but protecting her from here could be done. I'd just have to be flexible. As Emma headed for the car, Michael came over and waited for his instructions. "We're going to need a new safe house," I told him.

"Sir?"

My home wasn't safe. The Bartels knew about it. If we were staying here, everything had to be new.

CHAPTER 15

Emma

Today was going to be a great day.

As soon as I woke, I remembered I was going to spend time with my sister today. After heading home, Carter had gotten a new phone I could use to text with her, and we'd started planning.

We were going to meet for breakfast, then go to a bookstore, followed by a lunch. For the afternoon we'd booked a salon, and then we'd end with dinner. All our meals would be at Carter's establishments. He'd also approved the bookstore and the salon. Every move we made had to be planned out, and we had to wear disguises. The guards would be doing their blending thing, and they were going the extra mile. Instead of wearing their usual black suits, they'd be dressed like normal civilians.

When we picked Andrea up, she looked at the guards and gave me a rueful grin. "They're less intimidating now."

I didn't respond. Their usual intimidation was conscious, but now they needed to be camouflaged, like me. I'd asked Carter if I should say anything about the Bartel war, but he told me to pretend it wasn't there.

"Get to know your sister," he'd said. "If you talk about the war, that could get between the two of you getting to know each other."

I followed his advice, but after perusing the bookstore, when we sat down for lunch, she brought it up.

"Ummm…" She unfolded her cloth napkin and didn't look at me. As she placed it on her lap, her head remained focused there for a beat. Then she looked up, and I saw a different look in her eye.

She was about to introduce a real topic, not the casual conversation we'd been having all morning. I readied myself, putting my hands in my lap.

"The bomb," she began. "I…" She stopped and tucked some hair behind her ear. "Kevin is making me bring this up. I—oh boy—I loved meeting you last night. I know it was unconventional, demanding to see you like that. To be honest, I'd had a little too much wine. I was very brazen until the guards showed up. Then all that liquid courage left me, but…" Her hand returned to her lap. "The bomb. You—you're okay after that?"

I froze. The less she knew, the better. "Yeah. I'm good. I don't watch the news. What are they saying about it?"

"That a previous employee did it. Someone who was fired and got angry. That club, that wasn't one of Carter's was it?"

"I don't believe so."

"Good."

She sounded relieved. She didn't know it was owned by the Mauricio family. I wondered how she would've reacted if she'd known that tidbit. This was dumb. I was pretending my life was normal and that I could get to know my sister the way normal people would—that we could spend time together, laugh together, maybe even tease each other or fight. We'd have months and months of being around each other. But we wouldn't. Here we were trying to force it in a couple days. Carter had never said a word, but I knew that's all I was getting. A few days to cover a few decades of history. It wasn't enough time, and I couldn't pretend otherwise.

"What's wrong?"

I refocused on her. "Hmmm?"

"You made a sound. Is something wrong?"

"Oh." What did I say? *Be honest.* That was the only way. I clutched my napkin as I prepared to speak. "Andrea—"

"Call me Andy," she interrupted, her eyes sparkling.

"What?"

"He called you Alley Cat."

"Andy. It's what my friends and family call me. Andrea's the uptight socialite persona." She grinned to herself, rolling her eyes. "I have to play that part, but this is nice. I can just be Andy with you. No charades or anything."

Except for mine. I twisted the napkin around my hand. If it had been made of cheap material, I would've ripped it in half by now. "Ah, yes. That is nice."

"So..." She leaned forward to grab her glass of wine. "You were going to tell me what's wrong."

"I was. Yes." I couldn't play pretend anymore. "You obviously know about Carter."

She went still in her seat.

"I don't know what you know or what you think," I continued. "But I can't talk about that stuff. If you want to get to know me, it's just me. There will be times when you're not going to see me or you can't get through to me. That's just how it is."

Her eyes darted to Thomas, who stood closest to us. She jerked them back to me.

"After meeting you last night, I wanted to cram the whole day with getting to know each other. I think I wanted to pretend this was normal, that we were just two friends who hadn't seen each other in a long time. But that's not the truth. The truth is that I shouldn't even be here."

"You shouldn't?" Her voice dipped low.

"No, but not because of you. Because of other things. And as I'm saying this to you, I'm realizing how wrong I am to have pushed for this. I should go." I started to stand. Calling Carter, making things right was foremost in my mind now.

"Wait." She touched my arm. "Wait, please. Sit. *Please.*"

I did, but slowly.

She swallowed and reached for her glass of wine again. Her hand trembled. "Yes, I've heard the rumors. I'd be living under a rock not to know who Carter Reed is, and like I said before, everyone back home is buzzing about you. They all know who he is, too. I'd be a liar if I sat here and told you I didn't want to know about him. That's not the truth. I'm curious, yes, but I think anyone would be."

She paused for a moment and took a breath. "However, I'm more curious because he's a part of your life. It's you I really want to know. We don't have to talk about him or anything that makes you uncomfortable. I promise. I won't even bring up AJ. Kevin made me realize last night that maybe I'm wrong—jumping to conclusions. I don't remember our mom that well either, so it's possible something bad happened with her. Maybe AJ was saving you. I don't know. I've just been looking for you all my life, and he's the one I blamed for taking you away."

"AJ was good to me." No one would take that from me.

"I can see that." She seemed cautious. "I can, and you're right about forcing the day together. I want to get to know you too, but I got a sense last night that now isn't the time for that to happen. Maybe we could finish our lunch and then promise to get in touch when the time is right? How about that?"

I nodded, feeling all the tension leaving me. "That sounds wonderful, actually."

"Good." She lifted her wine glass. "To getting to know one another. And if it takes a long time, that's completely fine, too."

I laughed, clicking my glass to hers. "That's perfect."

"Cheers to us then."

"Cheers."

This would work out. I could feel it. Everything would be fine. Once things were safe, I could go to her town, or she could come to mine, and we could spend more time together. I glanced at my phone. I knew I should text Carter, let him know it was okay to leave, but Andy started telling a story about her adoptive parents, and I tucked the phone back into my purse. I'd text him when we were leaving.

Carter

Cole was in the warehouse waiting for me when I walked inside. Without being told, the guards had stayed outside. This conversation was just for Cole and me. As he saw me coming, he switched on a high-force fan. If anyone had stuck a recording device anywhere, our conversation would be drowned out.

"What was your phone call about last night?" I didn't waste time. "Did you decide to move against the Bartels?"

Cole flashed me a grin, scratching his forehead. "You know better than that. I can't until I know who I can trust and who I can't. I called the meeting to gauge their reactions on some things, and I need your help."

"I won't spy on anyone in the family."

"No. I didn't mean that. I need you to start laying traps for the Bartels. I want to know their safe houses. I want to know all of their businesses. We know most of them, but there are always extras that no one outside of the family knows about. We need those."

I nodded. "That information's already been compiled."

"It has?"

"For back home." Just thinking about the change in plans, I wanted to curse. "That's what I was doing when I left before. I thought I'd take Emma home, and I was going to protect her there. I didn't think our fight would be in New York."

"You got all that information in that amount of time?"

It was my turn to flash him a grin. "I'm still in business with the Bartels. I got a lot of information about them, and the rest I found myself."

"You did all that?"

"With two of my men. It's easier doing recon when you're alone. I had no backing from the Mauricio family. That's what they found out when they made a few phone calls. To them, I'm acting alone. Now, I can't tell you what they're thinking since the bomb. Emma was either the target, or she was too damn close to it. I haven't reached out yet to test their reaction."

"Speaking of that, why are you still here? I meant what I said last night. I thought you'd be long gone."

"Emma has a long-lost sister who's reappeared—"

"The timing is suspect."

"—and she wants a few days to get to know her. And yes, I find the timing very convenient."

"Have you looked into her?"

I grimaced. "Not as much as I would like, no. But I will now. If there's a connection, I'll find it. She really is Emma's sister, so if they found her, that means they went searching for her and they've been planning this move for years."

"True. Finding a long-lost sister would've taken some time." His head tilted to the side. "Unless they just got lucky."

"Maybe." I shrugged. "Right now, I'm treating her as if she is a long-lost sister and not another weapon against Emma. It would be nice to have some firm intel on whether they're moving against me through her or not."

"I know, and I'm working on that. I have to run these tests on the elders. I need to know who I can trust. If I go into a battle with an army that's disloyal, we're all dead."

My impatience burned in me. I wanted to know now. I wanted to make my move. This was how I used to feel all the time. I was a caged panther, and I wanted out of the cage to protect what's mine. But I couldn't. Not yet.

"If you take too much time, there won't be any Mauricio family to test," I warned. "The Bartels have gotten away with enough already."

"You're telling me?" he shot back. "They came for me. They killed two of my friends, and they're the reason I even came back. Trust me, Carter. I am more than aware of how long this is taking. I'll move against them as soon as I know who's actually behind me and who's against me."

I understood that. It was a good battle strategy, but I didn't play politics well. I led my own army, and in times when I couldn't, I used to kill on my own. "It's taking too long, Cole." That was the truth no matter who was behind him. "If you need to cut them out of the action, cut them out. You need to make your move soon."

"What would you do?"

I fell silent. I hadn't expected that question. "What do you mean?"

"Come on, Carter." He smiled, shaking his head. "You've worked your way into a powerful position with both families. I know you're the lone wolf. You do your own thing, but you're the smartest guy I know. You think seven steps ahead of everyone else. If you were me, what would your first move be?"

"My first move would be to find out if that bomb was meant for Emma or not."

"And after that? What if it weren't, and it was a bomb sent against your family. What's the next step?"

"You need to gather information. Find out all the key players and the alliances between them. Know them better than they know themselves."

"And if that was currently being put together? What's the step after that?"

"Find out all their businesses. Everything. Even the houses where they take their mistresses."

"Already being done. After that?"

I shook my head, grinning. "Why are you picking my brain? You're making all the right moves."

"Because I'm missing something, and I don't know what it is. But I think you do. I think there's a difference—one small step—that I'm blind to."

I knew what he was getting at, but it was simple. He made it sound complicated. It wasn't. It was just a quality I had that Cole didn't.

I shook my head. "Cole, you can plan all you like. You can set up all the targets and hope you'll hit them when you shoot, but there's a point where you can't plan anymore. I plan. I set up safeguards, yes. That's what I was doing at home, but eventually you just have to strike the match."

"What do you mean?"

"The difference between you and me: I'd go in there and kill them all myself. And no matter how much I've trained you, that's a quality you don't have. You're smart. So am I. You plan. So do I. But while you wait to make sure the whole team will back you up, I'm already in there and doing it no matter who's with me and who isn't."

He wasn't going to make the first move. His method of testing the elders would take too long. This war, if it spilled over to me, was going to be my own. I wasn't going to wait for Mauricio family approval. I would do the same thing that had happened after AJ. If they came for mine, I'd go for theirs—all of theirs.

"So I should stop wasting time? That's what you're saying?"

Suddenly I heard Cole's measured words. He was watching what he said and being very careful about it. It all clicked, and I wanted to hit him. "You're an asshole."

"What do you mean?" he asked, but I could tell he knew I'd figured it out.

"I'm your weapon, aren't I? You're waiting for me to get fed up so I go and do your work for you. That's your genius plan?"

A bright smile stretched over his face. "It was until you figured it out."

"You're a dick."

His eyebrows raised, but I didn't yell. I didn't curse. I didn't lunge at him. I was pissed, but he was doing what was right for the family. He was utilizing the best weapon in their arsenal, and that was me.

"I'm not doing a thing unless I know they intend to hurt Emma."

He nodded. "I can respect that." He watched me, still waiting for anger.

"You can't control me," I told him.

"I know that."

"Good." Then I moved. My fist was up and hitting him square in the jaw before he saw me coming. As his body dropped to the ground, I knew he was unconscious, and I turned to leave. I had been a weapon for the family before, and if Cole wanted to go that route, fine by me. But if I was going to be used as that weapon, he'd have to deal with the damage I inflicted.

I wasn't sure if he was ready for that.

As I got into the car, my phone buzzed in my pocket. Pulling it out, I found a text from Emma: **Coming back. We can go home. I'll get to know Andy when it's safer.** A second text buzzed through as I watched: **I love you.**

Emma

The car was spinning.

No, that was me. I groaned as I leaned forward. The car wouldn't stop spinning. I could hear it laughing at me. It was taunting me, calling me a lightweight. Then I realized that wasn't the car. It was my sister. She sat next to me, patting my back and laughing to herself.

When I looked up at her, she convulsed in laughter again, covering her mouth with her hand.

"Sorry," she sputtered. "So sorry."

She wasn't. She kept laughing. Her entire face was a bright red.

I scowled at her, or I would've if my fourth glass of wine wasn't threatening to spill out. "Too much wine. Way too much."

"I know." She couldn't stop giggling and shook her head. "I'm so sorry."

"That was four glasses ago. Theresa stopped doing wine nights. I'm out of practice."

"Oh, Emma." Her hand rubbed circles on my back. "But we had fun. Who's Theresa?"

The car hit a pothole, and my stomach lurched into my throat. Oh no. Not good. Chunks were going to blow. I struggled to keep the wine down as I tried to focus on what Andrea had just said. Who was Theresa? That was it. I answered in a mumble, "She's the one who trained me in wine drinking. I could've matched you glass for glass tonight if we hadn't stopped."

"What happened?"

"We went to the gun range instead." Another pothole. The car lurched to the side, and my stomach went right with it. Clamping a hand over my mouth, I felt it coming. I wasn't going to be able to stop it. *No, no, no. Carter spent too much money on these clothes.* That was it. I was wearing my own clothes when I got back. Screw how they felt. They were cheap, and I could drink the best wine in them.

"Oh, yeah. Kevin told me about that." Andrea began petting my hair. She sounded content. "Who would've thought this? I'm in the back of a car with my sister, and we're both tipsy."

I held up a hand. "I'm not tipsy. That can be fun. I'm sick. That's not fun."

"You know what I mean. I feel like we're eighteen. We snuck out of the house and got drunk on wine coolers. Did you ever have those?" She sighed, leaning back in the seat. "I did. Some of the other girls and I would do that. We'd tell our parents we were sleeping over at each other's houses, and then all of us went up to Beth Anne's cabin. Of course, it wasn't a cabin. It was a log mansion, but it was fun. Wine coolers, gossiping, and swimming. Then we'd wait for the guys to crash our party. Oh, man. I miss those days. It was so simple back then."

My stomach stopped doing somersaults and settled. Her words were another reminder of how different we were. Andrea snuck out of her house to a log mansion. I snuck out of my foster home. She got tipsy off wine coolers. I got arrested. She got to go back to her adoptive parents. I went to a new foster home. Same face. Different lives.

I forced a smile. "I'm suddenly sober now."

"That's good." She gave me another dreamy smile as she patted my arm. Her eyes had glazed over. I could almost see the fond memories. "I can't wait for you to meet my parents. They've been supportive of me finding you—"

"Andrea," I started.

"Nope. I told you. Andy. I'm Andy to you."

I removed her hand from my arm and cringed. "Andrea, we promised to wait to share our past with each other." I didn't want to hear any more about her loving family, not when she seemed to want to take away the only family I'd had growing up: AJ.

"I know. I'm sorry. I just…" A wistful look came over her. "I found you. I still can't believe it. And Carter." She started fanning herself. "My god, that man. I couldn't believe it when I first saw you. You were with him, and even though he didn't look at you, I could tell he loved you—like, really loved you. You were going from a car to a hotel or something. And those guards were all around you. You were so beautiful, Emma."

I was a trophy to her.

That was how her words made me feel. I couldn't help but wonder if I'd be so alluring if I wasn't with Carter Reed? Would I still be so beautiful?

Stop, Emma. She's your sister. Get to know her. Love her. She's family.

I could almost hear AJ's words in my head. No matter what she'd said against him, he would've wanted me to know her.

I think. But why had we been separated? That was going to plague me. I had to find out the answer.

"Andrea." I lifted my head.

She stopped patting and straightened in her seat. Her mouth turned down. "Why won't you use my nickname? All my family and friends do—"

"Because I'm not," I snapped. "Sorry. I didn't mean it to come out like that, but I'm not your friend or your family. Not yet, anyway. We have to go slow. I meant what I said before. I don't trust easily, and I can't pretend we're close sisters. We're not even close friends yet. My life is complicated right now, and I can't handle the pressure of forcing this."

Her voice grew soft. "I thought that was okay, though? We've established that we'll take our time."

"I know. I know we both said that, and I know you're excited about finding me. But why were we separated? Our mother was a drug addict. Was she dangerous? Why did AJ take me, if he did take me away? And I won't hear you talk bad about him anymore. He loved me. He took care of me. He tried his best to raise me the right way, but he died. You grew up in this beautiful life. I grew up in foster care. I had no one to depend on during those years, and you, it sounds like you had an abundance of people who cared for you."

She had turned away. I had made her cry. Of course. I spoke the truth, but I had hurt her in the process. I sat back. Was I supposed to comfort her now? Was that my place? I couldn't. Instead, I just continued talking. "I just need you to slow down." So I could breathe. "Just slow down."

She looked back at me, and her eyes had softened. She started to smile, but the car swerved to the left. The force of it was so abrupt that we both pitched against the side.

I saw it in slow motion.

As I felt myself falling forward, Andrea's eyes widened. A look of pure terror washed over her as she flailed backward. She was trying to grab something, but her head was going to hit the door.

I reached for her. My hand was in the air, extending toward her, but then my seatbelt snapped tight. I heard the thud as the back of her head hit the door. She slumped forward immediately.

She was unconscious.

After that, everything happened so fast. I was barely able to understand.

There was shooting.

My door opened.

There was a struggle beside it. Thomas fought someone with a black mask on. He raised a gun, and Thomas brought his arm down in a chopping motion. The gun fell to the ground.

Get it!

I tried to lean out of the car to grab it, but the guy hit Thomas again. They were wrestling each other, and the guy kept trying to throw Thomas out of the way so he could reach inside for me. As they grappled with each other, Thomas' foot hit the gun. It went sliding underneath the car.

Seatbelt. Seatbelt.

Panic rose up in me, but I needed to remain calm. I needed to help. *Get that gun.* That phrase repeated in my head. *Get the gun.* I reached for my seatbelt with stiff fingers, and I fumbled trying to release the latch. Finally my finger hit the button with enough force. The belt released, and I almost pitched forward off the seat.

Oh, Andrea. She slouched forward, her seatbelt holding her in place. And her arms lay beside her like noodles. Her head bobbed back and forth, moving with the motion of the car as it was jostled by the fight outside.

Carter. I needed Carter.

No, get it together, Emma! I yelled at myself in my head. Taking a shuddering breath, I felt fear climbing through my veins. My body started to shut down as more and more gunshots sounded outside. I wanted to curl up in a ball and close my eyes. Maybe everything would go away. But no. It wouldn't.

"Come on, little girlie."

The voice was high-pitched, with an evil twinge.

I huddled further in my bed. My mom was coming. I couldn't hide. She was coming for me, not Andy. Andy was too small. She'd been hurt the day before, and she was still crying in her bed. It was my turn. I wanted to pull the blanket over me. I imagined it was a fortress. Once I was inside, no one could get through to me. I was safe.

My daydreams never helped me. The light outside my door changed to darkness with her shadow. She was right there. She was coming in.

"I know you're in there, Ally. Come on, little girl." She was trying to whisper, but she was giggling. The shadow weaved back and forth. "Honey, it's your mommy. Do you want a bedtime story? We can act out the stories. How about that, Alley Cat?"

The doorknob started to turn.

I had locked it, and I waited, holding my breath. She was going to get mad. She always did. Then she'd have to teach me what was right and wrong. Locking Mom out of the room was the wrong thing to do.

I didn't care. I kept locking it. She could keep hurting me, but... The doorknob stuck, and I heard her angry hiss from the other side of the door. Tears rolled down my face as I stared at the door. I couldn't run anywhere. She'd found me in the closet last time. She was even madder because of that.

"Ally!"

I almost screamed, but I turned to see AJ at the window. He motioned for me. "Come on. Open the window."

If I did she'd be so mad.

If I didn't... I climbed out of my bed and went to the window. Once it was open, I whispered, still crying, "She can't find me, AJ. She can't find me."

A fierce determination flashed over his face. "She won't. I promise, Alley Cat. Come on."

I crawled up and held my arms out. AJ scooped me up, jumped down from the tree, and ran away. I wrapped my little arms around his neck and looked back. The light in my room turned on, and then I heard her screech, "Ally!"

I closed my eyes and pressed into AJ's neck. I burrowed against him, trying to be as small as I could.

Right now the little girl in me wanted to hide. I shoved that person aside and crawled over my sister. I reached for the other door. The gun would be there. I knew it. But as I pulled on the handle, something wrenched me backward.

I found myself in the front seat, and a body clambered over me, pushing me down to the floor. I scratched and clawed at the person on top of me until I realized it was Thomas.

It was Thomas.

He shielded me as he shot at the person trying to come into the car.

Bang! Bang!

Two shots rang out. Then there was silence.

Thomas' body went limp. His arms fell back onto the seat beside us.

Emma, flatten yourself.

It was like Carter was there. I could hear him telling me what to do.

Make yourself as little as possible. They're coming in. Thomas is lying over you. They might not think you're there. You need to be still.

I started trembling and closed my eyes. I wanted to scream. I wanted to fight back. I wanted to run away. I wanted to find a gun and start shooting. But I didn't. I listened to what I know Carter would've told me.

I needed to be calm. I needed to be rational.

I closed my eyes and lay there. Then I escaped. My mind left my body, that car, and whatever was going to happen. I remembered Carter. I remembered AJ. I remembered a good memory from when we were kids.

"Come on, Emma," AJ called from the living room. "Movie night, and you're on popcorn duty."

A normal teenager would've grumbled. Not me. Movie night meant a full night with my brother and his best friend in the house. All night. They weren't out doing whatever they did. They were safe. Carter was safe.

My body warmed. I was going to see Carter for the next few hours. A surge of adrenaline had me buzzing as I got off the bed, put my book away, and walked down the hall. I could hear them talking. They were laughing about something, some guy named Dunvan. AJ called him an idiot. Carter laughed, but not as much as my brother.

My knees were a little unsteady. I was always like this. AJ said it was puberty. It was because of Carter, though. Then I stood in the doorway to the kitchen. AJ had his arm up, making waving motions in the air. "I don't need to worry about him. Dude, I'm primed for a win. Seriously. We should pool our money together. Dunvan's all talk. He won't do shit. You know that. He's been threatening the same crap for years now."

As my brother talked, Carter leaned against the counter. His eyes slid past AJ to me, and he grew somber.

I usually looked away. That's what I did. Everyone liked Carter at school. All the girls talked about him, and when he looked at me, sometimes it was too much. I was no one. But that night, feeling brave for some reason, I stared back at him.

There was a bruise on the side of his jaw. He'd been hit at the corner of his eye too. My eyes fell to his hands, and I didn't know if I should be relieved or not, but I was. His knuckles were swollen and red. He'd fought back. Whoever had hit him, Carter had stood up for himself.

Good.

He smiled, still holding my gaze, as my brother began talking about something else.

I wasn't listening. I don't think Carter was either.

I could hear what was happening around me now, but I stayed in my memory. I was happy there. I was safe.

They were in the car.

Two men were saying my name and cursing because I was unconscious. But I wasn't. I was hiding. I was pretending.

A seatbelt unclicked, and I heard a thud. Then they were gone.

I could hear them running away.

There were more shouts.

More gunshots.

I could hear the cars careening away.

Then more shouts.

More people running.

And someone was back in the car. He yelled, "In here!"

"Come on, Carter." AJ laughed. "You can't tell me you're not interested in Molly Hobalt. That girl is hot, man."

Thomas' body was lifted. I sucked in my breath. I was exposed.

Carter stared at me as he responded. "You're right, AJ. She's very beautiful."

I knew he wasn't talking about Molly Hobalt. I blushed and looked away, but I still felt the weight of his gaze.

"Oh my god," a man exclaimed above me.

Carter watched me the rest of the night, instead of the movie. I had never felt more beautiful.

I opened my eyes. The man was pale as he stared at me, his mouth hanging open. Then he snapped to attention and yelled again, "In here! Now! Cole!"

Cole…

A second later, Carter's friend popped his head around the door, and relief flooded over his face. "Holy shit. Emma."

I looked for my sister, but she was gone.

Carter

It was time.

My insides were stretched thin. My fury billowed inside me. It had become my friend again. As I moved, it went with me. It filled me up and it remained just under my surface. For now.

As soon as I stepped off the elevator, I saw her on the floor. A pillow had been stuffed under her head and a blanket covered her. Cole had sent me directions to an abandoned building, but no one knew I was there. I could hear their voices in a back room, but for that moment, it was only her and me. I couldn't look away.

She looked peaceful. I reached out. A strand of her hair had fallen into her face, but I caught myself. I wanted to tuck it back, but no. She needed to sleep. God. She'd been through too much already.

"Carter?"

Cole stood in the doorway. The voices halted behind him, and I looked up. His eyes widened, and he shifted back on his heel before he caught himself. He stuffed his hand into his pocket and straightened up. "The men didn't notify me you were on your way. I would've met you, if I'd known."

"That's because they didn't see me."

Emma was on the cement floor. She shouldn't be there; she should be home and in bed. But I couldn't demand for him to do better. There was no furniture. They were hiding. I recognized the men who filed into the room behind Cole. He'd gone back to the streets. He'd brought in the men he grew up with. He trusted them.

"We were following—"

"Who was it?" The storm raged in me, ready to strike. I contained it. Barely.

"We were following the Bartels' crew."

I nodded and bent down to scoop up Emma.

"Carter." Cole got into the elevator with me.

His men moved to come with us, but he held a hand out, stopping them. They looked at me, and I saw their concern. But those weren't my men. They were his, and they didn't know me. They only knew of me, and they thought I was a danger to him. *No, not Cole. Not him.*

"We didn't know who they were following. We saw the attack from behind, and once your guards began shooting back, we went in to help."

My men were dead.

My woman could've been.

I didn't care about the details.

The elevator doors slid open, and I walked out, cradling Emma in my arms. His men were guarding the bottom floor, and at the sight of me, their hands went to their guns.

He barked out. "Stop! Put 'em away."

I strode past them.

"Wait, Carter." Cole jogged to keep up with me. He grabbed my arm and pulled me to a stop.

I looked over his shoulder. His men could hear us, and I said, "Leave."

They melted backward.

"Look—"

"I'm not in the Mauricio family," I said, stopping him. Emma was hurt. She was bruised. She had bled. I would not let them break her. "This is me, only me—"

He shot a hand up. "Would you shut up? I'm trying to tell you something. I'm trying to tell you it's fine. Whatever you're going to do, I will back you. And I know the elders will, too. It's you. They went after your woman. You can go and do whatever you want to do."

When I said nothing, he rolled his eyes. "I'm sorry, Carter. I know we talked about you being my secret weapon against them, and yeah, a part of me was considering just waiting for them to piss you off enough so you could do the dirty work. But after we talked, I changed my mind. I realized that was wrong. So I got these men. These are guys I grew up with. I went to school with them, and I trust them. They'll do whatever I tell them, and they're yours. If you need them, let me know."

He glanced away, his voice softening, "I know you had most of your men guarding her. They knew that. They had other cars with them. Shit, Carter. They had a fucking army to go against yours, and I know you still have a few men, but they can't be enough."

Emma moaned in my arms. I held her tighter, wishing I hadn't let her go this morning. "You're not using the Mauricio soldiers?" I asked.

"I can't. Not until I know who to trust. And that's the other thing I needed to tell you. Those men will follow you too. The elders will follow you. They might not trust me yet, but they do trust you. You're the glue in our family right now. Whatever you need, we'll help you."

I nodded, then turned and left. When I carried Emma to the car, there were no guards. Most were dead. The few left alive, I had let go so they could return home, mourn their brothers. As I bundled her into the seat and walked around to the front to drive home, the solitude felt oddly comforting.

When I got her home, I didn't expect to see anyone. Instead, Michael, Peter, and Drake met me. They weren't in their suits, but had dressed in dark sweatshirts and jackets with jeans.

"I told you guys you could go home."

Drake moved forward and motioned to take Emma from me. When I didn't relinquish her, Michael spoke up. "He'll just take her to the bedroom. That's all."

"I'll tuck her into bed, boss."

Reluctantly, I allowed him to take her. I wanted to go with them. I wanted to be the one to tuck her in, but they were right. I needed to remain behind. They deserved my time, and I raked a hand over my face. "Guys, I'm sorry—"

"You pay us," Michael cut me off. "We're not here because you're our boss. We're family, too. We follow you because we respect you."

"We lost so many today."

"Not Emma. Or you."

Peter cleared his throat. He wasn't as tall as Michael, but he was broader in the shoulders and thicker in muscle. "Our job is to protect both of you," he said. "We know the consequences of our job, the risks that are part of it. We die to protect you."

Drake returned and nodded. "I agree with them, boss."

"They weren't just our coworkers, they were our brothers," Michael said. "We want to help you. Tell us what to do."

"I need to know everything. I need to know their businesses here, their warehouses, any side deals they have, everything. I want to know their mistress' information, the playgrounds for their children. I want to know every hiding spot they're going to use."

"Got it." Drake and Peter nodded. I gave them instructions on what to do if they ran into trouble, and they left.

Michael remained behind, taking a position next to the door.

"Michael," I said.

He looked at me.

"You're not my bodyguard anymore."

"What do you mean?"

"We're a team now. This place is guarded. I have alarms set. If you'd like to sleep, go ahead."

"But Emma." He gestured toward the bedroom. "I figured you'd want to be with her."

"I do, and I will be, but we take shifts now. Go and rest. I'll stay awake for this shift."

"Sir?" He still seemed confused.

"Go. Rest. It's my turn. If anyone comes near the building, they'll trip the alarms."

"Drake and Peter?"

"They know the codes to get in. They'll be fine."

He nodded slowly. "Okay, sir."

"Michael," I called again.

He turned.

"Move into one of the main bedrooms," I told him. "We need to be in closer proximity now, and it's not sir anymore. I'm Carter."

Another nod. "Yes, si—Carter." Then a corner of his mouth lifted in a smile before he headed to grab his stuff.

I checked all the locks, the codes, every inch of our home. Everything was secure. Emma was still sleeping, and I wanted to go to her, but safety was first. Grabbing a coat, I walked the perimeter of our building and checked all the alarms I'd set there as well. After that, I checked the next block over and repeated the same routine. I was thorough. Then I went back.

We were safe. No one knew of this location. Noah knew I had a place in New York, but he didn't know of *this* place, and Emma had never been here. This was my safeguard for the war. Not even Cole knew about this place, or Gene. The Bartels would find us. I knew it was a matter of time, but when they did, they would have a fight on their hands. Until then, I'd take the fight to them.

Michael had taken the bedroom closest to the entrance doors. I checked in on him, and he was indeed sleeping. Good. He'd need it. Then I moved to my own bedroom.

Emma had curled up in the sheets. She had them tucked under her chin as she balled into the fetal position.

I stopped now, for a moment, and let the reality crash over me.

I almost lost her.

They almost got her.

My jaw hardened. Never again.

Emma

When I woke, I didn't need time to remember. It had been plaguing me while I slept. They killed Thomas and took my sister. It was like Mallory all over again, but this time I knew my sister was in danger from the start. I had only realized the true danger of Ben when it was almost too late.

And Thomas…

I squeezed my eyes shut. Someone else was gone because of me. Someone who was a friend. Feeling the threat of tears, I bit down on my lip. I couldn't feel it, not now so I rolled to my back. Carter was perched on the edge of the bed and watching me. He wore a black sweatshirt and black pants. His dark blond hair seemed darker, and I realized it was wet. As I sat up, I saw the concern in his wolf-like eyes. A shiver wound its way through me as I held his gaze. He must have known what had happened to me, what had happened to my sister. But there was no reason to go into hysterics. It was what it was.

Thomas was dead. My sister was gone.

I'd feel later. I welcomed the physical pain and I had plenty of that. My body was sore. It was still hurting from the bomb, and now it had new aches and pains from last night.

I didn't care.

I needed Carter. I needed to remember we were alive. It was the two of us. I couldn't lose him, no matter what happened.

I cupped the back of his neck and pulled him close.

"Emma?"

I shook my head. No words. I didn't want to talk. I didn't want to feel the pain, not yet. I wanted to feel *him*. I wanted to feel love instead. I wanted to taste. I wanted to be alive. As if sensing my unspoken need, his eyes darkened, and he lifted me up to straddle him.

I closed my eyes and held the man I loved. Resting my forehead to his, I placed my arms on his shoulders as he held my hips. His thumbs rubbed back and forth. *This. Right here.* He was the most powerful man I knew, and he was all mine.

I had what so many women wanted. They were drawn to him because he was powerful and deadly. It wasn't a mirage. He was dangerous, and that same shiver took hold of my spine and burrowed deep, melded with me at a cellular level. It was the good shiver, the delicious kind.

I leaned back, tipping us down to the bed, and I wound my legs around his waist, pulling him down between my legs.

Dangerous. Yes. Carter was dangerous. I raked a hand up his arm, curled it around his chin, and pulled him down to me. But he was *my* danger. He was *my* protector. And he was *mine* to protect.

"Are you su—"

I fused my lips with his. A tingle raced through me. I wanted to keep feeling sensations like this, not the other stuff. And as Carter rolled me beneath him, he helped me forget. For a little while he made me feel only him.

Afterwards, much, much afterwards, Carter slid out of me and moved to his side. He kept one hand on my stomach. "Are you sore?"

"Don't." I rolled to my side to face him and shook my head.

"Don't what?"

"Regret this. Yes, my body is hurting, but it's because of the bomb, because of the assault on the car. That's from them. They inflicted that on me, and I won't let them have power over me anymore." I ran a hand up his arm. He was so strong, his veins corded under his skin. "I won't let them take this away from me."

His face softened, and he tipped my chin up. "I love you."

"Always," I replied, and my eyelids lowered as he bent closer, his lips grazing over mine. It was the gentlest of kisses.

He whispered against my lips. "I'm sorry about your sister."

"Me, too."

Pulling back, he let out a soft sigh. "I'll find her, Emma. This isn't like your roommate. We'll get her back. She'll be safe. I'm not as entangled with politics as I was then. I don't have to wait this time. Last time everything had to be discussed and approved. This time, I'm out. I can do whatever I want, but I know Cole will back me. The elders will, too."

"Why did they take her?"

"Besides the obvious?" His thumb brushed over my forehead in a tender motion.

"They think she's me."

"Yeah. I'm assuming. And I'm hoping that when they figure it out, they'll use her as a bargaining chip instead of getting rid of her and coming for you again. They've messed up twice. They'll be braced for retaliation this time."

Retaliation. I looked at the clothes I had shredded from him earlier. He'd been dressed to blend in with the night and do his vengeance. People were going to die—people already had—and there was going to be so much more. I was terrified of what else was going to happen, but the war was here. I was involved. I wasn't going to hide this time.

"What about the police?" I asked.

"What about them?"

"Should we report her missing? Or has that already been done?" Another question came to the tip of my tongue, but at the tightening around his mouth, I held it back. "What?"

"If the police are involved, that means questioning. That means hours spent being interrogated. That means they'll watch us. That means we can't do what we need to do."

"So no one knows? Your men, Carter."

"My men will be traced to me, yes, but it'll take them a while. None of them are in the system. They weren't allowed to hold any identification, and anything they did have on them, guns included, will be traced back to a shell company. Eventually they'll get employee records and go to the families, which will have them looking for me, but that'll be then. Not now. I'm hoping to be able to deal with this quickly, then go and tell the families myself."

"If you can't? If the police get there first?"

"Then I'll apologize to them for that injustice as well. I can't leave this war, not yet."

"I know," I told him.

His hand slid back down the side of my face, and I leaned into his touch, moving so I could kiss the palm of his hand.

"I want to help," I said.

He pulled his hand away and sat up.

The distance those words created between us was frightening. I sat up as well, holding his gaze. The sheet fell away from me, but I didn't care. I had to be firm. I had to sound strong. He couldn't see any shadow of doubt in my eyes.

"I mean it," I added.

"No."

"Carter—"

He stood and reached for his pants. "No."

"Carter—"

"No." He zipped them and reached for his shirt.

I watched as he finished getting dressed. He was putting on some shoes when I tried again. "Carter—"

"I *just* got you back." He whipped back to face me, his eyes seething. "A bomb, Emma. A *bomb*, then this car. They were trying for you. If your sister hadn't been there, they would've found you. They would've looked for you, and the first place they would've searched would've been underneath the big bodyguard. I am sorry your sister was taken. I will get her back, but if she hadn't been there? You. It would've been you." He gritted his teeth as he finished, and his shoulders were tense, so rigid. "I would already have a body count in the thirties by now, if it had been you. Heaven and hell. That's where I would go for you. So, no, you *cannot* help."

Going to the dresser, he pulled out a 9mm and stuck it into a shoulder holster. He reached back inside and paused, and a moment later he pulled out another handgun. Meeting my eyes, his harried and haunted, he placed the gun onto the edge of the bed.

"I'm not a fan of Theresa, but right now, I could hug her," he said quietly. "You know how to use this."

It wasn't a question, but I nodded anyway.

"This is your friend. You wear this everywhere. You get so used to it that you feel naked without it. Got it?"

"Got it."

He paused, studying everything about me. He was testing me. A year ago, I would've been scared. Now, I was just wary. "I'm fine, Carter."

His eyes narrowed. He didn't believe me.

I pulled the sheet so I was covered and looked down at my hands in my lap. They weren't shaking. They were calm. I held them up. "See. I'm fine. This isn't our first time here, and I feel like we've been getting ready for this forever. *War. It's coming.* Those were your words and well, it's here. I'm not shocked. I'm scared—I won't lie to you—but I'm here, and I'll help in any way—"

A warning flared in his eyes.

"—Any way you'll let me," I finished. "Whether that means holding down the fort here or going out to fight side by side with you, I'll do what you say."

At my words, his shoulders dropped, relaxing. "Do you mean that?"

"I do."

I did, until he was threatened. Then all promises went out the window. I'd protect him with my life. "You have to promise me one thing," I added.

He grew wary now. "What?"

"Be. Safe." I swallowed over a lump. "I know you're the Cold Killer, but it goes both ways. You love me. I love you back. I'll be safe, but you hold up your end, too. Be. Safe."

He let out a deep breath. The lines around his eyes seemed to deepen, and he crossed the room to me. Bending down, he cupped my head and pressed his lips to mine. At the slight contact, I surged up and wound my arms around his neck.

He gave me air, for that small moment. Once he left, I'd be holding my breath until he returned, and I knew the process would repeat over and over again until he found my sister.

I wanted to pull him back down. I wanted to stall him and keep him with me a moment longer, but I didn't. I sat there as he turned and left.

I could hear conversation a beat later, then a door shut. It wasn't long before one of the guards cleared his throat outside the room, the door still closed between us.

"Miss Emma?"

"Drake?"

"Just letting you know Peter and I are here. Michael went with Mr.—he went with Carter."

The lump doubled in size, but I called back as if it weren't there, "Thank you, Drake."

Michael. Peter. Drake. Carter. Me.

That was all that was left.

CHAPTER 18

Emma

Carter returned in the morning, but he hadn't found her. The next day was the same. Then the third day. The fourth. Fifth. The days blended into a week, then into the second week. All the same results. Nothing. They couldn't find Andrea.

The next few weeks felt like we were living in an alternate universe. There were no friends to spend time with. There were no paparazzi in hiding because *we* were in hiding. No one knew where we were. No wine nights. No gun range nights. No nights at the club. Even the guards—we all protected each other. Carter kept looking for Andrea, and as the weeks progressed, a routine started for us.

Peter and Drake would go out during the day. Their job was to gather information, so they followed the Bartels like ghosts, wherever they went. They identified all the men who worked for them. They figured out all of their schedules for each day of the week.

Each night when they returned, they'd meet with Carter and Michael. Sometimes I joined the meeting. Other times I couldn't stomach more bad news. They never seemed to get any closer. Then, after the meeting, Carter would leave. Most times he went alone.

Sometimes he took Michael with him, but every time he came back, he was covered in blood.

When he came home, sometimes in the middle of the night and other times in the early morning, he walked past me in the bedroom, stripping off his clothes. He always left them in a pile and spent an hour in the shower.

In the beginning, I got in with him. He'd stand there, letting the shower rain down on him with his head bent, his eyes closed, and his hands clenched as the blood ran off him. Even after I'd cleaned him, he would remain in there.

Then I realized he was remembering everything he'd done. He was, in a way, washing away what he had done as he let that water rain down on him. So I began leaving him alone. As he showered, I gathered up his clothes and washed them. Carter never spoke of it. All he would say, later in the morning, was that he'd cleaned out another area the Bartel family controlled. That was all. No one asked, but we all knew.

The Cold Killer had returned.

Carter was killing men, and he was doing it alone. I could only assume he had Michael go with him if there was too much danger, if he needed backup for certain places.

The news was on in the kitchen when my sister was declared missing. Carter had returned a couple of hours earlier, and Drake was making toast as we all sat down at the table for breakfast. Michael brewed the coffee, Peter had grabbed a newspaper, and I made the eggs.

"Breaking news today. Andrea Nathans, daughter of prominent hotelier Edward Nathans and his wife, Cherise, has been declared missing. The police issued a statement not long ago that she was last seen in New York City where she went to reunite with a long lost sister. Andrea Nathans is twenty-six years old and described as slender, with brown hair and brown eyes. She is a known marathon runner. As more details are released, we'll be updating you with the latest."

The anchor turned to her cohost, and they began chatting about my sister. Was there more information? Did the police know anything? Were they sharing that information with the public? When and where was she last seen? They kept discussing Andrea, but they had no more information than what they'd already shared.

Then the pictures started.

The first image showed her alone. She smiled at the camera with her hand reaching out to the photographer. A second was of her in a graduation gown, and a third with a group of friends. Their faces were blurred out, but she leaned over with them, drinks in their hands. In the fourth picture, she was standing with a couple. The other faces were again blurred, but she looked so happy.

Those were her parents. I could tell.

She looked loved. She *was* loved. I could see it in her eyes.

Carter's phone jarred me. Its ring was loud and harsh, but I realized I hadn't heard it for a long time. As he answered it and headed to the back for privacy, I frowned. He must've been in contact with others, but he never talked about the life we'd all left behind to hide.

When he came back, he looked at me for a moment. No words were shared, but I knew he was leaving again. He grimaced as he glanced at Michael. "That was Cole. He needs to meet."

Immediately, Michael and Peter reached for their guns and checked whether their clips were full. Drake did the same, but Carter stopped him. "No, Drake. You need to stay with Emma."

"You sure?"

Carter nodded. "Yeah. This is just business. I've been watching the news, but nothing's been leaked about the Bartel losses. I'm assuming Cole's been getting in there to clean up after me." He pointed at the television screen. "It's about that. The police know

Andrea was here to see Emma. They found the last restaurant she visited." He gazed at me again. "There's footage."

All eyes focused on me.

"They're looking for Emma now?" Drake asked.

Carter nodded, up and down, like the weight of the world had just crashed down on his shoulders. "Yeah. I'm positive."

So my face would soon be up on that screen, too. I laughed, though I didn't realize it until I heard the sound for myself. It sounded like someone else. Hysteria, anger, bitterness, and panic all mixed into my laughter. And it just kept coming. More and more until I laughed so hard I cried.

No one said a word.

They seemed to be waiting until I finished, but I didn't. I couldn't make it stop. I bent over. My stomach started to hurt, but I still couldn't contain it. This, this whole thing—my sister had been kidnapped and now I was going to be "famous" once more. For being the reason she was gone. Me. It was all my fault.

If she hadn't come into my life, she'd still be with those people who loved her. She'd still be happy. She'd be with her parents.

But nope. I came into her life, and look what happened. Instant travesty.

That was me. That was my life. Everyone I loved went away. Everyone I let close ended up hurt. It didn't matter by whose hands. They were still gone. AJ. Mallory. Andrea. Thomas.

Carter was the only one who hadn't—as that thought entered my mind, my laughter finally stopped. It choked me instead. My god, Carter. I couldn't lose him.

Then instead of laughing, I was crying. Uncontrollably. My cheeks felt wet and tears landed on my arms. I couldn't do a thing. I could only stare at him.

Nothing could happen to him. Not like Mallory and Andrea. Not like my brother. Nothing meant nothing.

"Emma?" Carter approached me, his voice soft. He reached out.

I backed away. It was my fault. All of this. "No," I whispered.

"Emma, whatever you're thinking, stop. You're not being rational right now."

I wasn't. But who was? Everyone was dead. These four men were going to die, too. I felt it in my bones. I was going to be alone— alone and condemned.

"Emma." His hand touched my elbow.

I tried to shake it off, but he gripped me harder. He pulled me to him and shielded me from the others. It didn't matter. They knew I was losing it. I shook my head and lifted my hands to Carter's chest. He was trying to protect me, but didn't he see? He didn't need to. I was the one who should've been protecting them. It was me, only me. I was the reason they were going to die.

"Emma." His voice dropped so he was barely speaking. I could hear him, though. His voice was right next to my ear, and he wrapped his arms around my body, hugging me to him. Suddenly, he dipped and scooped me up, cradling me against him.

I should've stopped him. I should've kicked, maybe tried to leave. If I ran away, they'd live then? That made perfect sense, but I didn't have the fight in me.

Carter swept out of the room and took me to the bed. I knew he had to go. As he laid me down, I expected him to leave, but he didn't. He scooted in behind me and held me. I felt completely spent. No tears, no laughter.

I was numb.

Carter

"You've been busy."

Cole greeted me as I approached him in the warehouse a little later that morning. There were no men around. I'd called and asked if he would station them at a distance. He had hesitated before complying, and I knew his worry. A person asked for something like that when they didn't trust the other one. But that wasn't the case here, and I needed to make sure he knew.

"The less people who know about what I'm doing, the better," I explained.

His head tilted back and he studied me a moment. "I see."

"It's not that I don't trust you." I gestured to the emptiness around us. "It's that I don't trust your men."

"My men or the Mauricio soldiers?"

"Your men."

His nostrils flared slightly. "You trust the Mauricio soldiers, though?"

"You're still fighting with the elders?"

"More of them are willing to follow me. And it's not just lip service, but I know there are still a few who won't support me. I'm close to filtering them out."

Ah yes. With his surveillance of his own family members. He was still playing detective while I was out there taking lives. Yes. Mauricio politics didn't seem as important anymore. I couldn't hold back a disgusted sound. I was growing impatient with him.

Cole narrowed his eyes. "You disapprove?"

"Yes," I said simply. "You should be fighting your enemy, not your family."

"I offered to help you—"

"I don't need backup when I go into one of their warehouses. What I do need is for you and the elders to get your sticks out of your asses and start hitting some of their businesses yourselves. Going from one building to another, then finding their new hideouts is exhausting. It's taking time, and Emma's sister may not still be alive."

"She is." Cole looked down. His tone turned wary. "Whether you realize it or not, I *am* helping you. I'm holding down the fort while you're creating a shitstorm. If you'd give me a heads up, I'd appreciate it. As it is now, I send my men out to try and find what places you've hit during the night. We've been able to get in there to clean everything up so that the police aren't called. We've been able to keep this quiet, but you're not making it easy. So far only the Bartels know they're being annihilated. Carter, we're going to miss a place that you hit. If you tell us—"

"No."

"Why? Why won't you trust me?"

I opened my mouth to explain that no one could know, I couldn't run the risk of anyone leaking the information, but he held up his hands.

"I get it," he said. "You're being smart. Still. A clue would help, and you could only give it to me. I can have my men dispatched." I shook my head, and he let out his own disgusted sound. "My god. I know, I know. You can't trust anything. Well, you're making them scramble. That's for sure." Cole sighed. "My men have been watching them too, and they move every night now. They can't catch you, and they've been trying. Half the city is a ghost town because they're out there, wondering which place you're going to hit next."

"Do you know where they're holding Andrea?"

He didn't answer, and that was my answer in itself.

"Carter, I'm sorr—" he said.

I cut him off, shaking my head. "Don't. I'll keep looking."

"If it's any consolation, they're not sure if it's you or if it's us. You haven't left anyone alive to spread the word that the Cold Killer's back." He grinned.

I did not.

He sighed again. "Okay, yeah. I get it. I'll make some moves on my end. I've no doubt that the Bartel elders are meeting every night.

If we found one of their meetings, that'd help. They'd know where she's being held. I'm sure of it."

"You said she's alive. How do you know?"

He barked out a short, harsh laugh. "Because they're trying to ransom her to us. A new picture of her comes in the mail every other day. We're trying to find out who's delivering the pictures, but they come from all different angles. Different elders get them in their mailboxes. One was delivered to one of the kids in his backpack. His teacher found it and went into hysterics. We bought her silence. They haven't demanded ransom yet, but I think they're trying to scare you off through us."

"Is she intact?"

"Yeah. She's thin. It looks like they're beating her, but she's got all her parts."

I didn't ask what else they were doing to her. I couldn't think about that. If they did that to her, they would've been doing that to Emma. My blood turned cold, just imagining. I forced my mind away. "So you have been helping me."

"Yeah. I have. Or I've been trying. I'll keep trying too, and I'm close to fortifying the elders. I promise. We'll be much more effective once we've weeded out those who won't support us. They might not turn on you, but they'll turn on me."

"I know." He didn't need to keep explaining. "Have the police been in touch with you?"

"Yes. You know that's why I called."

I nodded. "What are they asking?"

"They want you. They want to talk to Emma. They know she's with you, but they don't quite know why you're gone. They don't know about the killings yet. They're still in the dark, and I think they've reached out to some of your colleagues, that other friend of yours. Everyone's covering, saying they've talked to you and you're busy. But, Carter, once they know the Bartels are losing people, they're going to swoop in. They'll come fast and hard."

"I know."

"They're watching us, too. Every day we see a new cop following. It's tense now. They know about the bombing. We covered everything up with the car attack, but they have to be wondering if a mob war is going on."

"Just keep doing what you're doing," I told him. And I would keep doing what I was doing. Nothing would get solved until I found Andrea, or—I couldn't think about the alternative. After Emma's breakdown, I don't know if she could handle it.

"We will. I needed to know what you wanted me to do about the cops, but we'll keep covering for you."

"Thank you, Cole. And I'll call you when I'm done with each spot." I held my arm out, and he grasped it, linking our forearms. We held each other's arms for a moment before letting go. We hadn't done that since the early days of my training him, so long ago when he first went into hiding. I had started again with Michael, Peter, and Drake, and it felt good to have that stronghold back in my life once more.

"Are you okay? With...what you're doing?" Cole asked.

No. It was cold out there. I shrugged. "It doesn't matter. I have to find Emma's sister."

"And when you do or they—"

My eyes flashed in warning, and he heeded it, not saying the words I didn't want to think about, not yet.

Revenge and rescue. Those had become my two missions over the last few weeks, but he was right. It was coming to an end. Either I would find Andrea, or they would kill her. I had to start thinking beyond what I was doing now. To me, the end was always with Emma and the Mauricio family, but now things were changing. I was tired of this life. I was tired of killing.

I needed out. Emma needed out.

"I don't know." That was all I said, for now.

Carter

I heard her in the gym as soon as I stepped inside. Michael was washing dishes. There was no greeting. He knew where I was going, and he pointed down the hallway, even though I didn't need to be told. I dumped a bag of weapons that I'd picked up from my old place on the table and headed past him.

When I got to the gym doorway, I heard a small *thump, thump* as she hit the punching bag. Hunched over, her arms up next to her face, she looked fierce. But when her hand hit the bag, that ferocity left immediately. The bag didn't move an inch.

"Are you using your whole body?" I asked.

"Yes, and my whole body is laughing at me." Her hands fell to her sides as her shoulders slumped. "I survived a bomb and a potential kidnapping, but my body is weak, and I hate it. If my body's going to be weak, fine, but I have to be sharp up here." She lifted a taped hand to her head. "I broke down, Carter. I can't do that again."

"And you think hitting the bag will help you with that?"

"No, but sitting around doing a Sudoku puzzle will just put me back to sleep. I figure it's the two birds with one stone thing." She nodded to the bag again. "Thought it would help both my body and mind."

"Emma," I said as I stepped inside and shut the door. "You need to rest."

She shot me a look. "You're not resting."

Because I couldn't. Because there was no time. "Emma."

"Stop." She rolled her eyes and resumed the stance to punch again. Arms up. Feet apart. Shoulders back. "I'm useless right now, so let me do this. It makes me feel helpful, at least."

"Emma, you have to rest. That will make your mind strong again."

"No." She closed her eyes and seemed in pain as she lifted her hands to press against her temples. "You don't understand. I—fuck it. They took her, and I can't—" Her face contorted. She looked in agony. "They took my sister because of me, and I can't do a damn thing about it." Rearing back, she punched the bag in a savage motion. "My sister—because of this." Her hand curled up and shot toward her face, like she was going to punch herself.

I grabbed for her, but she stopped just short of hitting herself. She looked at her hand, a hair's width away from her nose, and a sickening laugh left her. Tears rolled down her face as she bent over, still laughing, still crying.

"Emma."

She looked up. "I'm miserable, Carter. They're torturing her because of me."

"No."

"Yes. *Me!*"

"No." I grabbed her and hauled her close. "They're torturing her because of me, because I love you, because I won't let you go. That's why." My pulse raced. I loved her, and I was almost crazy because of it. She couldn't blame herself. "Me, Emma. It's my fault. Not yours. If you want to punish someone, punish me. I should've let you go a year ago—"

Her eyes went wild, and she surged up on her toes, moving against me. "No."

"—but I couldn't." I gentled my tone. I needed to get control of myself. "I couldn't. I'm sorry. I couldn't let you go."

"No, Carter." A whimper slipped out as she shook her head. "No. You can't say that."

"It's the truth."

"I love you. This was my fault—"

"Stop it!" I shouted.

She kept hurting herself. I saw the pain that flashed in her eyes as she cast blame on her actions, on her being herself.

"She's your blood family, and you can be curious about her," I said, trying to be calm. "You can want to get to know her. That's normal. That's the right thing, a person should be able to do that. But you can't, because of me. All of this is because of me. My god, you're allowed to want to have a family. That's what she is. That's what I did. That's the whole reason we're in this mess, because I couldn't be alone. AJ was dead. You were safer away from me than with me. So I let you go, but I went to the mafia. Because of that choice, your sister was taken."

"Carter," she whispered.

"Stop, Emma." She was breaking down, and I couldn't stop it, any of it. Every day she broke a little bit more—every time I came home without her sister. She wasn't eating. She wasn't healing. This was because of me. "This is my fault. *Never* yours."

"Carter."

She wanted to fight. Fine. I'd teach her how to fight. I gestured to the punching bag. "Show me your stance."

"What?"

"Show me. If that was me, how would you stand against me?"

"I..." Her eyebrows furrowed, and she tilted her head to the side. "What do you mean?"

I moved around the bag to stand beside it and gestured for Emma to square against me. "I'm a Bartel. I'm coming at you. How would you fight me?"

She raised her little hands, already formed into fists.

"No," I said.

"What?" She lowered her hands.

"Raise them up again."

She did, and I swept an arm around her, tucking her against my side. I walked in a small circle, carrying her. She couldn't kick me. Her arms were trapped against my body. Her only weapon was her teeth. She could bite me, but that wouldn't kill me. After setting her down, I asked, "Do you know what you did wrong?"

"Besides doing what you told me to do?" she retorted. The tears and hysterics had ceased. The fighting spirit had come back to her, putting color in her cheeks again. She blew a short puff of air, cooling herself. Her hands went to her hips, and she struck a defiant pose. Her chin lifted. "Okay. Show me what I did wrong."

She was challenging me. Good. "You failed my test just by being in front of me. If you're going hand-to-hand with a guy, especially someone who knows how to fight and is bigger than you, you won't win. You come sideways. You come from behind. You catch him off guard."

"How do I do that?"

"Distract him."

She looked down at her boobs and puffed out her chest. "With these? It's you. Besides taking my clothes off, I don't know how to distract you."

"Not me." I fought back a grin. "Though your girls look especially good right now." They strained in her sports bra and sweat-soaked shirt. They perked up even more under my gaze.

She cursed. "Stop it. Teach me how to fight."

"Know your opponent." I tapped the side of my head. "Get in here. Figure out what he wants. If it is knowledge, attention, his ego stroked—whatever it is, you give it to him. And you get a weapon. As soon as his guard is dropped, you hit him hard. You put all your weight behind that weapon. You have to make the first contact successful. He needs to be knocked unconscious, or he's ready, and he's pissed. If you don't have a gun, he'll get you. That's a guarantee. Don't set yourself up for failure."

She sighed. "That's easier said than done. I don't know the Bartels—"

"Yes, you do. What do they want?"

"Me."

Ice plunged through my veins at her answer. *Hell no.* That wouldn't happen.

"So use that," I said, forcing my voice to stay even. "Use me. They want me. They want information. You can give that to them, but once the wall is dropped—"

She nodded. She was so eager. "I got it. Disarm. Weapon. Crack. Knock him unconscious. I can do that."

I should have taught her some moves, maybe some kicks, lunges, how to twist and evade, but as I kept looking at her, the idea of teaching her faded fast and the idea of taking her to bed quickly replaced it. *Fuck.* I wanted her. Every day. Every night. She was mine.

Her chest heaved up and down. The rest of her body was soaked in sweat, and she'd even taped her hands, like I did. She'd gone through so much, and the idea that she was training to go through more knotted my own hands into fists.

She noticed my reaction. Her eyes lingered on my hands. "Carter?"

"You shouldn't have to learn how to do this." My voice dipped low and hoarse. It was my job to protect her. I wasn't doing that job well enough. "I'm so goddamn sorry for this."

"Stop." Her shoulders dropped, and she came to stand in front of me. Her hands rested on my hips, and she looked up at me. Her eyes were warm and soft. Her lips opened, and she swallowed. I saw concern in her eyes. "Carter, I'm not in the life because of you. Stop blaming yourself. I came to you. Remember? My roommate was being raped. My brother was killed. I killed Jeremy Dunvan. Me. You wanted me to see past Ben's manipulations, remember? I did. I saw the other side of the world, and I've gotten myself prepared. All of this isn't because of you. You're forgetting one thing. I wouldn't have my sister if it *wasn't* for you. She found me because the media is obsessed with you. I have *you* to thank for my sister."

There was still a bruise at the corner of her eye. It was tiny and yellow, but it was there. It shouldn't have been. "Emma," I whispered, dropping my head to rest my forehead against hers. "I'll get her back. I promise."

"Stop." Her hand went to my lips. "Stop."

Her eyes darkened, and the need for her spiked in me. I reached for her without thinking and hoisted her in the air. Her legs parted as I peeled off her shirt and bra. She fit against me, like she was made for me. Grasping the back of her head, I pulled her lips down to mine. One touch from them, and I was in a desert. I needed more, just more of everything. My blood was damn boiling. As I backed her up to the wall, Emma arched backward, pushing her breasts against my chest. I reached out to lock the door, and after that, it was just her. All of her. All of me.

I kissed everywhere. I caressed all over her. My god, I loved this woman. Cupping her breast, I ran my hand over her nipple. It sprang up, and she gasped.

"Carter," she moaned, grinding into me.

I knew. I *know*. I needed to be in her. She was beautiful. So damn beautiful. I wanted to savor every time with her. I wanted to relish every inch of her. Setting her against the wall, I knelt and kissed my way down. Her lips. Her chin. Her throat. Her chest. Between her breasts. Each of her breasts. My tongue swept around her nipple, and I sucked before continuing down to her stomach. My hands cradled her hips, and I felt her starting to tremble as my mouth lingered there.

She grabbed a handful of my hair and held on, like she was guiding me. A jolt of pleasure surged in me, and I lowered her shorts, then took her in my mouth. She bucked under me and another moan came from her. Her whole body shuddered now. I kept licking and sucking. I loved this woman. I was going to love every part of her.

"Carter." She tried to pull me up. "Please."

I thrust my tongue inside her, but she'd had enough. She jerked on my hair again, so I stood and used my fingers. They thrust inside her, going deep, and lifting her off the floor. One of her legs wrapped around my waist as I leaned over her, my fingers going in and out. I held her weight and kept her still. I kept moving. In and out. Deeper, then pulling out, plunging back in.

I looked up to see that she was watching me. Her eyes were lidded, darkened with lust, but I saw the love she had for me. I groaned. I couldn't stay out of her anymore. "Fuck it." I hoisted her up one more time, and Emma was waiting for me. She was ready. Her other leg wrapped around my waist again, and then I was in her. All the way.

We moved together.

I kept thrusting, and she grinded against me. Our hips strained against each other. I didn't think I could get more inside her, but she changed our angle, and suddenly, I was there. I was so deep. As I kept sliding in and out of her, I closed my eyes and just felt her. She trailed a hand down my face, tracing my lips.

That small touch. So gentle. So loving. That was Emma. Then she took hold of my hip and began matching my movements. She pounded down on me, as hard as I was going. We were screwing and making love, all at the same time.

I felt my climax coming. I didn't want it to. I wanted to hold out, and I slowed, gripping her hips so she slowed as well. As she did, she held herself still, and my hand went to her entrance. I began rubbing over it, applying pressure and then softening as she gasped. Then, when I felt her body starting to tense, I began moving inside her again.

She was coming.

I kept touching her, kept thrusting in her.

Her legs suddenly convulsed, wrapping my waist in an ironclad grip, and I felt her come. Her entire body lifted, arching against me. She kept trembling, and I waited, going a little slower. As she started to subside, I watched. I waited. Then her eyes opened, and she bit down on her lip, nodding to me.

It was my turn.

I began pounding into her. Harder. Deeper. *Shit.* I would never have enough of this woman. Ever. Emma worked with me, holding my hips as an anchor while she lifted her body up and down, too. I leaned a hand against the wall above her head, my other hand grabbed her thigh, and I kept going. I was going to come. It was nearing. I closed my eyes, once more going into her, and it washed over me. Waves of pleasure rolled through me, leaving me weakened and satiated. No, that was Emma. No other woman made me feel like this. It was her, only her.

Opening my eyes, I found her watching me and smiling as her chest heaved for air.

"I love you," she murmured.

Goddamn. I kissed her and whispered against her lips, "I love you, too."

"Carter."

She sounded so sad. I pulled back and waited. A hand always punched through my chest when I heard that tone from her, when she was hurting.

"I'm scared you won't get her back."

That hand was still in my chest, and it rammed further down, all the way to my gut. I shook my head. The hand kept ripping through me, but I said, "I will find her. I promise."

A voice in my head warned me not to lie to her, but I told him to shut up. I would, but I couldn't promise to find her alive. I prayed Emma didn't push that. I couldn't say those words. I couldn't lie to her.

She didn't.

She nodded and leaned against me, letting me hold all of her weight. I was grateful to hold her there, just enjoying the feel of her in my arms. I would hold her till my last breath, if I could.

"Uh..."

We tensed, hearing Michael clear his throat on the other side of the door.

"I don't know what I'm interrupting in there, but I have to interrupt," he said. "I'm sorry. I'm sorry. I'm sorry. I'm going to keep apologizing because, again, I have no idea what I'm interrupting, and I have to do that. Interrupt. That's what I'm doing right now, and I'd punch a guy for doing this to me—"

"What is it?" A growl formed in the back of my throat.

"Uh. Yeah. Peter and Drake are back." He paused. "They found Andrea."

Emma gasped, shoving me back. She dropped to the floor and ran for the door, but I caught her arm, swinging her back to me. "What?" A snarl twisted her lips.

I grabbed her shirt from the floor and pushed it against her chest.

"Oh." As she covered herself, I pulled up her shorts. She glanced down and another, "Oh," left her lips. "Yeah. Thank you."

I zipped myself up, grinning down at her. "You're mine. Not theirs."

She reached up and pressed her lips against mine. "You're mine, too." Then she had the door open and ran through it, asking, "Where is she?"

Emma

Peter and Drake had found her. That information was cemented in me, securing my hope. She was alive. She had to be. I was ready to go with them, fight beside them, but Carter wouldn't have it. Peter had been shot as they got away. They were going to regroup, but I had to stay back and tend to Peter.

At first I refused, but I saw the warning from Carter. If I didn't, he said he would lock me in the bathroom and be damned the damage I would do as I tried to get out. *Fine.* I told him I would stay back. I would dress Peter's wound.

That was what he wanted to hear. So that's what I said.

And now, after seeing that the bullet had gone all the way through Peter's shoulder, and after finishing his bandages, I had another item on my agenda.

Spying a bungee on the floor behind his chair, I pulled it through a loop on his pants, tying it in a firm knot to the chair where he sat. It wouldn't stop him, but it would give me the element of surprise. That was all I needed. I waited another second, but he wasn't paying attention. It was now or never.

"Peter."

I secured the end of the bandage over his wound and stepped back. He'd put his gun on the counter behind us. I knew what I was going to do, but I was an idiot. Still, I didn't see another way around him, and with my decision finalized in my head, I stepped backward. He inspected the bandage as I took one more step backward and reached behind me. My hand closed around the gun's end.

"Hmm?" He lifted his arm to look. "What'd you say, Em?" He looked now.

I held my breath. He didn't know what I had in my hand. He just saw the set of my jaw and the determination in my eyes.

"No, Emma." He shook his head. "Let them handle it. It's for the best."

It wasn't. My alarms had been going off since he got back. He'd been wounded. Drake had been taken. Carter and Michael left to rescue him, but it was all wrong. Why let him go? Why now? It was a trap. Carter knew it, too. I could tell by the way he seared me with a look, but he had to go. They had one of his men, and Drake was family now. He had to go, but so did I.

"No, Peter." He didn't understand. "Where are they?" I was going.

His eyes narrowed, and I watched as he realized he didn't have his weapon. He remembered where it was, and he knew I had it.

My arm dropped from behind me to my side, and I moved over, out of reach.

"Emma, I'm serious. You can't go after them." His eyes trained on the gun in my hand.

"Okay." *Let's lie about this then. Let's do it that way.*

I put the gun aside and held my hands up, making a show about it. "Fine. I won't go, but I still want to know where they are." I had to know. And he didn't know about the bungee cord behind him. I was banking on that.

His gaze centered on the gun; he was thinking it over. I hoped his thoughts went along this route: what would it hurt? He could grab the gun faster than me now. He looked me up and down, and his head lifted a bit. *Oh, yes.* I was smaller than him. He was quicker than me. If I did anything, he could get the gun and hold me off. Easily.

I needed him to think all of this over. I held up my hands again. "I won't go. I promise. Just tell me where. Tell me, Peter. What if something happens? I can call someone, Cole maybe. I can send him there. Just..." *Please God, tell me.* "Where are they?"

"Emma, if I told you—"

"I won't go," I barked out and moved another step away from the gun. "I'm promising you, but I have to know where they went." My hand pressed against my stomach. "This doesn't feel right, Peter. They had you, and they let you go? You didn't fight to get away. They. Let. You. Go." Why wasn't he just telling me?! "Think about it!"

"Emma, I—" He stopped himself. He knew I was right. I could see the dots connecting in his eyes. He was going to tell me. I could almost see it on the tip of his tongue. I stepped forward, my hands in the air, as if I could pull it out of him. Then he gestured to the gun and started to stand. "Okay, but give me—"

My voice rose. "Just tell me! My god!"

He sat back, stunned. A look of sympathy filtered across his face. "At sixteen-oh-one Bezzaleen Road. It's by Uni—"

I knew enough. I whipped around, grabbed the gun, and turned back to him.

His eyes were wide. He tried to stand and stop me, but the bungee contracted and jerked him back down. He began to twist around, a question on his lips. "What the—"

I whipped the end of the gun across his face as hard as I could. He fell back. I needed to hit him once more, so I backed up and ran at him. At the last minute, I jumped in the air and put all of my body weight behind the gun as I hit him again.

His body slumped. I caught him before he fell out of the chair, pulling it over top of him because of the cord, and I tried to slow his descent to the floor. It wasn't smooth, but I lessened his fall a little bit. Before his head hit the floor, I caught it with my foot. And then—it was all over.

Peter was unconscious, but safe. I was good to go.

I didn't waste time. I grabbed another gun and shoved it into my pocket, then I grabbed a Taser for my other pocket. Weapons, weapons, weapons. I could almost hear Carter's urgings in my head as I forced myself to think clearly. I was going in. I was a girl. I was at a disadvantage, so that meant I needed to equal the power, and that meant as many weapons as possible. Fuck it. I grabbed another bungee and tied it around my ankle, securing a third gun there. I did the same around my waist, pulling my shirt over so it hid the bulge.

I had four guns, a Taser, and—I reached for a handful of knives and a leather case. I put the knives inside, then looped the strap around my head. It looked like I had a wallet as a necklace. Whatever worked.

I left.

I took my own car, and when I got to the block Peter had mentioned, I parked the car and began running down the sidewalk. I must've looked a sight, but I didn't care. As long as I got there and could slip in—that was my whole plan. Sneak in. Help where I could. Get Carter out. Those three things.

When I got to the house, the front door had been kicked open. Well, it looked blasted open, but no one was standing guard, so I walked through.

That's when I heard the gunshots.

They were in the back of the house. I had come in at the end. As I hurried through, I stepped over bodies and kept looking from room to room. I didn't know who was hiding out, or if Carter, Michael, or Drake had been left behind. Sweeping through the bottom floor, I found only dead bodies. Most were bleeding from the chest, though some bled from their heads, but all of them had that vacant look of death in their eyes. That was fine by me. So many.

I didn't want to count them. I couldn't. I knew Carter had killed them all.

I circled up to the second floor and began hearing small moans. The men up there were still alive. As I moved from room to room, I grabbed their guns or kicked them out of reach. They couldn't roll over and shoot me in the back that way. I dropped all the weapons into the toilet and locked the door so no one could get in there.

There was one more room to check before I went down the stairs and explored the back side of the house.

I stepped back into the hallway and stopped.

I saw her foot first.

She wasn't wearing her boot from that night in the car, and her toes were bloody and swollen, but I knew it was her. With a sinking feeling in my gut, I nudged the door open. It slowly revealed my sister tied in a chair. Her legs were spread, and she would've fallen over, still tied to the chair, if it hadn't been secured to a big bed behind her. Her whole body slumped forward. Even before I touched her I could tell she was unconscious.

As long as she wasn't dead.

Holding my breath, I moved closer. I felt like I was sneaking in, my heart breaking, but there was no one around to catch me. It was her and me. My god. *Be alive. Be alive. Please, be alive.* I prayed silently as I neared her. I took in the matted blood in her hair, the black and blue bruises all over her body, the way her shirt and pants had been ripped away, and I reached out. But what was I doing? How do you waken someone who's been tortured because she took your place? *No.* I shut that voice down, and my finger touched her head.

I pushed her, and kept holding my breath.

She didn't respond.

I closed my eyes, crying silently. I pressed my fingers to her neck. At first, there was nothing, and I opened my mouth in a silent cry. But then I felt a beat, beat, beat. I almost fell down. She had a pulse. She was alive.

"Andrea," I whispered.

Bending down at her feet, I looked for what held her captive. Her hands were in plastic ties. I needed to cut through them. *Scissors*. I looked around the room—nothing. A lone dresser stood against one wall, but the drawers were open. Nothing in them. I glanced at the pillow and bed. Nothing. The sheets were torn off and thrown on the floor. There were only two empty hangers in the closet.

Nothing. I couldn't even fucking cut my sister free.

The leather case hit my arm as I swung around in frustration. I heard the clink of knives.

Cursing my stupidity, I rushed to her and sank to my knees. Taking a knife out, I began cutting away the ties. "Andrea, Andrea, Andrea. Please. Andrea, Andrea, Andrea. Wake u—" I chanted.

My knife tore the last of the plastic, and she fell over. I scooted back—had I hurt her worse?—as she gasped awake. Her body twisted to the side as she woke, and I stood to step back, pressing my hands, with a knife clutched between my fingers, against my stomach. I could only wait and see her reaction.

She looked at the other side of the room, then scrambled to sitting. Her eyes were wild, and her mouth gaped as she saw me. "Emma?" she gasped.

I knelt next to her. "You're okay?"

"Wha—"

A blood-curdling scream sounded from somewhere in the house. We both jumped.

She asked, "Who—"

"Come on." I gestured for her to stand. "We have to go. Now."

"Em—" But she pushed herself up. Her legs were unsteady, so I grabbed her arm, helping to balance her. The scream sounded again.

"Wha—who was that?"

Not human. At least, it didn't sound human. The high-pitched scream made my stomach roll over. I only shook my head, though. "We have to go. Now," I said again.

"Okay." She held onto me. "Okay. Thank you, Emma. Thank you."

It was my fault. I couldn't say anything in return. My fingers clutched her arm, and I clasped a hand to her shoulder. Together, like that, we made our way down the stairs. She gestured ahead. "Through the kitchen. There's a back area."

I nodded.

As we came to the kitchen, I made sure she could stand alone, and then I stepped inside. I needed to go first, in case someone was there. I would fight back, not her, but no one was there. A door was off its hinges behind the stove. I could see a small walkway back there. I gestured for Andrea, and she scurried behind me. She took hold of the back of my shirt, and I edged forward, holding a gun in my hand. The scream came from that way.

They were back there.

One step at a time, we inched forward.

The walkway was small and narrow. I could see lights below it. It led into an area that seemed to be underground. There was shouting below us.

"*No! Ahhh—*"

Others yelled, but all of them were interrupted as a gunshot sounded. Whatever was below, or whoever, they were killing the people yelling.

"You fu—"

Another gunshot.

The person silenced.

"Emma," Andrea whispered. "We should go."

Carter was down there. I shook my head. "No."

"Emma." She tugged again. "You don't understand. These people—"

Bang!

We both jumped. That shot was so near that my eardrums echoed from the deafening sound. Holding a hand over my ear, I stepped to an open doorway. Then my heart sank, again.

A man stood with his back to me, and he held a gun, aimed at Carter. Drake was on the floor with blood spilling from him. I scanned his body. The gunshot was in his shoulder. I hoped the bullet had gone clear through, like with Peter.

Carter saw us, but averted his eyes right away.

This was life or death.

I untangled Andrea's hand from my shirt and edged forward. When she realized I was leaving her there, she shook her head. But it had to be this way. She had to stay. I told her this silently with my hand, then held a finger to my mouth. She also needed to remain quiet. Her head bobbed up and down. She seemed to understand what I was going to do.

"Stay right there," the guy ordered Carter. He held the gun steady and stepped closer to him. Two steps. His back was rigid, his shoulders tense. He wasn't steady and didn't really seem in control. At any moment, he could shoot.

I wouldn't let that happen.

Slowly, I edged inside the room and raised my own gun.

My arms were straight, and I aimed carefully.

Carter watched me now. His eye twitched. I didn't know why— then I said, "Put it down."

The guy tensed immediately. He began to turn around.

I moved forward. "Put. Your. Gun. Down." My gun was right behind him. My heart pounded so loud I could barely hear myself. "Put it down. Now."

"Emma," Carter said.

I couldn't hear anything else. My pulse was deafening. The guy still hadn't done what I said, and I gestured to the floor. "Drop it. Now."

He didn't. He turned and pointed his gun directly at me—then all hell broke loose. As soon as his gun cleared from Carter, I heard Carter yelling, "*Get down!*"

I sank to the floor. The guy wavered, confused at seeing Andrea behind me. I twisted around and yelled at her, "*Get down!*"

She gasped, then fell to the floor.

At the same moment, Carter lunged. His elbow came down on the guy's arm, and he yanked the gun from his hands before ramming his elbow into his head. The guy fell to the floor. His hips landed not far from me, just as someone else ran into the room. The shooter reached behind him, even as he was falling, and pulled out a second gun. I recognized Michael just as the shooter pointed his second gun at him—

Bang!

The shooter went limp. His gun fell from his hand and skidded across the room. Standing above him, with his gun cupped in both hands, was Carter.

He'd shot him.

The guy was going to shoot Michael, and Carter killed him instead.

We were all safe.

A gurgle came up my throat. I was relieved, terrified, and joyous all at the same time. I pushed myself to sitting, but Carter was there.

He swept me up, picking me clean off the floor and wrapped his arms around me. He buried his head into my shoulder. "Oh my god." He trembled as he held me. "Oh my god." His hand stroked my hair. "You're alive. Thank god."

I was alive. So was Andrea. Peter. Drake. Michael. And Carter, too. I leaned back and framed his face. "I love you so much."

Tears covered his face. He pressed his lips to my forehead, then my mouth. I didn't care what happened after that. Carter was safe. We were all safe.

Emma

The police were suspicious, but Andrea corroborated our story.

She and I had been on our way home from a restaurant nearly two months ago. We were attacked. They took her, and my life was in danger, so I hid. Carter got a tip, went in search for her, and that was the showdown they found when they were called to the building. It hadn't been long before the cops and medics showed up. Andrea was found. We could no longer hide.

When I was cleared after I gave my statement, I walked through the police station and saw Carter in an interrogation room. Our eyes met and held, but neither of us showed any reaction. I was thankful he was alive. I had to trust him with everything else.

So I went to the lobby and waited at the desk. I needed to find out which hospital Andrea was at. As I stood there, a man approached.

"Emma?"

I didn't recognize him. He wore a black sweater over jeans, and a detective's badge hung around his neck. He gave me a half-grin. His dark hair was cut short, almost a crew cut, which seemed to fit his athletic physique. His face looked too weathered to be classically handsome, but he was rough and cute at the same time.

"I already gave my statement."

"I know." He glanced down, saw his badge hanging in view, and tucked it under his shirt. "Sorry about that. I forget half the time I have it on. Uh, no. I don't work at this station. I'm—"

It clicked. Amanda's boyfriend. Brian.

"—uh, you and I have a friend in common..." He trailed off as I nodded.

"Is Amanda here?" I asked.

"No." He gestured to the parking lot behind him. "They, uh, heard about your sister, so they're there with her. I don't think they've been able to see her, but Amanda said you would want them to check on her first."

I nodded. That sounded right. "My sister is okay?"

"From what I've heard, I think so. Amanda asked me to give you a ride over or just to be here when you got out." He looked around, but no one else had appeared. "We didn't know who they would detain and so forth. You know."

"The others are still being questioned?"

"Well, Carter and the other guy, Michael. The guy who was shot, he's at the hospital."

Drake. I nodded, my mind buzzing. What about Peter? Was he still—

"Amanda said another guy is at the hospital, too," Brian added. "She didn't know his name, just said she recognized him from your security team."

I pinched my forehead, feeling a headache coming on. "Right." Peter was safe. Everyone was safe. "I'd like to talk to Amanda."

His eyebrows went up. "Pardon?"

I held out my hand. "Your phone. I'd like to call Amanda."

He reached for his phone, but was slow bringing it out. "Because..."

"Because." I smiled at him. "You don't think I'm stupid enough just to get in a car with you? There are a lot of people who know a lot about me. Anyone of them could spin a nice web for me to believe.

Give me your phone. I will dial her myself, and then maybe I'll get in a car with you." He started to press a number on his phone. I stopped him. "No, no." Taking it from him, I waved toward the desk. "I'll call from over there. Thank you."

"Uh..."

Taking the phone to the front, I called to make sure it was Amanda. At the sound of her voice, my knees gave out. I grasped the desk to keep from falling.

"Emma?"

My throat wasn't working. "He—hey." Damn, I had missed her. "You, uh, have a guy here on your behalf?"

She laughed, sounding relieved. "Yes. That's Brian. We were all going to wait, but he didn't want us there. He said he didn't want me waiting around a police lobby unless I had to, so when he found out which hospital your sister had been sent to, we came here—Theresa and Noah, too. We all wanted to rally around and support you guys. How are you? How's Carter?"

I sucked in a breath. The tears were coming. Just hearing Amanda's voice had opened the floodgates. I tried fanning myself. I was tired of crying. "Uh, we're okay, I think. Have you guys been able to see my sister?"

"No." She was moving somewhere, and suddenly her voice was clearer. "I'm in a closet now. I can hear you better this way." She sighed. "No. They won't even let us on her floor. Theresa snuck up, though. She said there were cops outside her door, but they caught her and escorted her back down here. Noah knows the hospital's administrator, but even he couldn't pull strings. We're stuck. From what we've been able to overhear, though, her parents are flying in soon. She got quiet. "Emma, are those your parents?"

"No. Andrea was adopted."

"Oh."

Yeah. My throat burned.

"Okay." She kept her voice at a whisper. "I saw one of Carter's guys here, too. He walked through the lobby to the elevator. Theresa tried to slip into the elevator with him, but he didn't let her. We don't know if he went up to see your sister or if—"

"No. Drake's there. The medics took him and my sister to the hospital. I'm sure Peter is there for him."

She was quiet for a moment.

"They're the security guards you just mentioned," I explained.

"Oh. Gotcha. I didn't know all their names."

I nodded to myself. It felt so good to hear her voice, hear her laughing again. A lump formed in my throat. "Okay," I rasped. "I'm assuming your boyfriend is a safe driver."

"He's a cop. He tends to speed sometimes, but yeah, I think he's safe." She laughed. "I'm glad everything's okay. I've missed you, Ems."

The lump grew, and I whispered back, "I've missed you, too." I had missed all of them, even Noah. "I'll see you in a few then."

"Okay. See you."

It felt weird getting into a car with Amanda's boyfriend—and no one else. For an entire year I had been surrounded by Carter and his men. Being with a stranger brought old memories to the surface, back when I traveled alone—before Carter came back into my life and I was living with Mallory. I realized if she had seen me with this guy, she would've wanted to date him. And Amanda would've hated it. I chuckled.

"What's that?" Brian asked, merging with the traffic.

"Nothing. Just 'another time, another place' sort of thought."

"Oh yeah?"

"Yeah." *Amanda's boyfriend.* I shook my head. "It's nice to officially meet you." I was going to make her leave him. If someone made me leave Carter—I would've left them instead. "You love her?"

"I do."

I nodded. "Good. She's a good friend."

"She's a good person."

"Yes, she is."

He glanced at me before looking back to the road. "She cares about you a lot."

I cared about her, too. My gaze fell to my lap, remembering the bomb that night. I had chased after her so she didn't end it with him. "She really loves you."

"I know," he said. Then he cleared his throat. "Listen, uh. I'm not a fool. I know how tight you are with Amanda. I know about you, her, Mallory, and some guy she always describes as a pain in the ass."

I smiled. Amanda had hated Ben more than I had.

"I know there's history, and I know you're in love with Carter Reed," he continued. "I'm a cop, but I'm just trying to show you that I get the complexities of this situation." He coughed again, shifting in his seat. "But, uh, I'm in it for the long haul. I don't know how to say this. I guess, well, I never want Amanda to get hurt." He held a hand out to emphasize his point. "So…you know… I—we can leave it at that. If you know what I mean."

I wasn't sure, but I bobbed my head up and down. "Oh. Okay."

"I came to New York while she was there. She told me that woman on the news was your sister. Well, okay. That's a lie. I saw the woman on the news, and I know who you are. You could be twins. Amanda kept quiet. I don't know if she was going to tell me or not, but I came out because I wanted to support her any way I could."

I snuck a peek at him. He wasn't looking at me. His head moved up and down like he was talking to the traffic as he drove. He tugged at the collar of his shirt and his hand would wave in the air from time to time as he spoke.

He was nervous.

For some reason, that settled the nerves in my stomach. He clearly loved Amanda. I could hear it in his voice and I saw it now, in the way he tried to appease me. As he kept talking, I stopped listening, but I was glad I hadn't made Amanda break up with him

"Carter said you were an honorable guy," I told him.

He stopped mid-sentence and looked at me for a moment. "Really?"

I nodded and looked back to my lap, wrapping my hands around each other. "He did."

"Oh."

Before he said anything else, I murmured, "Treat her right. Always."

"Oh." This 'oh' was much quieter than the first one. "Yeah. I'm hoping to. The *always* part, I mean."

"Yeah. I got it."

"Not that you should—" He lifted his hand in the air again.

I cut him off. "She'll say yes."

"Oh," he said a third time, but this one was breathless. His hand dropped to his lap. "Wow. Okay, I mean. Yeah." He nodded to himself and sat straighter in the seat. "All right. Thank you."

One more nod. My neck muscles were protesting from the continuous up and down motion. "Yep." The sign for the hospital came up, and I pointed. "There's our exit."

"Oh, yeah." He swung to the right lane, and it wasn't long before he pulled up to the entrance, and I got out.

He held a hand up. "I won't be long. She said they're in the seventh floor lobby now." Then he pulled away toward the parking ramp.

The doors slid open as I approached and walked inside. Right away, I heard, "Oh my god, Emma!"

Amanda and Theresa rushed for me. They threw their arms around me, and I was engulfed in the tightest group hug ever. Noah stood back and gave me a little wave.

They were here. I still couldn't believe it.

"Emma." Amanda cupped the back of my head, as if shielding me. "We've been so worried. Your sister—We can't—"

"Our daughter was brought in earlier." A high-pitched voice spoke from behind us to someone at the reception desk.

Amanda and Theresa went back to hugging me, but a nagging feeling tugged at me. That voice… I looked over to see a woman and a man, both wearing winter coats. The man had a hand to the woman's back as they waited for the clerk to respond.

"Your daughter's name?"

I knew. Before they said it, I knew. These were Andrea's adoptive parents.

I pulled away from Amanda and Theresa as the man answered the clerk, "Andrea Nathans."

Her name hushed conversations in the lobby.

Everyone knew. The news flashed Andrea's picture, already reporting that she'd been found. The clerk's eyes widened, but she leaned forward and wrote the information down. Andrea's mom and dad glanced over their shoulders.

As they did, I saw the wrinkled lines in Andrea's father's forehead. He had bags under his eyes. He might've been in his late fifties, but he looked like he was in his seventies. I saw the sadness there, too—the way his hand lifted to hold onto his wife's shoulder, the way he moved closer to her, as if he was worried more about her than himself.

The clerk slid a piece of paper across the counter to them and pointed down the hallway to the elevator. As Andrea's mom took the paper, the clerk lifted a remote and changed the television channel. A cooking show replaced Andrea's photograph.

"Thank you so much." Andrea's mom held the paper to her chest as they left for the elevators.

"I…" I felt panic rising as my heart longed to follow them, but also to stay with my friends.

Luckily, Amanda and Theresa understood. They stepped back. Amanda gestured after Andrea's parents. "Go, Emma."

I didn't waste any more time. I hurried after them, but I didn't have to worry about them noticing my face. They kept their heads down and seemed to want attention about as much as I did. When the doors slid open and they got in, I entered and watched to see what floor they hit. Sixth floor. Then I scurried back out. Riding up with them, walking right behind them into her room—I didn't think I could be that close.

Because, after all, it was my fault. Their daughter had gone to find me. The guilt sat on my shoulders, weighing me down, so I took the next elevator.

When the doors opened on the sixth floor, I heard them down the hallway. They were arguing about something.

"Stop it, Gail," Andrea's father said. "We can ask those questions later. We have to make sure she's healthy first."

I started for them, but that voice... I recognized that voice. His tone. His pitch. The softness with a hint of authority underneath. Everything about him was familiar, and I froze in the hallway. My feet had a mind of their own. I couldn't move. I held a hand to my stomach as memories flooded through me, one after another. All of them came at me with lightning speed, and I shook my head. I couldn't handle all of them at once. They weren't making sense.

In my mind he argued with my mother.

He shouted at her, threatening to take both the girls. My mom shrieked back. Ally was hers. Andy was his.

Wait. That didn't make sense.

Then another memory—I was hiding behind a door and knew AJ was coming to see me. I was so excited, hugging my knees with my backpack ready to go. He didn't come, though. He was delayed, and when I had waited as long as I could bear, I went to the window to see if he was there. He was. He'd been there with this man. They were involved in a heated conversation, their arms waving in the air. AJ looked upset. The man looked tired. He was crying, and as AJ looked over at the window where I stood, I saw that he was crying, too.

A third memory—I could hear AJ saying to this same man, *"She's my sister. You can't take her from me."*

The man said, *"Neither girl is safe with Coralea. We both know that. I'm taking Andrea with me. Cora won't fight me. She knows she'll lose, but Ally. Ally's her big sister."*

"She's my sister."

"You know what I mean. We shouldn't separate the girls. They should live together."

"You just said Cora would fight you on that."

"Yes, but Aaron, we both know you have no rights to your sister. You're not an adult. You have no guardianship over Ally."

"We have the same dad. Isn't that enough?"

"Not against her mother. If you fight Cora, Ally will go into the foster system."

"Whatever. She might be better off there than anywhere else."

"Let me fight for her. I have the money. I can petition the court to take both girls, not just my daughter."

"No. Ally's my sister. She belongs with me."

"She's not with you. She's with Cora. We both know that's a disaster waiting to happen. You can visit your sister. I'll make sure she's taken care of—"

AJ yelled, *"I said no! I know what you're planning. You're going to take her out of state and hope she doesn't remember this place. You're not going to take me with you, and I can't afford to go myself. Any way you slice it, you're taking my sister away from me. I'm not on board with that. Stop asking me to do it."*

"Wait," I spoke without realizing it.

The man stiffened before turning to look at me. His wife turned with him, a confused frown on her face. But there was no confusion on his face. He knew me, just like I knew him.

I pointed at him, and a deep swirl of emotion began twisting inside me. He—this guy—he knew AJ. He'd spoken to him. He was… I looked at him closely. He looked the same except his hair had twinges of silver in it now, combed to the side, and he'd put on a few pounds. He'd seemed so old to me then, but looking at him now, I realized he must've been in his thirties. He had been my age now.

"You're Andrea's father."

His wife gasped. Her hand pressed against her mouth.

They both looked middle class, but I remembered the headlines. He was a wealthy hotelier. "Andrea said she was adopted," I said softly. That couldn't be true, though.

"Oh, dear." His wife sounded stricken. She looked up at him. "Edward, she remembers you. You said she wouldn't."

He touched her shoulder and squeezed it. "Because I didn't think she would. That's a good memory of yours," he said to me.

I was still filling in the pieces. But the more he spoke, the more memories came to light. They had started to fit into place.

"I couldn't remember Andrea because she didn't grow up with me, did she?" I asked. "You took her early. When she was little."

"She was five. That's when I stepped in. I had to. Cora was abusive, and I tried with you, but your brother wouldn't allow it."

AJ. Relief crashed over me, but a surge of anger was on its tail. "You—she came to me declaring that AJ had kidnapped me. You knew better. You let her think that."

He shook his head.

My voice rose. "Don't lie to me. She took away his memory. He cared for me and loved me. He did the best he could. He should be honored, not disgraced, and you could've stopped all of it. You could've—you offered to take me. Why didn't you bring him, too?

Why did you keep all of us apart?"

"I…" His voice cracked. "I couldn't, Ally."

I hissed and stepped back at that name. I felt slapped across the face.

He didn't seem to notice. He was still shaking his head, a hand cupping the side of his face like he was in pain. "Aaron was in the system. He was a lot older than both of you girls. If he'd come with me, it would've been years before everything was approved. His dad—your dad too—he was long gone, and Cora had kicked Aaron out. She denied he was hers, though it was plain as day. All three of you—Aaron, Andy, and you—you all had the same dark eyes. They all came from her, but I couldn't stay. If I'd waited too long with Andy, she would've changed her mind. Once I got the go-ahead, I fled. Aaron couldn't come with us, and he wouldn't let us take you without him… So we left you behind. We always wondered what had happened to you. Went back every year or so, but you were already gone."

"Andrea thinks you adopted her."

He lifted a shoulder. A defeated air hung over him. "It was easier to lie to her about the whole thing than admit the truth. She would've looked at me like you're doing now."

"And what was that lie, exactly?" A voice behind them spoke up.

Andrea had gotten out of bed. She'd wrapped a blanket over her shoulders, and she clutched it in front of her.

Her hair was still matted in blood. Her skin was pale, but she looked at her father with the same heated emotion that I had. The strength of that anger brought some color to her cheeks, though she swayed on her feet for a beat.

The nurse stepped close to her, and at the same moment her parents did. Andrea shot out her hand and hissed, "Don't. Don't touch me."

The nurse held her arm as her parents stepped away.

"You're my father? For real?"

He looked at the floor. "Yes." His voice was thick. "I'm sorry, honey—"

"Stop," she hissed again. "No more lies, Dad. This is my sister, and thinking over everything, you were never supportive of me finding her. You told me she was probably dead. That's what you— you tried to convince me of it, but I knew I had a sister. She gave me a drawing, and I had that. There were two sets of thumbprints. Mom, you told me it was a friend, but I remembered it wasn't. All this time, you guys were trying to bury Ally. That's why I couldn't remember her, because I was gone. I thought..." She closed her eyes and shook her head. "No. And her brother. I was convinced he took her from us. You told me you knew there was abuse. But it wasn't him; it was our mom. You *let* me think it was him."

She looked at her father as if he'd plunged a dagger into her back. A tug of sympathy rose up in me. She felt betrayed, and she had a right to, but this was her father. He was her flesh and blood. I'd give anything to know who mine was. No. I'd give anything just to have AJ back for five minutes.

Clearing my throat and watching all eyes swing toward me, I asked, "Is she still alive?"

"Oh, no." The wife began sputtering.

He shook his head, eyes panicked. "No, no. I won't let you look for her."

So she was.

She was alive.

"Is she still there?"

Andrea's mom paled even more. Her hand went to her chest, and she whirled to her husband. "Edward, they cannot—"

He touched her arm, quieting her plea, and looked at me. "Young lady, you cannot go looking for her. Corelea was a spiteful and dangerous mother to you then. I shudder at the thought of what she'd do now, if she could get her hooks in you."

"Or me, you mean." Andrea moved forward to stand beside me. She tightened the blanket around her. "You mean if my mother had her hooks in me? Because we have money, Daddy. *You* have money. I have an inheritance. How would you feel if all of that was squandered away? Everything you worked for, all your life, was ripped away? How would that make you feel?"

She lifted her chin, but her lips trembled. A disgusted sound mingled with her words. "Would it piss you off if I did that? Gave my mother money that you'd earned, like the truth you took from me? My sister. You could've—" She started to fall.

Her mother rushed forward. "Andrea."

"No." She pulled her arm away from her, but she faltered again. She was so weak. The nurse rushed to support her other side, and I reached around her, trying to help. It didn't matter. Andrea fell to the floor with a thud as her head made contact with the tile. It was a good, hard smack.

I felt sick.

"Andy!" her mother exclaimed, falling to her knees beside her daughter. A group of medical staff swarmed around her, and in the rush, I was pushed backward.

They hoisted Andrea onto a gurney and wheeled her down the hallway. Her mother followed behind, hugging Andy's blanket to her chest.

Then the only people left were her father and me. He stared right at me. I readied myself, but I saw no anger there. I thought he would've blamed me, the way I could tell his wife did. There'd been an accusing flash in her eyes. But not with him.

I felt a pang in my chest.

He looked...sad. "I've always known it was wrong to lie to Andy," he said quietly. "The truth would come out. I knew that, especially once she was convinced she had a sister and went to find you. The day she told us she was taking a semester off of graduate school to find you—that was the day my lies were going to be over. It was only a matter of time. That was years ago. I thought I'd have all this time to prepare what I was going to say to you. But here you are." He took a deep breath. "And I still have no idea what words I could utter to make anything right with you again. I am truly sorry, Ally."

"Emma," I murmured.

"What?"

"Emma." I cleared my throat. "My name is Emma."

"Ah. I see. Yes. Emma." He tried to smile at me. "That's a lovely name, too."

Yeah. Lovely. That was not the word I'd use to describe anything in that moment, much less my name, but it was the name AJ gave me. It was the name I would keep, no matter what.

"Emma!"

Theresa waved at me from the elevators. She frowned, studying Andrea's father beside me, and asked, "Did you find her?"

I forced myself to nod. *Look normal. Act normal.* Maybe then everything would be normal? That was a lie, though. Nothing was normal for me. I should've been used to that. Never hope for normalcy. Maybe then I might get it? But no. I skimmed a glance back toward Andrea's dad.

He patted me on the arm before turning away. "I'll be seeing you, All—Emma. You take care." Then he took off in the direction his wife and daughter had gone.

"Hey." Theresa stood in front of me now. She smiled, but there were questions in her eyes. "You okay? Who was that?"

Who was that? "No one." Was I okay? "I will be okay."

Her eyebrows bunched together. "Huh?"

"Nothing." I linked my elbow through hers, heading for the elevator. "I just want to go home."

As we got on the elevator, she hugged me against her side and pressed a kiss to my temple. "I'm glad you're okay, Emma. I missed you." She cupped my face with her palm and pressed my head down to her shoulder. "You deserve a year-long vacation after the hell you've been put through. Just think of all the gun ranges and wine nights we could have."

I groaned, my mouth moving against her shirt. "I'll need another year to recuperate from that."

She laughed, jostling her shoulder underneath my head. "Oh, Ems. That's what Carter's for. He'll help you with all the rejuvenation you need." She tightened her hold on my arm pressed against her side. "Now, let's get home. We have a few wine nights to catch up on."

I almost started laughing. Yes. Yes, we did.

Carter was still with the police and after checking in with Peter and Drake at the hospital, I went back with them. Peter told me to wait with my friends until he came to get me. He and Drake were going to be questioned by police soon and he didn't want me around them. So when we got to Noah's place, Amanda threw her coat off and headed for the kitchen. I lingered in the hallway, wanting to call Carter's phone just in case I got him, but Theresa yelled from the kitchen.

"Come on, Emma! You're here. You're back with us. We're going to toast to you."

"Toast?"

Noah came from behind me and went straight for the refrigerator. Amanda held a bottle of wine and wiggled her eyebrows at me. Theresa came from the cupboard with five wineglasses. I'd just finished counting them when Brian filtered in and went to the wall. He leaned against it, tugging at his collar as he shoved a hand inside his pocket. He seemed content to sit back and watch the entertainment. He pulled at his collar again and his gaze skirted mine before jumping to Amanda.

I thought he was content. Maybe not.

"No," Noah said, distracting me as he shut the fridge door with a bottle of rum in one hand and two beers in his other. He slid a beer over the counter to Brian, who caught it and tipped it toward him in salute. Noah nodded back, then plopped the rum in front of Amanda and Theresa.

Theresa's mouth hung open, and her eyebrows had shot up. "Uh—what?"

He nabbed the wine bottle from Amanda, flashing her an apologetic smile, and put it back in the refrigerator. With his beer, he turned to face me. He held his bottle in the air. "No wine for you ladies tonight. You're drinking the hard stuff because tonight—" He smiled at me, "—we're celebrating one of our own coming back home."

"What?" I could feel the tears forming behind my eyes. "What do you mean?"

A slow smile spread on Theresa's face, and she grabbed a carton of juice, filling three glasses. As soon as Theresa moved the juice to the next glass, Amanda poured rum into it.

Noah waited until all three of us had a glass in hand. He gestured to me. "Come on, raise it up. This is for you, you know."

I felt my face getting warm. "What are you guys doing?"

"Our sister is home."

I looked at Amanda. She'd said that so softly and eloquently. She spoke as if it were a fact, as if she were declaring what we all knew. I sucked in my breath. I hadn't known. I hadn't—I'd thought it and felt it, but the fear of being abandoned was always there. Because of Carter, because of who I loved, I thought they'd someday turn their backs on me.

"I second that." Theresa looked like she was bursting at the seams. She bounced up and down, waiting for me to lift my glass. "Come on, Ems. You're back with us. You're safe. Your sister is safe, and hey—you have a sister! A true blue sister. That's amazing. Don't get me wrong, though. I do not want to know what all happened out there because, you know—" She winked in Brian's direction. "But you're home. You're alive, and we missed the hell out of you."

The tears weren't going to stay hidden. One slipped down my cheek, and I felt more coming. I tried to swallow the emotion, but I knew my smile was watery. "You guys… Thank you." I couldn't. The words weren't coming. This. I really felt accepted by them, no matter what happened or what would happen. I flicked some of the tears away. "You have no idea how much this means to me."

Theresa frowned. "Because we're drinking rum instead of wine?"

"We love you, Emma."

I heard the tenderness from Amanda again. When I turned to look, she held my gaze and continued to smile softly at me. She glanced to Brian, then back to me, and her smile lifted up a notch. I knew what she was trying to convey to me then. No matter what happened, we were family. I nodded, and that broke the dam. I couldn't stop crying after that.

"Oh, Emma." Theresa came around the counter and hugged me, glass still in hand. Amanda laughed as she joined us, with her glass, too. "Wait." Theresa raised her glass. "We should all take a sip like this."

"What?" Amanda frowned at her.

"I mean it. I know it sounds stupid. We're mixed up in a knot here, but let's try it. It can be a new thing, like a bonding, sisterly-drinking thing. If anything, we'll all look really dumb together."

"Oh my god." Amanda rolled her eyes.

"Hush it." Theresa shot her a look, but she was trying not to grin. "This is what memories are made of. When we act stupid, we know we're going to act stupid, and we do it anyway. Now drink, woman." She lifted up on her tiptoes, straining toward her glass.

Amanda and I did the same. My lips barely touched my glass, but I tried. Amanda screamed and began laughing. She started hopping up and down, jostling me. "Hey," I said. My lip was almost there. I could just feel it when my glass tipped. I had one second to register what was coming, and I closed my eyes just as the liquid rained down on me.

"Oh my god." I laughed, extracting myself. I was wet, and a little cold, but everyone laughed. Peeking out through one eye, I could tell Amanda and Theresa were in similar states, both drenched. Noah and Brian stood by with the emptied glasses in hand.

The three girls shared a look, and as one, we launched for the guys.

Theresa leapt for Noah's beer, but he lifted it up and out of her reach. Instead of jumping for it, she darted around him, opened the fridge and pulled out a champagne bottle. Noah's eyes got big once he saw what she'd grabbed, and he began backing away. It didn't matter. She sprayed it all over him, shaking the bottle up and down.

"Theresa."

"You asked for it!" she yelled. "I'm giving back, Noah."

Amanda and Brian were tussling, too, and I stepped back to watch both couples. Seeing what Theresa had done, Amanda bypassed her boyfriend's beer altogether and grabbed the rum.

"Hold up," I called.

"Good thinking." She set it back down and grabbed the juice container. Instead of shaking it like Theresa had, she climbed up the counter and tipped it over. Brian just stood there, letting her do it. He shook his head and fought back a grin.

When he saw me watching, he lifted his hands in a shrug. "What do you do? I asked for it." Then he twisted around, snaked an arm around her waist, and plucked her off the counter.

Amanda shrieked, but it wasn't from terror. She was excited. *No, I corrected myself*—she was happy. As he swung her around in a circle, I saw that she was genuinely happy.

Good.

That warm emotion settled in my gut. It was firm, and it resounded through me. Everything I'd done was worth it. Leaving them, hiding with Carter—all of it was worth it. Making sure Amanda had changed her mind? That was more than worth it. She wasn't Mallory. She had a future. She needed to live it as much as possible. And me? I felt my phone buzzing in my pocket. I had my own future.

I snuck away, but as I did, I glanced over my shoulder. Brian was ducking Amanda's tickling hands and watching me. We shared a look. I wasn't sure what message was in it, but he nodded and started tickling Amanda all over again.

He was distracting her so I could go.

I got to the front door, where I was able to read my text message.

There are men downstairs for you.

I frowned. It wasn't a number I recognized. **Carter?**

A second passed.

Another.

Then my phone buzzed again. **This is Cole. Carter is coming here.**

I stared at it for a moment. That was odd. Why didn't he—

"Is that Carter?"

Brian stood behind me, his head tilted to the side, hands in his pockets. When I kept staring at him, he bobbed his head forward, indicating my phone. "I just know there's not much that would pull you away from Amanda and Theresa."

I narrowed my eyes. What did he mean by that?

He backed up a step and held his hands up. "Again. Wow." He scratched behind his ear. "I can interrogate a serial killer, but you, you scare the crap out of me."

I did?

"I just..." He closed his eyes and his head fell back. He groaned, then stared at the ceiling for a moment. "Man. What is it now? Three for three? Four for four? I'm striking out all over with you. Four walks, and I gave a run away. I'm going into foul territory."

I could hear Amanda and Theresa laughing in the kitchen. Whatever feelings I had for this guy, I had to put them aside. I gestured to them and said, "That sound."

He looked at me, traces of a frown on his face.

Amanda laughed again.

"Right there," I said. "She's happy."

"Because of you—"

I shook my head. "No, because of you. Yes, I hate that you're a cop. You know why. We all do. But she loves you, and I love her, and that's what matters."

"Yeah," he murmured. "I'm not like normal people, Emma. I can read the small print. She's happy. You're happy that she's happy, but I'm a cop. I'm with her. You're with a criminal. I know that you're going to pull away. You have to. I get it. I do. Carter Reed is your number one, and no matter how we try to make things sound pretty, the bottom line is that—"

I didn't need him to say it. I said it for both of us. "—you're a cop."

"Yeah."

"She doesn't sound like that when it's just me around," I told him.

He frowned. "What do you mean?"

"You know what I mean. It's you. I love her like a sister. I do. But you're going to be her family. Not me." I held my phone up. "I have my family waiting for me. I have to go."

"Brian! She's still in the bathroom?" Theresa yelled from the kitchen.

I was leaving without saying good-bye. Again. In so many ways, this was wrong, but having to say good-bye to them again? They wouldn't understand. I didn't know how to explain it, but this was right. It had to be.

Amanda was happy. The reason for it meant I had to go now.

"They won't understand why I'm leaving again," I whispered hoarsely.

"They will."

I held his gaze, a lump forming in my throat.

"They just don't want to admit it to themselves, but they know why. They'd do it, too."

"I'm being comforted by the reason I'm leaving." I flashed him a rueful smile. "There's gotta be irony there."

He chuckled. "You would've left whether I was here or not. Amanda and Theresa talk about you a lot. I'd like to think I've gotten a pretty good feel for what kind of person you are, and you would've gone anyway, for them because you know the less they're around you, the less they're involved with that life."

He was right. I felt a tear slipping down my face again, but I had to leave. I had no words. And I didn't think I could talk anyway, so I turned and went.

I had no idea how I made it downstairs and into the waiting car. I got in, huddled in the corner, and bent my head down. I couldn't keep the tears at bay anymore.

CHAPTER 22

Emma

The car stopped, and my door opened. But when I got out, I wasn't at Carter's place. I stared up at a three-story brick mansion. Two large, white posts flanked the front door, stretching all the way to the roof. I glanced around me. Three large men now stood by the car, waiting for me to enter the house. They wore black winter coats and stoic expressions. The guy closest to me was still holding the car door, but he stared straight ahead. None of them made eye contact with me. It was like they were robots.

At that thought, a shiver went down my spine, but I was locked in. A brick wall surrounded the house, and a thick wrought-iron gate had closed at the end of the driveway. I couldn't scale it, and I didn't think I could climb over the wall either.

"You work for Cole Mauricio?" I asked them.

No answer. No one moved. Nothing. I shivered again, and a sick feeling formed in my stomach. I swallowed. This wasn't good. Wetting my lips, I started to get back in the car. Now the guy moved. He reached around the door and grabbed my arm as another guard rounded the back of the vehicle to help him.

I froze. My heart pounded against my chest. "Uh. I'd like to go back. Is Carter here?"

They didn't answer.

The guard picked me up and carried me to the front door. The other two followed behind him as the car pulled away. I tried to twist around. I wanted to see the car leave. Maybe there was a code for the gate? I could escape and use that to get out? But no. The car paused in front of the gate, and it opened a beat later. That's when I saw the camera. Someone had activated the gate. That meant they'd be watching for me, too.

As the guards and I entered the house, passing between the two large posts, I looked up and saw more cameras. I counted five, all pointed at different directions. This place was a fortress. And okay, my fear officially started to spread. The shivers had been a forewarning. Now, full-blown panic. My lips started to go numb, and my hands shook.

"Emma?"

Cole came down the stairs, frowning as he studied the guys with me. The guards holding me lowered me to the floor, but my knees sagged, and I couldn't stand. *Thank god.* My lips moved, and I thought those words, but they didn't come out. I couldn't talk, but I was so relieved to see Cole.

He stopped halfway down and tilted his head to the side, still studying the men. Then a wall came over his face, and he was unreadable. His hand lifted from the bannister, and his foot moved up a stair. He began moving backward, away from us.

"Boss?" the guy holding me said.

At that moment, a door down the hallway opened. A man swept out, followed behind by six more giants. They matched the giants around me—all robot-like movements, black coats, and staring straight ahead. The guy leading them stopped in front of me. He looked closely at me, his lips pressed together, and my eyes traced the scar that went across his forehead. Five of the other men went around him and walked past us to the stairs.

"Gene?" Cole didn't move any more.

Recognition flickered in my mind. This was Gene, a guy I'd seen with Carter before. I never liked him, and I thought he'd been killed. After Carter killed Frank Dunvan, this guy never came around again.

Instead of watching the robots around him, Cole focused on the guy in front of me. "What is this? What are you doing, and why is Emma here?"

"Because," Gene sighed. "This has gone on long enough. I must end this before it gets out of hand."

"Out of hand?" The men escorted Cole down the stairs. As he walked past me, he asked, "And Emma? Why is she here? You can't do anything to her. Carter will find out. He'll kill you."

Carter trusted Gene. I remembered that now. He was his mentor.

But he didn't like me. I had known that right away. Still, that couldn't be this guy. He'd been wary of me before, but now his features were cold, a look of impatience on his face—like he needed to deal with us before he could go home for the night, like we were a chore for him.

Saying nothing, Gene stepped aside and the men led Cole and me into a back room. He followed behind. The room was massive. Bookshelves lined the walls, with a set of couches and a chair at one end of the space, and a desk and two chairs at the other. A large window overlooked a backyard covered with snow. I searched for the brick wall that surrounded the house, but I couldn't see it. A row of trees blocked my view, further encasing this house. As I kept looking—there must be some way of escaping—Gene walked over and closed the curtains.

We were in complete privacy now.

The men shoved me into one of the chairs by the desk and Cole into the other. A flicker of sympathy flared in his eyes before he shut it down and turned to face Gene, who now stood behind the desk. Everything about Cole was stiff. Gene wasn't. He leaned forward, resting his hands on the back of the desk chair and let out a deep breath, looking from Cole to me and back again.

I didn't think this was the time to start yelling, but I wanted to. Every cell in my body screamed for me to run, try to fight, try to leave. It was useless. There were so many men between the door and me. And if there were cameras in the front of the house, there'd be more behind it.

I was a prisoner, whether I wanted to accept it or not.

Please, Cole. I prayed to myself. *All those training sessions with Carter need to pay off.* Surely he was preparing now, and when he fought back—that's who Carter would've considered a brother, someone who fought back, someone who would try to save me, too—I would do anything and everything to help him.

A weapon. I would need a weapon.

"What is this, Gene?" Cole asked in a low voice.

I scanned the room for a weapon, but paused and looked at Cole for a moment. He was so stiff in that chair. His hands were flat on his legs, and he stared right at Gene. His jaw clenched, and then his eyes narrowed.

Weapon. *Weapon.* I needed something.

Gene laughed. It came out as a smooth baritone, but I couldn't hear any amusement in the chuckle. "You, Cole. You're what 'this' is all about. None of this was supposed to happen." He shook his head as another bitter laugh trickled from him. "The goddamn bloodline prince. That's what you are. Your family was supposed to be wiped out, but nope. Carter saved you, and then he hid you from everyone. The fucking weapon I helped build did his job *too well.*"

"Weapon I helped build." I held my breath as those words registered. *Gene helped create Carter. "Did his job too well."* I glanced at Cole, who still showed no reaction. My god. Gene wanted Cole dead.

"You sent the Bartels to me," Cole said.

"Yes." Gene straightened from the desk and stood tall.

Neither man looked away. If Cole hadn't been so still, he would've seemed calm. He wasn't, though. I knew he was far from it.

"You were supposed to die, but you never did," Gene continued. "I'm not saying I organized the attacks on your family back then. I didn't. I wasn't even on the periphery of it. But yes, you were supposed to die along with your family. The elders were going to form a democracy. After a few years, I was brought in. I was educated, and yes, they blamed me for you still being alive."

His steel eyes flickered to me, then settled on Cole again. I felt singed from even that short contact.

His jaw hardened. "Carter was my assignment. They had me scout him. No, sweetie." He looked back at me and the corner of his mouth lifted, but it didn't form a smile. It sent fear through me instead. "He didn't just happen to come to us. We knew his old man. We'd been scouting him for a long time. Your brother getting killed was our lottery win. It was the right move, the right time to push Carter over the edge. Oh, yeah. Who do you think gave him those guns to clean house? I'd been talking to him long before that."

"You knew what Carter would do?" Cole asked.

As Gene swung his attention back to him, I felt like I could breathe. He'd been pinning me down, crawling inside me and poisoning me. This man—he was why all of this had happened. He was to blame. I felt another surge of fear, but I squashed it.

Fuck the fear. I was going to kill this man.

Gene let out another soft sigh. "We had no idea what he'd do. His old man was an asshole. We thought Carter would be, too, and then his best friend was killed and the kid turned into a nuclear bomb. When we saw what he was capable of, we scooped him up right away. He came to us, but we led him with crumbs. And yes, since then he has surpassed everything we thought he might achieve." He grinned and a genuine chuckle came from him. "We just wanted another street soldier, to be honest. Never could've predicted it, not what he's become." The amusement slid away, his eyes went flat, and his head lowered, like he was going to charge us. "And since then, he's become what we need for the family."

"What are you talking about?" Cole asked.

"You."

"Explain." Cole's tone was soft, but it was a command.

Gene laughed again, shaking his head. "Figure it out. You were supposed to be dead. I told them where you were. It took me three years to find you, but I did. You weren't supposed to live."

"They killed my friends." Cole's mouth flattened. "*You* killed my friends."

"Yeah. And I'm going to kill you, too."

"You set everything up. Finding me. Why?"

"I just told you!" Gene flung his hands in the air. "My god, are you that dumb? You were supposed to die, but you didn't. And after dealing with Franco Dunvan, the elders realized we needed to follow one man again. Democracy doesn't work for us." He stared at me. "Take a guess who was chosen."

"Carter." Cole cursed under his breath. "This was all about him. He's been out because of her—"

"—and she'll be the reason he'll come back in," Gene finished.

"You wanted him to be the leader, your man in charge, but you told him to stay out at first." Cole shook his head. "Carter told me you urged him to stay out."

"Why do you think? *You* had come back. You weren't supposed to. You were supposed to be dead. I needed time to clean up my mess, but then I realized Carter was like a dog after a bone. He wouldn't rest until you were voted back into leadership. I hated that. You have no idea. We were being force-fed your bloodline again after we'd done so much to get rid of your family."

"*We?*" Cole spat. His eyes were wild, and his chest heaved up and down. "*We?!*"

Gene grew quiet, pausing as his eyes lingered on Cole for a moment. "Well, me and a few others. We lost Stephen and Jimmy last year. They didn't know when to keep their mouths shut about something."

"So not all of the elders are involved?"

There was a beat of silence.

It extended to another minute.

Then I got it. Gene wasn't as connected as he'd made it sound. As soon as I figured it out, Cole must have too, because he started laughing.

"You're an idiot, Gene," he said. "A complete idiot. Have you thought this through?"

"You think you're so smart, Cole? You never would've figured this out. Ever." He waved a finger at him, a gleam of pride coming to his eyes. "If it had been Carter on that stairwell just now, he would've gotten it the second he saw Emma being held against her will. He would've launched an attack then and there. Hell, we'd probably all be dead if it'd been him and not you."

He puffed up his chest, as if he were boasting. "But no, lucky for us, Carter's still being questioned. The police want to pin everything on him. Who do you think he'll come to for help? To make sure nothing comes back to him? Me. The only thing that'll keep him out is…"

His beady eyes swiveled back to me. "…his woman. Thanks to the Bartels wiping out most of his security guards, we were able to scoop you up. We knew right where you were, and for once, you weren't protected. I can't let this opportunity go to waste."

"You're sick, Gene."

He shrugged. "No matter how much Carter tried to push you onto us, your place was deemed irrelevant the day your father died."

"So you're with the Bartels? You're working with them?"

"What?" His eyebrows lifted, but he was grinning. He enjoyed this. I saw it now—it was almost time. He bent down and opened a drawer.

I sucked in my breath.

He reached inside.

No…

He pulled out a gun.

"Are you? Are you working with them, Gene?" Cole's voice rose.

He was stalling. I got it then. My whole body felt drenched with ice. He couldn't fight them? Is that why he was stalling for time? If he couldn't—I couldn't. I wanted to see out that window again. I wanted to pretend I could find an escape route. Fighting was pointless. They had guns. One shot and everything was done. My pulse picked up. My vision began to swim around.

Gene had started to come around the desk, with that gun in hand. He was checking the clip.

"*Are you?*" Cole demanded.

He slammed the clip back into place and stopped, only a few feet from me. He held the gun like it was a phone. Like it was nothing to him. It was everything to me.

He smiled at me, but murmured to Cole, "You don't think I know what you're doing? You think I'm that dumb? Waste his time. Ask him his agenda. Ask him anything. Demand it. Make him mad. Make him upset. He won't think right. He'll start talking. He won't know what he's doing. That's your plan, right? Wasting my time, trying to stall. For what?" He waved the gun between us. "You're both going to die. You have to."

Talk, Emma! A voice screamed in my head. My throat wouldn't work. I couldn't get any noise out.

A high-pitched laugh started to build in my throat—no, that was my head. I could hear myself laughing. This was hilarious. This wasn't real. It couldn't be. Then I walked away from myself. I saw myself sitting there. She'd been screaming at me, but she waved her hands in the air now. Skipping. She was going away.

I began to slip away. My mind was leaving the room.

I heard Gene's voice from a distance. "That'd make everything better, would it? No. I'm not working with the Bartels. If they got some information, then…that's a different story. No, Cole. After you're dead, the Bartels will be wiped out. Carter's already eliminated half of them. They're hurting. They're wounded. You know how an animal can be, if they're backed against a corner? They strike out, and maybe not in the smartest way." He winked at me. "Maybe they kill someone they shouldn't?"

Me. The Bartels would be blamed for our deaths. I swallowed. Carter would buy it. He had no reason not to.

The gun was so close to my head. He was going to do it. Any second. My heartbeat raced. It was almost deafening, but I could still hear him. *Close your eyes, Emma.* I tried to make myself do that. I didn't want to see it happen, but my eyelids weren't obeying me. They remained open, almost glued to my face to keep from closing. I fought against myself. I felt my muscles coiling. My mind was leaving, but my body wanted to attack.

"If you kill her—" Cole seemed to snap. "You say you want Carter back in, and killing us will do that, but it's only going to launch a manhunt. Carter won't buy your story that the Bertals killed her. He'll find all of them, and he'll question every single one. He won't be satisfied until he knows for sure who killed her. He'll find you. He will." He softened his tone as he finished, "You're cementing your own murder if you kill her."

"No, Cole. You're wrong. Carter *will* come back to us. He *will* lead us and fine, if he needs to know the truth, I'll make something up. I'll pin her blood and hair on someone so he can kill him, knowing he's avenged his woman."

"You're wrong, Gene. You're so wrong."

I could feel Cole's anger then. He was furious. No, he was deadly.

There he was. There was the guy Carter had trained. And, just like that—just hearing that—I felt my mind coming back. There was still hope.

My pulse slowed, just a tiny bit.

There was still a chance to fight.

"If I kill her, Carter will be out for blood. He'll have no one else to turn to except his family. That's who we are. We're his family, and he'll come back to lead us. She was the only thing keeping him out anyway."

He aimed the gun at my head. His arm was so steady.

"He'll *want* to, Cole, because the *Bartels* took everything from him," Gene continued. "You…" He stepped close and the end of the gun touched my head. "And his woman."

Fight, Emma!

No, that wasn't just the voice in my head. Now I was the one screaming out loud.

I launched myself off the chair. Gene hesitated for a second, stunned, and I flipped over the chair, slamming it against the side of his head. After that, it was chaos. Cole flung himself straight for the guards. They'd been running at us, but he slowed them down. Then he was on his feet and fighting all of them. He was landing blows, blocking theirs, kicking them.

Gun, gun. Get the gun, Emma.

Gene was winded, bent over. He almost fell to the ground, but caught himself. But I had stunned him, and the gun had fallen from his hand. That was enough. I saw it behind the desk. I started for it. I needed to grab it. My hand touched it, and then I was jerked backward.

"No," I whimpered. I was so close. I almost had it.

Gene hauled me back and dragged me to my feet. He held me against his chest as he reached for the gun. I tried to kick it away, but his arm tightened over my windpipe. I gasped, feeling an explosion of pain in my chest. He picked up the gun and straightened back up. His arm loosened a bit, but I still gasped for breath. That pain wasn't going away. It got worse. My vision blurred as I sagged in front of him.

His arm hoisted me back against him, holding me upright.

Smack!

The sound of a body hitting the wall drew my waning consciousness across the room. Two of the men were down, and Cole still traded blows with the others.

I felt the end of the gun press against my ear.

"I'll shoot her," Gene warned.

Those three words sent terror through me. They paralyzed Cole, too. He stopped fighting and lowered his arms. The guards didn't waste any time. They grabbed him, and one slammed the back of his gun down on his head. Cole crumbled to the floor, unconscious.

It was just me now. I tried to gather some energy, but there was nothing. I could barely lift my head. Gene's arm pressed against my throat. It was the only thing keeping me from the floor.

"Fuck," he grunted against my ear. "I didn't think this would be so damn hard." He paused, held his breath.

It was coming. I had to fight.

I lifted my head and sank my teeth into his arm until I tasted blood. A surge of satisfaction flared through me, as he shoved me to the ground and howled in pain.

"Fuck! Fuck! You bitch!" He kicked me in the side and I doubled over, blinking back tears.

"Boss." One of the guards stepped over. "We'll do it."

"Yeah?"

"Go get cleaned up. We'll take the bodies to the car."

"Yeah. Okay." Gene sounded exhausted. "Thanks, Mitchell."

I watched his feet move toward the door.

The guard standing over me lifted his gun and aimed. Another guard stood over Cole. He took aim, too. I couldn't look. I couldn't *not* look.

Then Gene opened the door—and froze. "Wha—"

Bang!

His body dropped to the floor to reveal Carter standing there, gun in hand.

Carter

I'd heard him coming.

The timing couldn't have been more perfect, and when that traitor revealed himself, my gun was up. A look of shock and horror flashed over his face when he saw the 9mm in my hand. But it didn't matter. He was dead the second he saw me.

I still stood over his body and fired two more times as Peter and Michael rushed around me. Gene's men didn't stand a chance. In seconds they were all dead, their blood mixing with my mentor's.

"Carter!" Emma was up and running at me.

I caught her halfway and lifted her in the air. This was the fourth time I'd thought I'd lost her. I was chilled to the bone. This had come too close. He'd had time. He could've put a bullet in her head. A shudder wracked through me. *Never.* I was never letting her go again. Burying my head in the crook of her shoulder, I whispered, my lips pressed against her neck, "Marry me."

She stiffened, then choked out a sob and whispered, "Yes."

Thank god. We held each other even tighter after that.

"Carter."

Michael waited beside us as Peter rushed from the room. I knew what Michael wanted, but I was still reluctant. *Shit.* How many times did I have to get her back, hold her, and then release her right away? But I nodded at him and let go of Emma.

"Carter?"

She looked terrified and fierce at the same time. I didn't think I could love this woman any more than I already did, but I felt a whole new level deepening in me—a level I never knew was there.

Michael reached for her arm.

She frowned at him. "Carter?"

"You have to go with him," I told her.

Two more gunshots rang out from the back of the house. I had to go. A wall went up in me. It was time to kill, not love. I nodded to Michael. "Take her."

She jerked out of his hands. "What the hell are you doing? I'm not going anywhere."

"Emma, go with Michael. We need to sweep the house and see who else is here. Go with him. There's a car outside. You'll be safe there."

She opened her mouth. I knew she was going to keep arguing, so I cupped the side of her face. Her protests died down.

"I can't be distracted. Please. Go with him. So I know you'll be safe," I whispered, pressing my forehead to hers.

"I'm scared for you," she whispered back.

"I know. But I'll be fine." I gave Michael a look. "Take her."

"Ca—" she began.

But instead of grabbing her arm, he bent down and threw her over his shoulder. Then he was gone, and I knew he'd drive her to the house.

She was safe. Emma was safe. I had to keep telling myself that as I looked down at Cole, still unconscious. Hearing another gunshot, I left the room. We'd come back and pick him up. Peter needed me now.

Emma

"Where are you taking me?"

I was pissed. Goddamn this crap—making me leave all the time. I got it. I couldn't fight like them, but I was tired of being treated like I was helpless. I wanted to fight. No, it was more than that. I wanted to be there to protect my man. This wasn't just about Carter protecting me. It went both ways now. We were an evolved couple, damn it.

Michael had put me in a car waiting in the driveway and was behind the wheel and moving in an instant. There'd been a truck beside it, and I knew that was left for Carter and Peter. *Cole*—I remembered him and jerked upright in my seat. "We have to go back."

"No." Michael kept driving.

"Cole. We have to go back for him. We can take him to the hospital."

"Carter will take care of him." His voice was gruff. "And Carter and Peter will be fine. They can handle themselves. It's you we need to worry about."

"But—"

"Emma, it's not just Carter who cares about you." His knuckles were white as they gripped the steering wheel. His jaw clenched. "It's us, too. We care about you, and we're like a family now. So… you're going where you'll be safe. Okay?"

The fight left me. I knew they cared, but hearing it now—my eyes got misty. Goddamn, I wanted to go back so much, but hearing that, I couldn't do a thing. I leaned back in my seat, folded my arms over my chest, and said, "Well, I care about you guys, too."

"We know." He glanced out of the corner of his eye at me in the passenger seat. "We know."

I couldn't talk. My throat felt swollen. I loved these guys, too. *Family.* He'd said that word, and he was right. I looked down at my lap, but I couldn't stop thinking about that. A year ago, I'd had Mallory, Amanda, and Ben. That was it. And even then, we hadn't been the family I'd thought we were. We were always dysfunctional. But now, so many things had changed. A family closeness had formed among Amanda, Theresa, Noah, and me. Then there was my actual sister and now Peter, Drake, and Michael. A laugh slipped out. It wasn't just Carter and me after all. We had all these people loving us, worrying about us.

"What's funny?"

"Just...with all of this." I gestured around the car, but I was indicating our life. "The people trying to hurt us, you guys, with everything that happened because of Mallory a year ago. I have family. That's an amazing thing"

And I was an idiot.

"Take me to Noah's building," I told him.

His hand tightened over the steering wheel. "No."

"Michael, please. I left them before. I have to make it right."

"You're not safe there."

"Who's going to go against Carter now? I heard what Gene said in there. He's wounded the entire Bartel family, and now that Gene's gone? There's no one left. I'm safe. Please? I need to make it right with Amanda and Theresa." I had to. I hoped he understood.

He sighed. "Ten minutes. We go in and out. That's all the time you have. Ten minutes."

Ten minutes was all I needed. A smile stretched over my face. "Thank you, Michael." It stayed there until we walked down the hallway to Noah's place. We'd slipped in the building through the back door, but in an instant Noah's front door opened, and Brian stood there. When he realized it was me, he disappeared for a beat.

Amanda and Theresa appeared at the door. They took one look at me and stood side by side. Amanda's hands went to her hips.

Theresa's folded over her chest. They were like a scowling human wall, barricading me from further entry. Noah stood in the back, his gaze flickering from me to Theresa and Amanda and his frown deepening. But he seemed more wary of them than me.

Michael stood behind me and remained quiet. Yep. This was all me.

"You're not going to make this easy, are you?" I asked them.

Their faces remained unchanged, as if made of stone.

Not the right thing to say. I cleared my throat to try again.

"Right. Well. Okay. First off, I'm sorry. I'm sorry I left, and I'm sorry I didn't say good-bye or explain why I was leaving." *Oh, boy.* "This guy told me I have ten minutes before I have to get somewhere safer, but I want you to know I made him bring me back. He'll throw me over his shoulder if he has to, so I have to make this quick."

I let out a burst of air. How could I make things right in this short amount of time? I wrung my hands together. "I thought I was doing the right thing. I can't be around you guys. My life with Carter is going to affect you, and to be honest, if I hadn't been with my sister, I would've been with you guys that night she was taken. Something could've happened to you."

My chest felt so tight. "And Amanda, I can't put you in the middle. You're in love and happy, and there are going to be secrets. I can't talk to you anymore because if I let the wrong thing slip, then it's on you. You have to keep a secret from your guy, and what happens when you get married?"

Her eyes got big. "What?"

Brian's head poked out from behind Theresa, and he made a slicing motion.

Shit. "Uh…"

"What did you say?"

"I meant *if* you get married. What then? He's your family. I'm not and—"

"Whatever." Theresa rolled her eyes and opened her arms. "Get your ass over here. We know why you left. We're not dumb, but don't do it again."

"What?"

"Ever," Amanda piped in.

Were they serious? "It's that easy? No pitchforks?"

Theresa waved her arms, beckoning for me again. "Come on. We're not complete assholes. We know why you left. Brian—cop. Carter—not. We get it. We even understand, but you're family. Whatever happens, we'll figure it out."

More misting in my eyes. I blew out a breath and tried to fan myself. No more tears. I was so tired of crying.

"Emma," Michael murmured behind me.

It was time to go. Again.

Theresa and Amanda didn't argue. They understood his cue and came forward. All three of us stood there a moment, hugging each other.

"I love you guys," I told them as our heads bent together.

Theresa sniffled. "I'm a blubbering idiot half the time I've been in New York. It's your fault. I'm always worrying about you, and now crying because of this. I love you. We all love you."

"Yeah." Amanda had tears on her face. "No more leaving like that. Go and get whatever you need to finished, and then come back home. Okay?"

"We'll make it work. Somehow," I repeated.

"Somehow." Amanda affirmed, wiping my tears from my face. "We lost one sister. I don't want to lose another."

I closed my eyes for a second and thought of Mallory. It was time to go. I could almost feel Michael's insistence behind me. But I didn't want to let them go.

"Okay. Enough of this gooey, girly blubbering we're doing," Theresa huffed and pulled from the hug.

But as Amanda stepped back, Theresa wrapped her arms around me again. "Go kick some ass, then come back," she whispered in my ear. "We know you have to do what you have to do."

"I will," I promised, giving her one more squeeze.

"Be safe," Amanda said.

"I will," I told her.

As I pulled away, Michael had already started down the hallway. He held open the back stairwell door, and I gave the group a wave before darting after him. I didn't look back over my shoulder, but when I heard their door click shut, I knew they'd gone back inside. I ducked under Michael's arm holding the door and headed down the stairs with him right on my trail.

As we moved to the bottom floor, we were silent, moving in sync. I wasn't the same Emma I used to be. As we reached the back exit, I knew what to do. I stepped to the side, Michael handed me a gun, and I took it, ready for him.

He opened the door and swept his gun around, making sure we were clear behind the door. I went right, my gun up and steady as I cleared the front of the door for us. With the pathway clear, we jogged for the car, side by side.

Carter

The house was empty.

As we checked the last room, Peter closed the door and grunted, "I just clipped that last guy, but Gene's men are long gone by now."

"They were in the back, you said?"

He nodded, looking grim as we returned to the library. "They were mounting another attack. There were three of them. But when I busted through the door and started shooting, they ran off. I'm sure they're safe by now and have warned the others. The elders…"

He trailed off as we stepped through the open door.

Cole sat up, leaning against the couch. His eyes were closed, and he rubbed his forehead. He groaned without opening his eyes. "I'm going to have the motherload of headaches, aren't I?"

"That's what you get for letting Gene get the jump on you," I told him.

He shot me a look. "Really?"

I shrugged. "The guy's old. You're a spring chicken compared to him."

"Nice. Thank you. I just escaped death, and you're giving me shit."

Peter and I shared a grin. Cole was lucky to be alive. We knew that. He would've handled all of them, I was sure, but Gene had Emma in the room. I didn't need to ask to know that Gene had done something to even the odds—maybe had a gun to Emma's head or something. But I didn't want to rehash it. I'd heard enough to know he'd gone rogue.

I held out my hand. "Come on. Let's get your head checked out, then plan our next move."

"Our next move?" Cole took my hand, and I pulled him up. He gave me a wary look. "Do I want to know?"

I was done. I had to be done. "We'll figure it out."

"Not all of the elders were with him. Just a small group of them."

"We'll find who it was. We'll take care of them."

"And then?"

I knew what he was really asking: what would happen to this family and me. I would find the traitors. I would kill them, and then I was done. But to him I said, "That will be talked about then."

I didn't want to talk about it anymore, and he respected my silence as we got into the truck and headed home.

I'd been frustrated at how long I'd been questioned. *Emma was alone*—that was all that had been going through my head. I hadn't left any orders in place in the event that she was released from the police station and I wasn't.

The cops at the station didn't have enough to arrest us, but that didn't mean they weren't trying to find something. It was self-defense. Both Emma and Andrea had given statements to back that up, and my lawyer threw out enough legal jargon to get the cops to back down. They'd wanted to pin something on me, but with no evidence to contradict what Emma and Andrea were saying, their hands were tied.

When I couldn't get Emma on the phone as we finally left, I called Drake, who said she'd been sent to Noah's place where they were planning on picking her up once the detectives left them at the hospital. Then a call to Noah told me what I needed to know. Someone had picked her up, and those men weren't mine. I went to the Mauricio house for answers. What I got, as soon as I walked through the door, was a betrayal.

I waited a few blocks before I asked Cole, "He didn't say who was with him?"

"He said a small group. He was quiet about it, but I got the sense that not all the elders backed him. I don't know if they knew what he was planning."

But we didn't know. That was the bottom line.

"Look, Carter—" Cole started.

I shook my head. Too much fighting. Too much blood. Too much death. "I'm tired, Cole. I don't want to keep fighting. If they weren't a part of it, then…" All those elders. All their families? Pain like I hadn't felt since AJ's death burrowed deep in me. "They were my family, Cole." After AJ. When Emma was in foster care. Before she came into my life. "They backed me up to help *her* out."

The thought that they would take her from me? After helping me keep her?

"Gene had a gun to her head." Cole was quiet as he said that. I heard the resignation, and I knew what he was saying.

"We have to make sure who was with him and who wasn't." I pinned him with a look. "We have to. All those lives, Cole."

He grimaced and cursed under his breath. Raking his hands over his head, he groaned and rested his head back against his seat. "We have to be unified. You and me. Nothing will work otherwise."

"We are."

He glanced sideways to me as Peter kept driving. He studied me for a moment, but then he nodded, and I could see the relief go through him. His shoulders relaxed, his head dropped, and all the fight seemed to disappear.

"Thank you," he said quietly. He laughed a second later. "She bit him, Carter."

"What?"

"Emma. That's why he was leaving. She bit him hard enough to draw blood."

I grinned. Of course, she bit him. She was a fighter, *my* fighter.

Emma

Four months later.

Amanda was quiet beside me. We watched from the car as Theresa and Noah went to the door and knocked. We'd been parked outside of Andrea's parent's home for a half an hour.

Finally Theresa had said they'd go first to scope it out, but the truth was I couldn't move from the car. I didn't know why. I just couldn't.

"Are you nervous?" Amanda asked.

I shot her a look. "If you were to guess?" Thirty minutes. That's how long we'd been there.

She flushed and grinned. "Sorry. I know. I'm nervous, too."

"Why?" I turned back toward the house. The question was more for myself than her. There was nothing to be nervous about. I'd been at Andrea's bedside every day she was in the hospital. We were still strangers, but we were a work in progress now. Her parents had come too, but our paths only crossed one other time. Andrea had wanted me to come in the afternoons, and her parents were allowed in the mornings.

She'd been in the hospital a week for monitoring, and I knew some of her stay hadn't been smooth. She'd fought with her parents, and she hadn't said much to me. We talked more about what we remembered from our pasts, about AJ and our mother.

I had no reason to be scared to go into her parent's home, but I was.

"I don't know." Amanda smoothed her shirt, then rubbed her hands over her jeans. "This is real, you know? I mean, her dad is her real dad. He could've been yours, or maybe he can help you find yours. Who knows? He didn't say anything about your brother?"

I shook my head. "Just that he asked AJ if I could go with him and Andy, and he refused. AJ's older than Carter and me—not that it matters—but I guess our mom kicked him out, and he was in the system already. It would have taken too much time to go through the legal stuff for him to take AJ, too. And my real dad took off long ago. That's what he said."

"Oh." She grew quiet.

"Yeah."

"Still. She's your real sister. I think that's good for you to have real family. You never did before. When it was you and me with Mallory and Ben, none of us did. That's what we bonded over. Mallory would've been happy for you."

I let out an uneasy breath. The knots weren't loosening in my stomach.

"It's a nice house," Amanda noted.

I smiled. It was. It was a mansion. It looked like it had three or four levels to it, complete with a pool around the corner in the back.

Amanda looked at the backyard, too. "Is that a tennis court on the other side of the pool?"

I laughed. "Maybe. Who knows? She said her family was wealthy. He's a hotelier, like Noah."

"Does Noah know him?"

I frowned. "I have no idea. I didn't think to ask."

"That'd be a trip, huh? If Noah knew your sister's real dad all this time?"

I didn't care about that. My hand flattened over my stomach, and I pressed down as if I could calm the nerves that way.

"What do they think of Carter?" Amanda asked after a moment.

I lifted a shoulder. I couldn't look away from the front door. Theresa and Noah were still waiting, and she rang the doorbell again.

"I…don't know. I only saw her parents twice, and the second time it was in passing. Andrea told me she forbade them to speak to me until she wasn't so furious with them."

"I think I kinda like your sister."

I turned, sharing a grin with her. "Yeah. Me, too."

"Emma, I think everything's going to be okay." She patted my hand. "You and Carter are back home. I have no idea how everything was resolved, but it seems like it was—and Carter and Brian even met. They seemed to like each other."

"They stood on opposite sides of the room the whole night."

"Still, Carter didn't shoot Brian. Brian didn't arrest Carter. That's a win in my book."

Hearing the amusement in her voice, I patted her hand back. Everything was going to work out for Amanda, even though Brian hadn't proposed yet. He'd assured me that night when he and Carter were both at Noah's for dinner that he had it planned. Just a few more months…

"Things are good," she continued, "really good."

I waved her off. "Stop talking. You're jinxing everything." Laughing, I tried to soften my blow, but she was making the knots tighten back up again. "Declaring that everything is great is the fastest way to mess it up."

"Oh, come on. You can't believe that."

I glared at her. "Mallory. Dunvan. My sister was kidnapped. Let's just…cool it with the declarations of happiness."

"Okay." She was still grinning. "Oh, look."

Theresa and Noah stepped aside as the door opened, and Andrea's father was there. He was dressed like Noah, in black pants and a sweater. Andrea's mother appeared as well, in a dress with pearls around her neck. Her hair was pulled back in a bun. They shook Theresa and Noah's hands, their movements tense and robotic. Theresa gestured to the car, and everyone looked our way.

They didn't move and seemed to get even stiffer.

"Pretty sure the nerves are on both sides," Amanda said. "They look like they're going to meet a death squad."

Andrea's mother lifted her hand in a small wave. I returned the motion, but I didn't open the door. I couldn't bring myself to leave that car. It was familiar. It was friendly. It was safe.

Then Andrea's head popped around the door. She said something to her parents, and her mom gestured to me in the car. Andrea turned her gaze my way, and a frown appeared. She stepped out, but paused and shook Theresa and Noah's hands before pointing inside. All of them nodded and turned to go inside. Andrea's father's gaze lingered on her for a moment before moving to our car, but then he went inside as well.

Andrea stood on the doorstep and motioned for us to come inside.

I let out a deep breath. This was it.

"Come on." Amanda squeezed my hand. "We're right there. You're not alone meeting them."

That wasn't it. I didn't worry about an uncomfortable dinner. If that was the case, I would've had Carter come with me. I was the one who'd suggested he wait to meet Andrea's family. Meeting me was one thing, but meeting Carter Reed was a whole other deal.

But as we headed to the house, I suddenly knew what I was scared of.

"Carter's not coming?" Andrea asked as we approached.

I shook my head. "No. He had something to do tonight."

"Oh." Andrea's smile was shaky, and she rolled her eyes. "You have no idea how relieved Kevin will be. The rumors and stories are getting to his head, and to my parents, too. I swear I think they were worried a mob hit would happen at dinner." She grimaced. "Kevin suddenly wanted to learn how to shoot a gun this week..."

She faltered, and we stood in silence. Abruptly, she thrust her hand out to Amanda. "I'm Andrea. I know we met in the hospital, but I was half out of it that whole time. Figured it wouldn't hurt to do another introduction."

"Oh." Amanda shook her hand. "Hi, I'm Amanda. Emma and I—"

"Go way back." Andrea held onto her hand and pumped it up and down. "She told me all about you guys. You and Theresa. My dad knows Noah. Can you believe that? Small world, huh? Actually, he doesn't like Noah, or he didn't until he found out he was coming to dinner tonight. The hotels are rivals. My dad's hotels aren't as successful as The Richmonds. Not even close. Don't tell my dad I said that, though. He'll disown me. Okay, he won't, but... Yeah..." She released Amanda's hand and took a step backward. "Sorry. I'm a bit nervous."

Amanda looked from her to me and began laughing. "It's official. There's two of you." She pointed to the door. "I'm going inside. The dinner smells delicious, even from out here."

Andrea smiled. "Yeah. Okay. I'll tell the cook. I don't know what my mother would do without Norma."

Amanda smiled back at her before slipping inside.

Once we were alone, Andrea let out a sigh. "Down to two, huh?" She flinched. "I'm sounding like an idiot. I'm sorry. No wonder you're not ecstatic about going in there—with me being a fool. I, just... My dad's an ass with what he did, and I'm sorry he left you—"

I held up a hand, stopping her. "No. That's not why I was in the car for so long."

"Oh?" She leaned toward me.

"You were kidnapped."

Her head bent down. "Oh."

"They had you for so long, and I know you were tortured. I saw when I untied you."

She stood there, frozen, like she wanted to disappear.

I could feel tears building. I could barely speak around them. "I am so sorry, Andrea. And I can't..." How did I make this right? My face. That's why she'd been taken. "I can't make any of that go away. I—"

Andrea's head came back up. Her eyes were stricken. "My dad left you behind. That's been eating me up inside since I found out. I can't, I can't make *that* right. He's been telling me more about our mom, and she sounds horrible. No wonder you can't remember your childhood with her, and thank god your brother got you away from her. I—*my* dad left you there, and knowing you grew up in the foster system after AJ was killed? That *haunts* me. I can't make that go away."

My voice was soft. "You were tortured."

"Not that much."

"Andrea—"

"I wasn't. Really. They left me alone most of the time. Yeah, they hit me sometimes, but they said it was for effect. They took a bunch of pictures, but then they left me alone." She stopped and drew in a shuddering breath. "They were angry every day. I could hear them. They were arguing about me. They kept saying 'it wasn't working'— whatever that meant. Some wanted to kill me and be done with it, but others kept fighting back. They kept saying I was their 'only leverage.' I knew right away they thought I was you. I never told them I wasn't."

"You didn't?"

"If I had, I think they *would've* killed me. They needed you alive for whatever they were trying to do. The cops keep asking me what I know, but I don't know that much. Have they…" She faltered again and bit down on her lip. "They keep thinking I'm lying about that last night, but I'm not. You untied me. We went to the room, and they were going to kill all of us. It was them or us. Carter defended us."

She'd been taken because of me. I would never let that burden go. "I am so sorry, Andrea."

"Andy."

"What?"

The corner of her lip turned upward. "Andy. Stop calling me Andrea. Please."

"Andy." I laughed. "Yeah. Okay."

"And for everything else, it'll be okay."

My eyes clung to hers. Was she being honest? Was that the truth? Would everything be okay? I wanted to believe her. I did.

She reached out and squeezed my arm. "I have my sister. Whatever bad things happened, it was worth it. I have you back."

My hand rested over hers, and I felt my head moving up and down. She was right. What happened, we'd deal with. I squeezed her hand. "I'm glad you came looking for me."

"Me, too." Tears slid down her face.

My face felt wet, too. I rolled my eyes, wiping my cheeks. "This is a great start to this dinner."

Andrea laughed, throwing her head backward. "Come on." She linked her elbow with mine and opened the door. "Our first family dinner. It'll be interesting to say the least."

As we went inside, she whispered in my ear, "I have so many friends itching to meet you and Carter. I'm the most popular one in our social circles because of you. I can't wait for you to meet everyone. Next time, bring Carter."

I laughed, but I didn't respond. It would be a long time before any of them met Carter. I wasn't ready to share my real family with this new one, not yet.

Carter

Cole and I stood side by side as we prepared to walk into the conference.

It was in a neutral building, in neutral territory, and we made damn sure it was the top floor. That way Cole and I could escape easier than any of the Mauricio elders. They were old and out of shape. We were far from that. The rule was no weapons. That was their condition, which made sense. I'd been their Cold Killer—but I hadn't earned that name with only my 9mm. My hands helped, but they were tucked behind me as we walked through the doors of the building. Drake, Peter, and Michael remained out front. I wanted them close, but not within shooting range if something happened.

As we'd walked toward the building, we'd studied the terrain. I saw nothing. No snipers, no Mauricio soldiers hiding in wait. We'd scrutinized every vehicle and saw no one. The only cars were the black limousines each elder preferred to use when attending meetings like these. They were more intimidating and were meant to indicate each elder's wealth and power.

Each limousine had a driver, and we knew there were men inside, but those were the elders' security detail.

And now, as we stepped through the double doors into the room, each of those elders sat waiting. The tables had been turned to form a U-shape with the opening pointed at us.

Cole had set up this meeting. After Gene's betrayal, he went underground. He already had men outside the family he trusted, but he scouted and recruited even more. When his army was big enough, he reached out to his uncles, and this meeting was the result. Because they hadn't struck against us, they either wanted peace or they didn't want to be killed. Standing before them now, I studied each one intently. I needed to see their reactions. I needed to gauge whether they were willing to follow Cole, or if they would have to die.

Cole started. "You all have come tonight because each of us has a wish for peace." He gazed at me. "We're tired of the killing, and I have no wish to murder my own blood."

That was unnecessary. The unspoken sentiment was strong enough, and I waited, making sure each of them registered the real meaning behind Cole's words.

None of them said a word, but they sat up straighter. A few grimaced and looked away. They got the meaning. I knew they had.

Cole continued. "As you know, I have my own men. With Carter beside me, we have enough holdings and assets to be a formidable enemy."

At Cole's mention of being their enemy, they glanced at each other. *Fear. Uncertainty.* I caught those two emotions before they could be masked. They quickly went back to being statues, but they were growing restless. One couldn't keep his hand still, so he tucked it under the table. Another's eye kept twitching, and he coughed, wiping his face to cover it up. A third leaned forward, his eyes even more intent on what Cole was about to say.

They needed the family. They couldn't go against both of us, not if we were together. I saw their surrender.

Cole paused and looked around the room. He was going to keep going, tell them about all the men he had, how I had built up my own security detail again. Every word he was about to say had been carefully picked to let the elders know we weren't to be taken lightly, that we were a real enemy, if they chose to go that route. It was either accept us back in, or be damned.

But I knew it was done. They wouldn't go against us, not after what I'd done to the Bartel family, who had all gone underground after we took Andrea back. So I cleared my throat. Cole glanced at me, his eyes narrowing for a second. Then he nodded and stepped back.

It was my time to talk.

I looked each elder in the eyes before I did. "You know what I did to the Bartels. I cut their family in half. If you touch Emma. If you betray Cole. If there is any attack on my loved ones, I will hold you responsible. I will do more than cut your family in half. Let me be very clear."

They were riveted. They knew I was speaking my truth. I would kill them, no hesitation.

"Emma is why I'm no longer the Cold Killer. If something happens to her, I will hunt each of you down. I will take from you what you took from me. I will do to you what I did to the Bartels, but it will be three times the damage. Do not think this is a bluff. You will die." I pointed at Cole. "He is the true leader. His bloodline is the true leadership of this family. You will uphold those traditions."

One by one, they looked from me to Cole, until all eyes were on him.

He stepped forward. He was their leader. I saw it. He saw it. They saw it. I didn't want to kill my own family. I had been praying, hoping this would be the result, and it was, but I had lingering doubts. If they'd betrayed him once, they could do it again.

Cole looked at me and nodded, a fierce determination coming from him. "I will fulfill my father's leadership, and my first order of this family is to release Carter from us."

A stirring sounded from the men.

I silenced them, holding my hand in the air. "Cole is granting my request. I asked to be released. After this day, all my business shares will be sold to Cole. He is taking my place in more than one way, but if he needs me, I'll be at his side."

They needed to accept that, and as they stood, coming around the table to me, I knew they had. A line formed, and each one of them hugged me before returning to his seat.

Cole was the last. No words were spoken. This was the end, and we knew it. I would go back to Emma, and I would live my life free, like I had before AJ was murdered. Cole would always be a brother, and he was the one they needed to fear. As I left, I heard him announce the other reason for this meeting. "There are three men among you who are traitors to the Mauricio name because they aligned with Gene. They supported him as he was going to kill me and Carter's woman. To show your loyalty to me now, those three traitors need to stand up."

I paused outside the door. Cole already knew who the men were. He'd searched for them, but the elders needed to hand them over. When I heard the first name spoken, I started forward. It was done. As I went to the stairs, I heard the last two names.

I was almost to the next floor when I heard the gunshots.

One.

Two.

Three.

It was done.

EPILOGUE

A woman stood in front of AJ's tombstone with a bouquet of flowers in her hands. Her head bent down, but I could see, even through the car window, that she had my build. Her shoulders were slender, and her dark hair whipped around in the wind. That was all I could tell. But Andrea and I looked so much alike that we must've taken after her.

It was the logical conclusion, but I wanted to know. A part of me didn't want to look like her. AJ had taken me away, and I couldn't remember most of my childhood. I knew that was because of her, and in some way, some small way, I blamed her.

If she'd been the mother we should've had, none of this life would've happened. AJ would've been alive. Andrea and I would have grown up knowing each other. But then there was Carter.

I glanced over my shoulder as he waited for me. I might not have known him. *No.* He was my soul, the other half of me. I had to believe we would've found our way to each other, even if things had been different. And gazing at him now, I knew that would've happened. Somehow. Some way. At some point, we would've found each other.

But life had turned out the way it had, bringing me right to where I now sat, watching a stranger who never should have been one.

Carter had awakened me this morning and told me there was something I needed to see. I didn't question him. I got out of bed, dressed, and followed him to the car. The guys hadn't come with us. Michael, Peter, and Drake opted to spend time with their families, so they weren't with us for the week. Carter was really out of *that* life, so they weren't needed as much as before. For a few days alone, just Carter and me, we'd get by just fine.

"That's my mother?" I asked now, but I knew. I think I just needed to hear it affirmed out loud.

"Yes." Carter nodded. "My guy notified me she was coming here today."

"How'd she find his grave?"

"I had her told."

"*What?*"

"She was my other reason for returning home when you were in New York. I had my investigator research your sister fully, and he found your mother. I meant to tell you earlier, but I needed to know what she was like. She abused you, Emma. I couldn't bear it if she hurt you again. I didn't talk to her, but I saw her. My investigator talked to her. He told her about AJ. She asked about him. She asked about you. He was instructed not to give her any information about you, but I told him he could share this with her."

He had known...I was glad he hadn't told me. "Why did you tell her about this?"

He looked at me, his eyes searching mine. "Because AJ told me he wanted her to know."

My breath caught in my throat. "He did?"

"A long time ago he did. He used to talk about your mom when he was drunk. I thought she was dead, so I never thought about what he was saying, but he said someday he'd meet with her again."

"What else did he say? If he ever met her again?"

"That he would forgive her." Carter's blue eyes darkened, and the sides of his mouth stretched tight. "I thought he was just rambling. That's what he did when he was drunk. If I'd thought your mom was alive, I would've found her a long time ago for you."

"No." I reached for his hand. Finding out about Andrea was enough, but this, but her—I didn't want to know her now. "It's good that he would've forgiven her, but I'm not going out there."

"Emma?"

I shook my head. "I'm not. I can't." I looked at him. "I don't want to know her."

"Are you sure?"

I nodded. "She had her chance. I don't remember what she did to me, and I don't think I want to. If my memories are blocked, there's a reason for that, but I can't get over what she did to AJ. She kicked *him* out. I don't care what AJ did, he stuck around. He still took care of me. He fought for me. She didn't. Any woman like that, I don't want to meet. She doesn't deserve to know her daughter." My pulse quickened, and I closed my eyes. She'd kicked AJ out. She tossed away one child, let another go with her father, and me she treated more like a toy than a human being. I wouldn't meet her. This was a door I wasn't going to open. "I can't, Carter. I don't want to."

He laced our fingers. "You don't have to."

"You said you didn't talk to her? When you came to find her before?"

"I didn't, but my investigator did. He said she was pleasant. She's been sober for a few years, and she's lived a hard life. He said she was polite, but he could tell she had demons still with her."

I leaned back, resting my head against my seat as I turned to face him. Carter let out a soft sigh and touched the side of my face. He tucked some of my hair behind my ear, his fingers lingering there, just resting on my cheek. It was such a tender caress, and I closed my eyes. I drew strength from him. I would always draw strength from him, and I knew what he was doing.

He was allowing me closure. Meeting my mother was the last door to my old life. In a way it was still open because of all the questions Andrea had awakened inside me, but being here now, all I could think about was what she did to my brother, what she'd done to me.

"AJ was a child then," I told Carter softly.

His thumb rubbed back and forth over my cheek. I knew he was waiting for me to go on. He knew I had more to say.

"Whatever he did, he was a child," I told him. "He was an innocent, and she turned him away. She may be a changed woman, but I have no obligation to her. I don't have to forgive her. There's nothing to forgive. I don't need to know her, and I don't need to remember whatever she did to me."

"Okay."

That was it. Carter leaned close and pressed a kiss to my forehead. "You can do whatever you want," he whispered, his lips grazing my forehead. "If you want to meet your mother at some time, I'll be there. I'm with you. If you want to get to know Andrea's father more, and her mother, I'm with you. You can decide. Everything is in your court."

I pulled back to look into his eyes. The love there took my breath away, and I felt my throat closing up. "Thank you."

We had gone through hell, and feeling like we were on the other side, like we'd gotten through everything and were still together—that was all I needed. I whispered, "I love you."

"I love you, too." His hand touched the side of my face again and he leaned in to kiss me. I loved the feel of his lips on mine, their soft touch as he held there, waiting to see what I wanted. He was letting me control this, too. It was a small gesture, but so much. I felt the hunger for him kick up in me, and I grabbed his shoulder and deepened the kiss.

He was mine.

He was home.

Carter pulled back and gazed down at me, a soft grin on his face. No words were shared, but I was ready to leave, and I nodded to him. It was all the signal he needed.

He sat back and started the car. As it swung around to head back home, I turned so I could watch her. She lifted her head at the sound of our car and looked in our direction. She did look like me. She had my dark eyes, the same heart-shaped face, and she even held herself the way I did. She seemed to recognize me right before the car completed its turn. Her eyes widened, and she jerked forward, but we drove away.

That was the first time I laid eyes on my mother. I knew I'd seen her when I was a child, but those were memories. Most of them were still buried, and the others were distant and vague.

I didn't know if I would tell Andrea about this or not. No. I knew. I *wouldn't* tell Andrea, at least not right away.

My sister was still too new to me. Getting to know her was going to take time. Her parents had already expressed their desire to get to know me more, but so far, the random dinner once a month was enough for me. I wasn't ready to take on a new family.

I glanced down at my hand, joined with Carter's. He'd left his family, while I seemed to have gotten some of my old one back. But after a moment, I knew that wasn't true.

Carter *was* my family.

He was the only one who counted.

Everything else would fall into place.

www.tijansbooks.com

ACKNOWLEDGEMENTS

Thank you to all the bad reviews I received from Carter Reed. I read them and they inspired some of the content in Carter Reed 2. I hope I did it justice. I tried, at least, so thank you. I want to say thank you to all the Tijanettes, Kerri, Eileen, Heather, Cami and Celeste. Thank you to Jessica, Chris, Paige, and Elaine. I love working with each of you. And Lisa! We had a whole other cover, and I made you do a whole new cover. I also want to say thank you to a couple special readers: Rhiannon King and Michelle Louise Drew. Thank you to all the readers who kept asking for a Carter Reed 2. You guys kept asking and I truly hope you enjoyed what you received!

A big thank you to Heather Wishnia, Eileen Robinson, Laura Hutton, Pam Huff, and Amy English. All of you guys are amazing and I'm so grateful to have your support. For real. Thank you from the bottom of my heart.

Thank you to The Rock Stars of Romance for helping me with my last two release blitzes. You guys are amazing to work with and thank you to all the blogs out there that have helped and supported me! I truly do appreciate it so much.

Jason and Bailey—I love you both.

CPSIA information can be obtained
at www.ICGtesting.com
Printed in the USA
LVOW04s2044061216
516057LV00011BA/1647/P